THE DAUGHTER OF OLYMPUS

THE GILDED GODS SERIES, VOLUME: 1

Cynthia D. Witherspoon

Previously Published as The Sibyl: The Oracle Series, Volume: 1

Published 2020 by Shadow City – A Next Chapter Imprint

Cover art by CoverMint

ONE

June 24th

Athens is burning tonight. You'd think I'd be used to the heat of a southern summer since I had been raised in Charleston. But Georgia heat isn't the same as it is on the Carolina coast. Where Charleston's humidity smothers you, Athens' sun boils you alive. The heat remains long after twilight. I imagine my blood bubbling beneath my skin every time I walk outside.

I shouldn't write that. Dr. Stevenson suggested I only put happy thoughts on paper. Lies scratched in black on white. Underlined with the pale gray print of my notebook. Maybe someday, I will convince myself that they are true.

"If you can't say the words, then write them." He had stressed. "Write them all down so you can revisit the good in you when all you can see is the bad."
He's right, I suppose, though I'd never in my wildest dreams imagine going to see a therapist. Funny. It was my dreams that drove me to his office in the first place.

I am getting ahead of the assignment. Perhaps, I should introduce myself first. That is the only way to begin a new relationship, after all. A name. A smile. A 'how are you?' and the rest unfolds with ease. But nothing is easy. Not really. Especially not relationships.

My name is Eva. That's not my birth name. That's not the name printed on my birth certificate, at least. The name printed on that scrap of government acknowledgement was too long. Pretentious. It was as heavy and hard as the memories attached to it. So I sliced it away. The extra letters were discarded until Evangelina became Eva.

It fits me better. Eva is a serious name. One that is quick and to the point without a flurry of bullshit hanging from it. So at nineteen, I did the unthinkable. I went against my mother's wishes and changed my name through the court. Evangelina Claryse McRayne became Eva Claryse McRayne. If I ever marry, I'll work up the courage to drop Claryse, too. It's too full of my mother's aspirations. The name itself literally means 'famous'.

I wonder how many baby name books she had gone through to find that one. A name so perfect to fit the dreams she had for me.

Dreams. That word again. I hate that word now. I had gone years without remembering them. So why now? Why did it take a college diploma to make me remember the scenes from my sleep?

I suppose I will tell you about them some day, but I am running late already. I am meeting a friend for drinks downtown and Elliot hates it when I keep him waiting.

I'd nearly dismissed his invitation. I was far too busy wallowing in my state of unemployment to spend money on alcohol. But Elliot promised he had a job offer lined up for me. He promised it was good.

We would see. I had an idea of the type of career Elliot had in mind for me. And I was sure I wouldn't like it.

I STARED at Elliot Lancaster as if I'd never seen him before. His eyes were too bright today. His hands were too animated. More than once, I was convinced the beer resting next to his elbow would go toppling over to spill its contents across the old wooden table. I interrupted his monologue about the amazing adventures we would have with a wave of my hand. It took a minute, but Elliot sputtered to a stop mid-sentence.

"You've lost me." I managed to pull my voice to the surface. It blended well with the country song that bayed from a jukebox in the corner of the bar. "Go back to the contracts."

"Not much I can say about them." Elliot picked up his bottle by the neck to take a swig. "You'll learn all you need from Connor."

"Whose Connor again? Why is he important?"

"Why-," Elliot breathed and I didn't know if it was the atmosphere or his breath that stank of cheap beer. "Did you not hear a single word I just said?"

"I was listening."

I was lying, of course. I'd tuned Elliot out when he started talking. I tended to do that when I was around him despite his status as my best friend. I can't tell you why I considered myself close to him. Perhaps, it was because he always found me on campus. Perhaps, it was because he had a hardness about him that I craved to have myself. He gave me a cold look now before he rewound his story. This time, I made sure to focus on him instead of the crude words carved into the surface of our table.

"Connor Garrison is the executive producer who agreed to take on this project."

"Ok." I studied him through the hazy air. Cigarette smoke hung between us like a curtain. "I think it's great that you got a gig on television, but I can't do this with you."

"Why not?" Elliot fell back in his chair. "Give me one good reason why you can't be on the show."

"You know why."

I didn't have to speak loud for Elliot to hear me. He knew exactly what I was talking about. He knew everything about me whether I wanted him to or not.

"Eva," He clasped my hand against the table until the words beneath it cut into my skin. "That's over. You're better."

"How do you know that?"

"Because you are." Elliot emphasized his words with a wave of his hand. "You can get a shrink in L.A. They can travel with us if it makes you feel better."

Nothing about this conversation made me feel better. Nothing about the decisions Elliot had already made for my life set well with me. The knot in my stomach tightened as the bourbon I had been sipping on threatened to bubble back up.

"How?" I used the break in the music to speak. "How can I do this? I've never been on television. I didn't grow up in that world like you did, Elliot. I have no experience."

Elliot smirked at my concerns. I thought they were valid ones. My friend made it clear he disagreed with me. He took another sip from his beer, swished the liquid around in his mouth, then swallowed. Elliot was pretending to consider my words, but he already had an answer. Elliot always had the answer.

"You don't need experience. You'll be a presenter, not an actress." Elliot began to gesture with the bottle. The table was so small, I stiffened as I expected to get smacked in the face. "This isn't any gig on T.V., Eva. This is our chance to travel the world. Maybe we can make a difference in people's lives."

"Let me get this straight," I caught the bottle before it connected with my nose then pulled it from his grasp. I took a swig and vomit rose up in my throat. The alcohol was too bitter. It stank worse up close than it had across the table. "You want to go to dusty old houses and talk about the scary ghosts who live there? How in the hell are you going to make a difference doing that?"

I kept it in the singular. There would be no 'we's in my responses. Television was Elliot's world, not mine. No matter how hard he tried to pull me into the abyss with him.

"Give me that." He snatched his nasty beer back. I went back to studying the table top. "If we can prove the existence of the paranormal, it would be monumental."

"How can you prove such a thing?"

"Belief."

"I don't understand." I pulled my eyes upward. Elliot looked distorted in the low light. He looked meaner somehow. "Belief can't prove anything."

"Belief is all the proof we need."

I squinted as I tried to see him. Someone put a quarter in the jukebox and Dolly Parton filled the silence between us. She sang a song about being hurt by love.

I didn't know about love, but I was intimately familiar with being hurt. Elliot let me sit there like a sulking child before he tried again.

"Our crew will consist of me, you, and a cameraman. Come on, Eva. I need you on this. Two friends, chasing down ghosts together. We'll have a hell of a time."

I began to tear his beer napkin into little squares. Most ended up in jagged shards that I pulled into a pile with a swipe of my palm. Flimsy pieces of trash that had once been wooden trees. Funny how the same material that made the table we sat at also created the trash in front of me now.

"Elliot, I just can't." I found the strength to refuse him. "There are a million girls who would kill to have this conversation with you. I'm not one of them. I'm sorry."

"Is this because-"

"Partially." I interrupted him. "I am starting to make progress, Elliot. What if I screw it up? What if-"

"Eva, stop. You're not crazy. You don't need a shrink. You need to get over it."

I couldn't breath as I stared at him. A strange numbness wrapped itself around me. I forced myself to grab a twenty from my wallet to cover my drinks. I tugged out the bill then pressed it on top of the trash pile.

"I'll be sure to tune in, Elliot. Sounds like a real riot."

I slid out of the rickety chair and almost ran face first into a couple stumbling past me. They were trying to make out and walk at the same time. The result was a laughing fit between them as they continued past. Neither had seen me.

I was as invisible now as I had ever been. A familiar ache filled my chest. It thudded along with my heartbeat until it settled in the pit of my stomach.

"The studio is going to provide us with a condo. A five figure salary to start."

Elliot finished his beer then stood. He hooked his arm through mine in an act of possession. When we first became friends, I had relished in the gesture.

Elliot saw me. He really saw me. We'd met in English 101 our freshman year at the University of Georgia. I was the haggered girl in the back corner. He was the charismatic student who had everyone swooning over him. The first few weeks, he ignored me as everyone else had done. But it wasn't long before I started spotting him everywhere. At the gym where I had cheerleading practice. In the canteen. The library. When he finally approached me, I called him a stalker. He told me I wasn't wrong then proceeded to take the seat across from me. He talked the rest of the night.

And that became the pattern of our friendship. Things had never blossomed beyond that between us. I became used to Elliot"s presence. He would come to the football games to watch me cheer. He would appear on my paths around campus. Come to my little apartment when he knew I would be home. I asked him once why he'd even bothered to approach me. Elliot had given me a magnificent grin of white pearly teeth.

"Because I decided that you are mine."

That was it. I had no choice in the matter. We weren't dating. Elliot liked his women to be easy. Fun. More than that, he liked them to be happy. Everything I was not. I was far too focused on school to attend frat parties or take part in the stupid games they played on the quad.

"Eva," Elliot tapped me on the nose as we stepped out on the sidewalk. "You're not listening again."

"What? Sorry. I was thinking about you."

"About me?" His face lit up. "What about me?"

"About how we met." I confessed. "What were you saying?"

"That the show is more than a job." He clasped my arms. I was so thin, his fingers were long enough to touch each other. "It's your chance to get away from Georgia. From your nightmares."

"Did your dad set up the condo? And the huge salaries?"

Elliot's face went dark and I opened my mouth to apologize. I was all too familiar with his fear of being under the shadow of his famous father. The great Joseph Lancaster who had founded Theia Productions. I can't tell you how many times I heard him talk about his fears of not measuring up to his father after too much alcohol. Usually, his confessions came before he passed out on my couch. His body relaxed by the liquor, his soul lightened by his impassioned speeches of failures and prodigal sons.

"Dad wrote out his conditions for hiring us, but the show is my idea." Elliot returned his arm through mine, mercifully forgiving my slip of the tongue. "I pitched it to Connor's team. They loved it. Now, all I have to do is get your name on the dotted line."

"I haven't agreed to this." I frowned at him as we passed beneath a streetlight. "I still have concerns, Elliot. I can't just dismiss them."

"Eva, everything here," He gestured to the row of bars across from us. "Everything in your past? It's gone. Start over with something new. Somewhere new. Let all of this just fall away."

"And while I'm at it, become a completely different person?" I snorted as I moved closer to him when a crowd of boys dressed in shorts and body paint raced past us. "Is that what you want?"

"I think it will be good for you." Elliot tapped my temple as a headache formed behind my eyes. "Hollywood changes people. It can make you or break you, Eva. I won't let it break you."

I wanted to believe him. I needed to believe him. A part of me wanted to do this. A part of me wanted to stay with Elliot so that he wouldn't forget about me. I'm pretty sure the alcohol had taken over when I finally gave him the answer he wanted so badly.

"Ok." I whispered. "Ok, I'll do it."

"Really?"

Elliot let out a whoop before he lifted me off my feet in a bear hug. The lights spun around me in thin streaks against the night so I shut my eyes.

"Put me down!" I smacked his shoulder. "Elliot! I'm gonna puke!"

Elliot put my feet back on the sidewalk and I stumbled forward when my knees decided not to work. Elliot caught me against him then wrapped me up in his arms. Even drunk, I felt nothing for him. No sparks. No pool of desire in the base of my stomach. Maybe I was too stunted to feel emotions anymore.

I pulled back with a muttered 'sorry'. Elliot, still on a high from his victory, grinned at me in the streetlight. He looked like a wolf with pointed teeth when the shadows hit his face.

"Tell me, Eva. What made you change your mind?" His grin grew wider. Almost grotesque. I shuddered and took a step away from him. "Was it my good looks?"

"It certainly wasn't your modesty."

I began to walk towards my apartment and chided myself for my thoughts. Elliot wasn't dangerous. He was my friend. He was there, wasn't he? He had stayed with me after...after the event. After my parents had returned to Charleston and my mind was still unraveled. I hated that it had spilled outward.

I thought of the little notebook I had left behind on my desk. I needed to write this out. I needed to plot and plan ways to hide the crazy in myself. I needed to become someone different.

Not Evangelina, but Eva. Not the broken girl scared of her own thoughts but a fighter who could survive anything that came her way. I could do this, I told myself. I would do this.

"Wait up!" Elliot caught up to me and fell in step beside me. He bumped me with his shoulder and I nearly took a tumble into the trashcan on the street. "I'm gonna crash on your couch."

"I'm not really in the mood for conversation." I cut my eyes up at him. I was nearly afraid I'd see the wolf in his features again, but there was nothing but a half drunk smile on his lips. "I'm going to bed."

"We leave for L.A. on Wednesday."

"Wednesday?" I squeaked out the word. "Are you serious?

Wednesday is two days away and I have so much to do! I'm not going to be ready by Wednesday."

"You'll be fine."

Elliot took my hand and I let him. The sweat on my palm was cold and made my skin feel clammy. To the crowd around us, we appeared to be a couple drunk from the bars and each other. I found that strange since there was nothing between us.

Nothing at all.

TWO

My mother called me today. To be honest, I was surprised to see her number when it flashed like a warning sign across my screen. Janet McRayne wanted as little to do with me as possible. Believe me when I say the feeling was mutual.

I considered letting her call go to voicemail. I was busy, after all. Busier now than I had ever been. Yet, the fear I felt for her remained coiled like a snake in my stomach. By the third ring, I snatched it up before I made myself sick from its venom.

"Hello," I sat forward in my desk chair. "Eva speaking."

"Evangelina." My mother's tone was cold and I winced despite the fact that she was three thousand miles away from me. "You should use your proper name now."

"According to the state of Georgia, Eva is my proper name." I busied myself by rearranging the pens in the little yellow cup beside my monitor. I was still on edge, still anxious from my thoughts of disobedience. "What can I do for you, Mom?"

"We haven't heard from you since you left for California and the girls at Society are asking about the show."

Of course they were. The 'girls' my mother referred to were a group of women suffering from empty nest syndrome and menopause. The Heritage Society had been my mother's most beloved project for ages, though I was sure they spent more time discussing the latest Hermes bag line than how to preserve the history of my hometown.

"Evangelina."

Janet McRayne's tone was one of perfected impatience. I envisioned her standing in the kitchen dressed in pressed slacks, heels, and a set of white pearls that were the true mark of a lady. Her beautiful face stoic, but her green eyes would be flashing with anger at me.

"Fine," I managed. "The plans for the show are going fine."

"You must give me more than that." A low tapping filled the air. Her perfect manicure must have taken the brunt of her frustration with me. "Have you met anyone interesting?"

By interesting, she meant famous. But my negative answer disappointed her. I was good at that, you see. Disappointing my mother.

"No, I'm sorry." I pulled out a red pen and began to doodle on the side of my notepad. Two harsh strokes. More. I needed to keep myself busy when I spoke with her. It helped my voice remain steady. "I am taking classes through Theia's studio. We are going to a conference tomorrow to announce the start of filming."

"An announcement? What sort of conference?"

"It's called Paracon. In New York."

"I can't very well call it by such a ridiculous name." She scoffed. "Isn't there another name for it? Something more grand?"

"No, m'am. I'm sorry." I bit my lip at my second apology in less than five minutes. I racked my brain to come up with something positive. "The condo is lovely though. It is two stories and on a cliff. I can see all of Los Angeles from my bedroom."

Elliot came into the office at that moment. I used him as an escape from my mother's phone call.

"Elliot is tapping his watch, Mom. I need to go."

"Very well. Call me when you have something exciting to talk about."

That was it. I shut down my cell phone and rested my forehead on my arms. Elliot gave me a curious look. I could feel his dark eyes boring into the top of my head as if he could see my thoughts through my skull.

"Janet?"

"Janet." I lifted my head and took in his t-shirt and jeans. Elliot didn't bother with a business casual wardrobe. He didn't have to since his father signed our paychecks. "She was just checking in."

"We've been in L.A. for almost two months and she's just now checking in?"

"Yup," I breathed out the word. I turned to my laptop then jostled the mouse so that the Google homepage replaced my screensaver. "She needed an update for the Society. I guess she's tired of being overshadowed by weddings and pregnancy announcements."

"You know she's excited about the show."

No, she wasn't. My mother wasn't excited about the show. She was excited about the fame she was convinced would come my way. She was excited about breezing into her Society gatherings then clutching at her pearls as the old bats chattered at her about seeing me in magazines. It didn't matter to her that most television shows never went past the Pilot. Evangelina would make her dreams come true or die trying.

"Anyway," Elliot ignored my silence. He ran his fingers through his brown hair and studied me. "We are going to head home in an hour. We need to pack for the flight tonight."

"I'm going to the coffee shop then." I swooped the mouse downward and clicked to shut it off. "I'll meet you in the garage in an hour."

"I swear, you work more in that hole in the wall than you do up here."

I snagged a pen, my messenger bag, and pulled my leather bound journal from my desk. I had promised myself I would catch it up. I hadn't been very good at making daily entries, nor had I gotten another therapist. Now was as good a time as any.

"See you in an hour."

"See you."

I headed to the elevator before Elliot could say anything else to distract me. He had a horrible habit of monopolizing my time. I had a horrible habit of letting him. So when I got my coffee order from the barista and snuggled into the plush seat of the booth, I silently congratulated myself for getting away.

I checked the date on my watch then sat back. I had two months of events to talk about, but I knew I would barely scratch the surface. I turned to a blank page and began to write.

August 24th

I have been in Los Angeles for almost two months now. The land of fake blondes and even faker body parts. The land of the stars and excess though I've seen more homeless people than I have celebrities. I always feel guilty as Elliot rushes me past them. I'm not invisible! Their eyes silently scream as they shake their cups at us. I'm a human, too!

I want to help them. I want them to know that they are not alone. That they are seen. Acknowledged. But I don't stop. I don't go against the tide that is Elliot Lancaster. He is the wave and I am the sands being tugged wherever he sees fit to lead me.

Any good shrink would tell me that I have replaced my mother with Elliot. I am so used to being controlled that I've never allowed myself the freedom to do as I please. They would say - with a furrowed brow - that I am repeating the harmful cycle that led to my hospital stay.

It is easier, I think, to do as I am told. There is no drama and everyone around me is happy. Because I followed Elliot, I now had a beautiful condo. I had a contract that promised more riches than I could have dreamed of. If the results are so positive, then why fight against them?

My first meeting with Connor Garrison went well enough. He had circled around me. Before I could ask him if he wanted to measure my waist and check my teeth, he had boomed that I was perfect. I was exactly what the show needed.

And so, my Hollywood career began. I was outfitted, pampered, and plucked until it became annoying. I had wanted to scream that if I was so damn perfect, then why did I have to go through this torture?

I didn't. I kept my mouth shut and appeared at every appointment. I went to every voice and blocking and equipment class. I smiled as I tried to be Eva, not Evangelina. I laughed or joked with everyone I came in contact with. This would be my image to the world. A happy, glamorous creature who charmed instead of cried. Eva McRayne would have it all. Evangelina could stay tucked into the back of my mind.

We have a cameraman. I met him the first day. The contract day. His name is Joey Lawson and his smile was infectious. Joey reminded me of every big brother I had ever seen on a sitcom. He's as tall as Elliot. Lean with a head full of dark curly hair and brown eyes that sparkle.

"Eva!" He boomed before he swept me up in a hug that took my breath away. "We're gonna have a hell of a time on the road!"

"Hi," I had stiffened until he released me. I took a step back but smiled at him. A fake smile that was tight and showed too much teeth. "You must be Joey."

"The one and only," He then straightened up and saluted. "Let's have dinner soon. Before you two leave for the Big Apple. Get to know each other."

I had politely declined. When I left Theia at the end of the day, I was far too tired to go out. I used my time to sleep, not explore the city. I had a feeling that I would need the rest to face the upcoming days.

And sleep I did. Wonderful, long hours of unconsciousness without the nightmares that plagued me in Georgia. The doctors had asked

Janet about them when I was in their care and she denied the events that terrorized me. In typical Janet McRayne fashion, she created such a fuss that the questions concerning my mental state were dropped.

Perhaps, it's for the best. Time and distance - combined with the hectic schedule of settling into a new life - had made them vanish. They faded away like smoke after a fireworks show, wispy until I could barely remember them. I'd like to think that my mother was right. That my mind had been so twisted by the stress of graduating college that I had imagined horrible visions. Vivid scenes that no one could have survived. Scars created by my own self-loathing because anyone who would do what I had done was capable of anything.

No. I don't want to talk about that. Happy thoughts, remember? So I will begin by saying how much I adore my new home. It is open and shiny. Peaceful and quiet. If I could, I would spend every moment in that space and be happy.

A home I now have because of work. Because of the show. We are leaving for New York to attend a conference called Paracon. Since Elliot wants the show to focus on ghost hunting, it was only fitting that we start to drum up interest with those obsessed enough with the paranormal to attend a conference about it. My only concern is what we will say about the project.

"Leave it to me," Elliot had laughed. "You just have to stand there and look pretty."

Look pretty. As if I were an ornament on a Christmas tree or a shiny toy on display in a store window. I kept quiet at his order as he went back to creating a spreadsheet of some sort. What could I have said? That I wasn't attractive? That I was far too thin and far too angular to play the porcelain doll he wanted so badly?

So this is what my life has become. A mess of pretending. Of ignoring the voice in my head screaming at me to run. I didn't like that voice. It sounded panicked. Scared. It was Evangelina's voice, not Eva's.

I would do the show. I would help it become a success even if that meant I did nothing at all except what Elliot demanded of me.

Look pretty.

I had never been to New York City before and I was enraptured by the life that flowed through this city. The small diners and carts that broke up the high rises. The bodies that pushed and prodded each other onward with their lives. I woke at dawn just to stand by the window in our hotel and watch the people below. Each person was in their own little bubbles of cell phones and business calls. Yet, they still managed to move together like the group of salmon I had once seen on a nature documentary.

Elliot and I were housed in the hotel where the convention was being held, so I didn't have the opportunity to join the masses on the sidewalks. I would have blended in with them seamlessly. As invisible as ever. The thought terrified me somehow because if one was invisible, did they truly exist? If man created their own realities based on their perceptions of the world, did that mean the people they didn't know didn't exist?

I was broken out of my thoughts when Elliot knocked on my hotel door. I took in my appearance as I walked by the large mirror propped against the entry way wall. I had chosen jeans for this. Hiking boots since I knew I was going to be on my feet all day. My honey blonde hair highlighted with streaks of white that contrasted bright and sharp against the dark blue t-shirt I wore. I was comforted by the sight of myself. I had always been drawn to the calming qualities of blue. I blamed it on the hours I had stolen from my studies to watch the ocean from my bedroom window. It's shades of blue and green and grey had been my inspiration. It's constant presence was a reminder that anything could withstand a storm.

Or a hurricane, which is what I felt my life had turned into. One large storm that tossed me around like a rag doll.

I opened the door before Elliot could knock again. His grin was so big, I was immediately suspicious.

"You look perfect." He clasped my hand and I used my free one to check my back pocket. I relaxed when I realized I had my driver's license and the room key. "Ready?"

"Yes." I responded as I closed the door to my room. "Lead the way, Elliot. I am right behind you."

THREE

"ARE you sure we have to go to this?"

I tugged at Elliot's sleeve like a child who was being forced to attend a doctor's visit. The closer we came to the area of the hotel where the conference was being held, the more I wanted to run. I became breathless with my anxiety.

I didn't like crowds. The bodies all smashed together, each content to share the same space until no one could move. No one could escape.

"I can just make something up. I feel pretty sick at the moment and you always said I was good with excuses."

"It's just nerves. You got nothing to worry about." Elliot pushed me in front of him as we joined a mass of people who seemed incapable of forming actual lines. Instead, they chatted and hugged and meandered their way up to a long table crammed with manila envelopes. "If you behave, maybe we can skip out early this afternoon. Be tourists for a while."

"Does that mean I can't laugh at how ridiculous this is?"

"That's exactly what I mean." Elliot clasped my arm just above the elbow. I felt as if I were his marionette. Tied to him with invisible strings that he manipulated to make me dance whenever he pleased.

"You have to at least pretend to take their beliefs seriously for *Grave Messages*."

Grave Messages was the name of our new project, though I wasn't sure what type of messages Elliot expected. If he wanted us to deliver the messages of the dead, I had no idea how he planned to do that. I hadn't seen any Ouija boards floating around the office. No tarot cards scattered across his desk.

"You know I can't make any promises." I was pushed towards the table by the crowd around us. I bumped into it when a man with a mohawk damn near fell over me in his haste to get to the front of the group. I managed to smile at the older woman handing out the name badges and shouted over the noise. "Eva McRayne."

"Welcome, Ms. McRayne." She handed me a manila envelope filled to the brim with papers and pamphlets. "Your name badge is inside as well as the schedule of events. I hope you enjoy yourself."

I nodded then stepped aside so Elliot could repeat the process I just went through. We stepped through a pair of glass doors when he had his envelope in hand and I could have sworn I'd fallen down the proverbial rabbit hole. Although it was only nine in the morning, the place was swarming with people. Most were in groups, going from table to table with banners proclaiming the names of ghost hunting societies and psychics willing to sell the answers to all of your questions. Other tables were filled to their edges with merchandise of all kinds.

I suppose such crowds were normal at a convention. It was the patrons who gave me reason to feel so disoriented. For every one person dressed in jeans, there were three more dressed as witches or demons. There were more than a few girls dressed in fairy wings and angel costumes. Elliot had to raise his voice so that I could hear him over the crescendo of voices around us.

"Well? What do you think?"

"I think I'm overdressed." I waved off a man in a silver alien costume handing out flyers as he started to approach me. "You didn't say I needed to visit a Halloween store before we left L.A."

He placed his hand on my lower back and led me towards an

area where the organizers had set up benches for the conference goers to rest on.

"Come on. I want to take a look at this schedule. It's packed."

I opened the folder and pulled out the papers the moment we sat down. Connor had emailed this same document to us several days before but neither of us had taken the time to look it over. Elliot was right. For every time slot, there were three to four classes being offered. Everything from how to sell your spells to spirit photography was listed. Each night had an event lined up so the convention goers could get drunk and socialize with those of their own kind.

"How long are we here again?"

Elliot stopped marking on his paper but he didn't look away from it. "Three days."

"Alright. And what do you suggest we go to?" I lowered the paper and studied him. I knew Elliot would take the lead on our schedule just as he took the lead on everything else we did together. "Choose wisely. I swear, I will punch you if you say you want to go to the session about flying through the astral plane."

"Today it'll be the history of spirit photography, then video." Elliot was back to making those marks on his paper. "And scrying. The presentation is led by Katherine Carter. It should be a very interesting day."

"Scrying?" I bit my lip to keep from laughing. "Sounds like a good way to clean your stove."

"Hardy har." Elliot smiled. "Look, Eva, I know you don't want to be here right now. But maybe, you'll find something to change your mind."

"Yeah?" I gestured towards the booth announcing that the Yeti had been found. "Like an authentic picture of a Yeti? Or the eighty-five year old woman who says she can give me the lottery numbers for a small donation?"

"Always go with the lottery numbers. Photographs can be altered."

I didn't realize he was joking until he grabbed my hand and

pulled me up from the bench. "Come on. Spirit photography starts in twenty minutes. I want to get a good seat."

"Oh, right. I can't wait." I mumbled as I let him drag me around the edge of the crowd. "Hey, did you know photographs can be altered? Maybe we should go get coffee instead."

"I've heard about that somewhere before."

When we found the conference room where the class was being held, Elliot broke the silence between us. "Remember, you promised to take part in this."

"I promised to promote *Grave Messages*." I made sure to stress my words as I collapsed in the first seat in the back row. "But you promised we could leave early if I behaved. A deal is a deal, Elliot. I'm holding you to it."

"Shush, it's starting." Elliot lowered himself into the chair next to mine as the man behind us shut the door. I shifted down into my own, preparing myself for the boredom sure to come from a man droning on about cameras, lenses, and lighting techniques.

I was not disappointed.

I was ready to go back to my room and crash by the time Elliot's scrying class was supposed to begin. He was in his element with these people whether he was sharing jokes or debating theories. I suppose I should have been happy for him. He did an amazing job talking about the show and I wondered more than once if he had been training on promotions with Connor.

I tried to copy Elliot's enthusiasm but it became increasingly difficult the longer I was being smothered by the crowds and their excited utterances. More than once, I found myself desperately searching for the exits. More than once, Elliot's grip on my elbow kept me planted next to his side.

Breathe, I would tell myself. *Breathe. You've survived worse than this.*

The source of my anxiety was easy to pinpoint. I felt trapped by the people moving in tangents around us. I couldn't breathe because there were far too many people smothering me with their plastic costumes and fake weapons and glued on smiles. I knew my thoughts were ridiculous. I knew that there was plenty of air and no one here was trying to actively smother me.

One more session, I promised myself. *One more session and you can escape this.*

This was supposed to be the fun lesson. It was an introduction into one of the methods people use to contact the spirit world. So I pulled myself together once again and followed Elliot into the same conference room we had been in just that morning.

This time, it was packed. Elliot had to nudge his way through the crowd so we could grab the last two empty chairs by the aisle on the front row. When we were seated, I leaned over so he could hear me over the noise of those around us.

"This one must put on quite the show."

"Katherine Carter is one of the most well known names in the paranormal field. She's been doing this for decades." Elliot leaned in until our heads were touching. "Scrying has been around forever. But it's making a resurgence these days."

"You mean these things can fall out of favor?" I raised an eyebrow and he pulled back. I released a breath I didn't realize I had been holding in when he put some distance between us. "I thought trends were only for fashion and stockbrokers."

"Not so, my dear. Not so." Elliot chuckled. "I have to say I'm proud of you though."

"Oh?" I smoothed out the front of my t-shirt then folded my fingers together in my lap. "For not ditching you to go back to my room?"

"Yes. I know you've been eyeing the exits all day."

He looked like he was going to say more, but he was interrupted by the small woman who walked up to the front of the room waving to her audience. I had to admit she had a commanding presence. What I couldn't believe was what Elliot had told me. The woman who turned to face us looked as if she were my age. Her thick black hair was pulled up in a bun on the back of her head. Her eyes were a strange golden color that gleamed as she looked us over. I wondered why she seemed so focused on us, but shrugged it off. We were right in her line of sight, after all. Maybe my day filled with all things spooky was starting to take its toll on me.

"When did she start scrying? In the cradle?" I whispered to Elliot before he could pull away. His only response was to nudge me in the ribs.

"Welcome, everyone." The scryer raised her arms. "It is my hope that I will be able to educate you on the ancient art of scrying. Many believe it to be a divination technique, but that is not it's only use."

I took the pose I'd adopted through these sessions so far, lowering myself further down into the seat as the woman began to pace across the carpet in front of us. She paused just long enough to be considered dramatic.

"Scrying is not simply for divination. Certainly some sensitives claim to use mirrors or glass during their own practice, but this is not the original purpose. Scrying can be traced back to the ancient Greeks who used it as a method to contact the spirits of the Underworld."

So this is why Elliot was so interested in attending this session. It wasn't for fun. It was for work. Did he honestly think he was going to try this at our locations? On film? I kicked at his foot. As my luck would have it, I missed Elliot entirely and kicked the stand holding a laptop and projector instead.

The laptop bounced off the carpet. The PowerPoint slide shining against the wall behind her went black.

The scryer stopped in mid-speech. She searched the front row and pointed towards me. "By Olympus, it is time."

"Oh my God," I knelt down to grab the laptop which had fallen against my foot. "I'm so sorry. I didn't realize how close I was to this thing. Let me see if I can put this back together."

The woman clasped her hands over her heart in an overly dramatic gesture. I raised an eyebrow in Elliot's direction before her next words snapped my attention back to the forefront of the room.

"You must be the one sent for me. Can you come up here please?"

I started shaking my head before she could finish her question.

"Um, I don't think that's a good idea. I apologize for the interruption in your presentation."

She gave me a patronizing grin as if she felt sorry for me. "Presentation. Yes, it is that. Don't be shy. You have been chosen. The gift of my long awaited death sent by the gods."

"I'm no gift, lady." I picked up my messenger bag then tugged the strap free from Elliot's foot. "I'll just leave so you can continue."

"Don't be silly." Katherine Carter's smile grew brighter. "Everyone in this room has come here to see me. I meet hundreds of people at these conventions. But you must be special. Are you a sensitive?"

"A what?" I desperately wanted her to turn away from me. I may have been afraid of becoming invisible, but now that I wasn't, the spotlight seemed to scorch me. The scryer had stopped in front of me and crossed her arms. "Look, I'm not being sensitive about anything other than the fact you are embarrassing me in front of all these strangers. Now can you please move? I'd like to leave."

"A sensitive. Someone who can sense things others cannot." Kathy uncrossed her arms, glancing down at Elliot before turning her strange eyes back on me. "No matter. Your knowledge will come with time. Will you stand up, please?"

I could feel my temperature rising the longer I stood there. Her harassment was becoming too much for me to handle. I started searching the walls for an exit sign. I spotted it one above the door in the very back of the room. Of course there would only be one. And of course, it would be blocked by the hordes of people.

"I really don't think that's necessary. Aren't you just going to give us your presentation and be done with it?"

"Oh, there will be a presentation." Katherine gestured for me to stand. "One of which you are a part of it. Please introduce yourself."

My so-called friend looked worried, but he didn't defend me. Instead, he took my bag from my grasp. "You have to, Eva. You were chosen."

Was he serious? I glared at Elliot as I stood up to face the room full of people who were staring at me with a mixture of awe and annoyance.

"Hello. My name is Eva. I am sorry I interrupted this session for you."

I made a move to grab my bag from Eliot's clutches, sure that the scryer's harassment would be over if I apologized to everyone. I figured Elliot could forgive me for not staying after all this.

No. Not even close. Katherine Carter took hold of my arm and pulled me up front to the table with her.

"Eva, is it?" Katherine reached over to the table to pick up a hand mirror. "The spirits are telling me you have been close to death twice before. They are intimately familiar with you. Is this true?"

I stared at the woman in shock. How could she...no. There was no way for her to know anything about me. Flashes of green walls and nurses who floated around as silent as ghosts exploded behind my eyes. I clasped my hand over the opposite wrist and she nodded.

"Many spirits can be deceiving, but these were not."

"I really need to get going." I tried to ease away from her, but this woman was quick. She grabbed my arm again to hold me in place just as Elliot had done throughout the day. I was overwhelmed with the need to cry as my anxiety began to churn in my stomach.

"Please. Just let me go."

"Look into this mirror." She handed it to me with the care one would preserve for a child. "The sooner you do as I say, the sooner we can all depart this place."

I wanted nothing more than to snatch the mirror from her hand and smash it against the carpet. Yet, I wrapped my hands around the handle and held it tight. My fingers remained glued to the gold handle.

"Alright, but only if I get to leave after this."

I was surprised at how heavy the mirror was as Katherine Carter released her grip. It was obviously old with carvings along the rim and handle. I flipped it over so the glass was facing me. I saw what I always see in a mirror. A thin and ragged girl who was better off in the grave.

"I see myself." I handed it back to her. "I'm not sure what you were trying to do, but I don't think it worked."

"Tell me you are willing to do this." Katherine Carter shifted from foot to foot before locking her hands in front of her as she refused to take the mirror back. "You must be willing."

"Well, I'm not." I thrust the mirror in her direction. "So take this back."

"Please," The scryer closed in the distance between her and clasped her hands over mine holding the mirror. "Just try. Be willing to try."

"Try what exactly?" I frowned. "You're not being very clear."

"I can't explain it. No human can explain what happens with mere words. Just please, say what I tell you to say."

Katherine glanced at the audience and I got it. She was using me to make her little presentation more dramatic. The scryer was making a scene to fill in the time gap since I broke her laptop and subsequently ended the PowerPoint she would have shown to us.

"Alright, fine." I tugged my hands free from the woman. "I'll play along with your act. What do you need me to say?"

"I bind thee, mirror, to my very soul."

I turned towards the audience and waved the heavy thing like a flag. "I take thee, mirror, to be my own."

The scryer clapped her hands together with obvious excitement. "Apollo, bless my eyes to make me see. Allow me to hear the words that are silent to the living so I can learn from the dead. I am your true daughter. Your messenger. Your servant for time immortal."

"Ok." I faced her and repeated her mantra. When I was done, I tried to give her the mirror once more. "Can I go now?"

"Close your eyes, child. Your world will change the moment you open them."

"Whatever it takes to get this over with."

I let out an exaggerated sigh as I closed my eyes. I felt the woman grab my hands, holding them so tight against the handle it was hard for me not to cry out as the carvings cut into my palms. Katherine Carter started whispering, her words getting lost to my ears as my hands began to burn. This time, I did cry out. But the woman had a grip on me. One she wasn't going to let go of easily.

I felt the heat rising up from my hands then travel up my arms. I was so focused on getting away from the scryer I barely heard the applause erupting through the room. The fire engulfing me didn't stop until it reached my eyes and my ears. The horrible woman started cackling like a wicked witch in a fairy tale just as the pain from the heat became unbearable. She released my hands as she called out so that the entire room could hear her.

"The reign of the Seventh Sibyl has begun!"

I opened my eyes to seek out Elliot's familiar face in this sea of strangers. Instead, my gaze was trapped by the mirror glowing red. The glass seemed to be reflecting the fire engulfing my mind. I wanted to look away. I needed to look away. Yet the colors captivated me as a strange white noise filled my ears.

Elliot pushed Katherine Carter out of the way. He took hold of my chin to force my eyes away from the strange shades of red and black. I could see his lips moving. I knew he was asking me if I was alright.

I couldn't hear him. I could hear nothing as the white noise shifted into a furious whispering much like what the scryer had done. I turned my attention onto the mirror as a face formed in the darkness. I knew this face was the one whispering to me. It was a man; young and strangely familiar. His golden eyes shimmered as he smiled. This was the voice filling my ears.

"You have returned to me, daughter."

I dropped the mirror just before I passed out.

FOUR

I HEARD the voices clamoring around me before my eyes fluttered open. Elliot was the first face that came into view as he pushed a man back who was knelt next to my head. I'd like to say that I sat up and asked the crowd surrounding me what the hell they were looking at.

Truth be told, I felt like an absolute fool and my head was killing me. Bright sparks of color broke through the black behind my eyes each time I closed them. Elliot was as astute as ever when he knelt over me.

"Don't movc, Evic. You had a nasty fall and-"

I lashed out to clutch a handful of his shirt and pulled him lower. Our noses were almost touching when I hissed out my next words at him. "If there is anyone at this fucking conference who can make me disappear, find them. Find them now."

Elliot's laughter caused another round of pain to bounce through my skull and he worked my hand free before he announced to the room that I was fine. Easy words for him to say as I rolled onto my side then pushed myself up to sitting.

"Go slow, little one." The stranger Elliot had pushed away helped me sit upright. "You had a nasty fall."

"Fine. It's fine." I winced when black spots danced before my vision. I turned to get my first good look at the man. His black suit was rumpled and he was a bit too interested in studying my eyes. I felt a flush rise up in my cheeks as I took in how attractive he was despite the wicked scar that ran through his right eye. "I'm ok."

"Eva, are you sure you're alright?" Elliot had returned to my field of vision. I didn't miss how his blue gaze turned to ice as he looked between me and the man. An awkward moment passed between the three of us before my friend took my arm. "Can you stand up? You really should get up off the floor."

I was in the process of doing just that when a scream filtered into the conference room. This time, it wasn't mine. The audience who had been watching me started to run out of the room. The drama of my collapse was forgotten in light of the screams. I started to follow them but something was holding me back. No, not something. Someone. The stranger was frowning at the door as he tightened his grip on my arm.

"Ms. Carter is no longer with us." His dark eyes flashed as he knelt down to pick up the mirror with his free hand. "It seems this now belongs to you."

"Oh, no." I took a step back away from his grip with my hands up. "I want nothing to do with that damned thing."

He shook his head. "You have replaced Ms. Carter as the Sibyl. I'm afraid you no longer have any say in the matter."

"The what? Replace her? "I mirrored his movement. "No. That woman attacked me with, well, something. I want her arrested or thrown out of this conference. Do whatever the hell it is that security does to people around here."

"Yes. Replace her." The stranger ignored my demands. "Ms. McRayne, Katherine Carter is dead. You initiated her passing the moment your spell was done."

"Who are you?" Elliot finally decided to join our little conversation. "If you're with security, then it might be best if you are outside looking for the woman who attacked Eva. If not, then our time with you is done."

"Elliot, am I still out cold on the floor and dreaming all this?" I turned to Elliot as if he had the answers. He was just as confused as I was. It was the stranger who answered me.

"I'm afraid there is nothing more which can be done for Ms. Carter. We have much to discuss, Sibyl." The man pressed the mirror's handle into my palm until my fingers closed around it. "Your life has been changed in more ways than you could ever imagine I am now assigned to you as your guard."

"No," I slapped the heavy mirror against my leg in frustration at the riddles the man was speaking. "I don't need to be guarded because of some woman's crazy mumbo-jumbo. Did Connor put you up to this? Is this some sort of promotional stunt? Because if it is, I remember what was written in my contract. Being knocked out on a hotel floor was not in there."

"Connor? Promotional?" The stranger had the decency to look confused for a moment. "I don't know what you are talking about."

"Wait, how do you know Katherine is dead?" Elliot interrupted. "She isn't here, certainly. But I'm sure there is a perfectly rational explanation as to where she has gone."

He was interrupted by the loudspeakers overhead and the faint sirens becoming increasingly louder outside.

"Dearest Patrons, please return to your hotel rooms. It is due to a most unfortunate accident the rest of today's sessions have been cancelled. Thank you for your patience and please forgive any inconvenience this may cause."

"Ok." I drew out the word as Elliot and I stared at each other. "That was just a coincidence. Wasn't it?"

I turned around towards the strange man. "Thank you for your help awhile ago. But I don't think I'll need your services."

"Come on." Elliot led us out of the conference room. "Let's get you upstairs. I want to take a look at the knot on your head."

"I have a knot on my head?" I tried to keep my voice calm, but thoughts of the handsome man seeing me at less than my best came to the forefront. "Where?"

"Here." Elliot stopped just long enough to brush his hand against the side of my face. His gentle tone changed into one of panic as he grabbed my shoulders and forced me to face him. "Eva, oh my god."

"What?" I pushed at his hands, but Elliot wouldn't let me go. Instead, he pulled me over to one of the large mirrored columns in the lobby. "Elliot, you're really starting to freak me out."

"Look. Just look." He turned me so I faced the mirror. "Your eyes have changed, Eva."

"You're being ridiculous," I gasped when I noticed just what Elliot was talking about. My green eyes had shifted color. They were now as golden as Katherine Carter's had been. I only got a second to see the difference before my reflection became someone else.

Katherine Carter, who had thrust her mirror upon me not thirty minutes before was standing in front of me. She had changed just as I had. The woman's image in the mirror wasn't the young and beautiful person who had embarrassed me. She was old. Her face was covered in blood. But her strange eyes were the very same. She was laughing. I could hear her words in my head. I knew without knowing how that she had thrown herself in front of a taxi.

"You have freed me, child." She took a step backward, the crazy grin still lighting her wizened face. "Take care of my son. I place his very heart in your hands."

I fell against Elliot so hard he almost toppled over.

"Hey!" He managed to keep us upright, but I refused to look at the mirror again. I threw myself into him then buried my face into his shirt. Elliot's voice softened as he adjusted his hold to pull me closer. "Eva, it's ok. Gold is the new green, right? I'm sure it's nothing permanent."

"She's here." I was shaking so hard my teeth were clicking together. "Katherine Carter. I just saw her."

"Where?" Elliot held me tighter as he tried to calm me down. "I don't see anyone."

"Behind me. In the glass." I tried to keep my voice calm, but I couldn't manage it. "She threw herself into traffic, Elliot. Tell me you see her too."

"See what? Evie," Elliot pulled back just enough to tug my chin upwards. "Who did you see?"

"Her!" I jerked away from him and pointed at the column. "The scryer! She's in there."

"Ok." Elliot breathed out the word as long as he could as he kept his arm in place around my shoulders. "Let's go upstairs. You need to lie down. I'll fix you a drink and you can sleep this off. "

"As I said, we have much to discuss." The stranger was still behind us, his arms crossed over his chest. "What you've experienced is only the beginning, Ms. McRayne."

"Stop saying that!" I glared at him from my position by Elliot's shoulder. "There is no beginning."

"Eva is in no condition to speak with you." Elliot snapped as he turned us towards the elevator. "Leave us alone."

I had no choice but to follow him. I didn't say anything while we made our way through the hotel. I did nothing but keep my head down as I tried to ignore the others passing us in the halls talking about the horrible accident out in the street. I wanted to scream at them though. It wasn't an accident.

Katherine Carter wanted to die. She wanted to be free of the shackles binding her to this life.

Shackles she had clamped onto me.

I fell into a sleep filled with whispers when we returned to my room. I don't remember most of them, but one word was repeated so many times I couldn't help but remember it when I finally woke up.

Cumae.

Elliot was sitting in a chair at the edge of my bed flipping through the channels as if I were suffering from a bad hangover instead of a psychotic breakdown. This was my rational explanation. I had snapped from the stress of moving across the country. It wouldn't have been the first time I'd had an episode that landed me in a hospital, after all.

Maybe I needed to pull my journal out. Write down everything that had happened so that I could get it out of my mind. I was still fragile. Still emotionally unbalanced. The fact that I'd had to stop my therapy sessions when I moved to L.A. had to have something to do with this. I'd simply cracked again. Except this time, I didn't go as far as I had back in Georgia.

My theory had holes in it, though. I kept seeing the Carter woman's bloody face in the back of my mind. I kept hearing her words through the cobwebs of sleep.

What did she mean, son? Who had she entrusted into my care? Was it the stranger who had helped me?

I knew one thing for certain. I had to get these thoughts out of my head before I started acting as crazy as she had. I mean, come on. Talking to dead people through mirrors?

I'd be locked away for life this time around.

"Hey." I sat up and cleared my throat. "Any good football games on?"

"No. The UGA game was hours ago." Elliot pressed a button and the screen went dark. "Are you feeling any better?"

"Yeah." I started picking at the blanket he'd draped over me. "I think so. I was having some really weird dreams."

"What kind of dreams?" His face was soft in the dim light. "Nightmares?"

"No." I frowned. "They were more annoying than scary. I'm in the dark and surrounded by whispers. I couldn't really make out what they were saying."

"Eva, maybe we should have a doctor check you out." Elliot's face was pale as he fiddled with the remote. "You might have done some damage when you hit your head."

"No!" I realized how harsh I sounded, so I tried to keep the annoyance out of my voice. I wasn't kidding about being locked up. It was bad enough when I spent time in the hospital before. "I don't need to see a doctor, Elliot. They aren't going to tell me anything other than what I already know."

"Which is?" Elliot tossed the remote onto the bedside table. It clattered to a stop right next to the edge. "A concussion is serious. It's possible you have one."

"I don't think seeing a dead woman in the mirror is a symptom listed for concussions." I shook my head. "No, I'm fine. I just got overwhelmed."

I flipped on the lamp beside me. I didn't know how long I'd been asleep, but the sun was going down. I could see little streaks of purple and yellow from the gaps in my curtains. "How long have I been out?"

"About three hours. Not long at all."

Elliot had turned his attention back to the blank television. Apparently, I wasn't the only one who was annoyed. His shoulders were tense and the look on his face became unreadable. Now it was my turn to ask.

"Ok, Elliot. What gives?"

"Cyrus is refusing to leave." Elliot frowned as he tossed the remote onto the side table. "He says he is tied to you now just like the damned mirror is."

"Who – or what – is a Cyrus?" I matched his expression as I swung my legs off the edge of the bed. "Don't tell me it's the guy from the scrying session."

"The very same." Elliot gestured for me to stay put and fixed me a glass of water. "Listen, you don't have to talk to him if you don't want to. He could be a stalker."

"Maybe." I sipped on the water. "Or maybe he knows something about this crazy Carter woman and what she did."

"Do you want me to let him in?" Elliot stuffed his hands in his pockets. "He's waiting outside the door."

I nodded and tried to straighten my messy hair while Elliot had his back turned to me. He opened the door then called out.

"Cyrus. She's awake."

Elliot returned as I sat down in the chair he had vacated. He took his place behind me when the stranger from the conference room entered.

"Ms. McRayne, I failed to introduce myself earlier. My name is Cyrus Alexius, Keeper of the Sibyl."

"I heard him call you Cyrus, so I knew that already."." I tilted my head towards Elliot. "I've also heard you refuse to leave."

"Unfortunately, our fates have been twisted together. It is not a matter of refusal so much as a matter of protocol and necessity. I am not allowed to leave." He stood in front of me with his hands clasped behind his back. "Tell me, how are you feeling?"

"Better." I frowned at him. "This isn't a social call, Cyrus. I want you to take the mirror back."

"I can't do that, Ms. McRayne." The stranger shrugged. "I can only advise you of the abilities you now possess."

"Abilities?" I laughed out loud. I knew it was rude, but I couldn't stop myself. "You have got to be kidding me."

"No, I am not." Cyrus glanced over to Elliot who rewarded him with a snarky smile. "It seems you were correct after all."

"Correct about what?" I glared at my friend. "What did you say about me?"

"Nothing bad." Elliot's smile became the picture of innocence. "I told Cyrus here you didn't put much stock in his...what did you call it? Mumbo-jumbo?"

I narrowed my eyes at Elliot when Cyrus spoke up from his position. I'd almost forgotten he was still in the room.

"What do you know of Apollo's Sibyl?"

"Absolutely nothing." I shook my head. "I'm not really in the mood for a mythology lesson either."

"So you recognize the name from mythology?"

"Yeah. How could I not recognize the name Apollo?" I shrugged. "But I didn't really pay much attention in my literature classes, so I don't know much about him."

"A pity you didn't, Ms. McRayne." Cyrus took his phone out of his pocket, pressing the side of it. "All myths find their foundations in history. You are now a part of that history. It is truly in your best interests to listen to what I have to say."

"I'm sorry." I was trying to be polite, but the laughter was bubbling up again. "Are you saying I've just become some sort of mythical creature?"

"Katherine Carter was no ordinary woman." Cyrus fiddled with his phone for a little longer. When he turned the screen towards me, there was a picture on it of an old woman partially under a cab. "This is a photograph of her body after she passed."

I shook my head as Elliot leaned over my shoulder. "No. That's impossible. She was so..."

"Young?" Cyrus smiled. "Yes, youth and beauty are only two gifts provided by Apollo to his Sibyls. Immortality is a third one."

"Obviously not." I frowned, tapping my fingers against the armrest. "I don't think immortality worked too well for her when she decided to play in traffic."

"Immortality fades just as quickly as beauty when the Sibyl is released from her oath." Cyrus leaned against the armoire the television was on. "Perhaps I should start at the beginning."

"No. I don't want to hear about this anymore." I stood then picked up the mirror from where I'd put it on the nightstand. "Do a spell. Chant a chant. Just make this go away."

"I cannot," Cyrus stayed put. "The only release is to pass the mirror onto a willing participant. At which point, you will cease to exist."

"But I wasn't willing!" I stamped my foot with frustration. "She forced me into this."

"You accepted the mirror." Cyrus's expression was one of pity. "You spoke the words just as she asked you to. It was at this point you made your choice."

"Then give it to Elliot." I started to hand the mirror to my friend, who backed away as if I'd threatened him with a knife. "Oh, come on, Elliot. You were the one who wanted to experience the unknown. Take my place."

"He cannot, Ms. McRayne." Cyrus locked his hands together as if I tried to force the mirror onto him instead of Elliot. "The Sibyl must be a woman. The Sibyl must be you."

"You are sounding awfully sexist right now." I frowned as I looked between the two of them. "So what am I supposed to do? Find another girl crazy enough to take my place?"

"It is an option, yes." Cyrus nodded. "But remember, please, to do so will also be your suicide."

"Suicide?" I felt as if there were a set of invisible chains tightening around me the more he talked. I didn't like it one bit. "Are you serious?"

"Deadly." He smiled at his little joke. "So you do have another choice after all, Ms. McRayne. You can be the Sibyl or find a new one, then die to release yourself."

"That's not much of a choice."

"It's not meant to be." Cyrus pushed off of the armoire. "Are you ready to listen?"

"We're listening." Elliot spoke up from behind me. When I turned towards him, he shrugged. "We need to know, Eva. I saw how you were when Carter gave you the mirror. I saw how you panicked when you looked in the column. Besides, you were talking in your sleep."

"I don't talk in my sleep." I snapped, but I had good reason to. This was a lot for me to take in and I hadn't even heard the full story yet.

"You did today." Elliot leaned over the chair, snagged my hand to pull me back down into my seat. "If we are going to find a way to break this Sibyl thing, we have to hear Cyrus out."

"Fine." I glared at Elliot and then Cyrus. "I'll listen. But only if you can give me a way out that doesn't involve suicide."

"There is no other way out." Cyrus tucked his phone back into his jacket pocket. "This is a long tale, Ms. McRayne. You may as well get comfortable."

"I'm fine." I crossed my arms over my chest. "I don't care about the history. I don't care about any tragedies or lost love affairs. Tell me what I need to know."

FIVE

I SUPPOSED nothing Cyrus could say should have surprised me. I mean, come on. I'd just survived the first day of a convention filled with weirdoes and con artists. I'd been attacked by a woman who committed suicide right after my encounter with her. And I'd hit my head hard enough to think I was seeing her ghost in a mirror. I'd changed my explanation in the half hour Elliot and Cyrus had been with me.

After all, who wants to admit they've had a psychotic breakdown? Especially given my own personal history with them.

My explanation made sense. It was rational. I'd hit my head. The fact some strange man was in my hotel room trying to convince me I had been given some sort of mythical abilities was the insane part. Cyrus started to pace across the room as he began.

"Sibyls are known as the messengers of the dead since that is their primary focus. Apollo is the god who grants them their gifts of immortality, beauty, as well as the ability to see and speak to spirits."

"Impossible." I interrupted him. "Ghosts, spirits, vampires – it's all a lie to sell movie tickets. You should be old enough to know this by now."

"Ah, but you have already been exposed to our world." Cyrus smiled. "Twice today. The first was the image in Carter's mirror. Apollo did speak to you, did he not? He has a tendency to be dramatic. Then Carter herself appeared to you. I was behind you the entire time, Ms. McRayne. I can see the spirits just as you can. Don't deny it."

"I," I paused long enough to get a sip of water. I needed to get my story straight. My thoughts were all jumbled. "I was delusional. It happens, you know, after you hit your head."

"True, but you said it yourself. Your fall was not so bad it would warrant hallucinations." Cyrus stopped pacing. "Shall I continue?"

"Why not?" I mumbled. Elliot squeezed my shoulder to let me know he was still there. "You're going to anyway. Who am I to stop you?"

"During the ancient times, Apollo was known for his conquests with women." Cyrus smiled as if remembering something. "Those who could afford to do so would lock up their daughters for fear the god would take notice of their beauty. Those who couldn't would leave offerings for him on his altars or pay his priests to ensure the god was blind to them. Yet, Apollo was still able to find women of his liking."

Cyrus resumed his pacing. I relaxed in my chair as I waited for him to continue. Mythology wasn't one of my interests. I liked facts. I could count on data to be reliable.

"The great god came across a beauty picking herbs in the woods of Cumae. As the account goes, she refused him. Day after day he would return to find her in the forest. Finally, he cornered her by a small lake and begged to have her. The maiden, flattered by the words of love from the god, set her basket down upon the sand. When she stood, she held a large mound of sand with both palms and told him she would grant him his wish if he would grant her one in return."

Cyrus stopped long enough to make sure I was paying attention. I was, but just barely. His voice was soft. Soothing. He was making me very sleepy.

"Of course, Apollo jumped on the opportunity. He promised her anything she desired. So she wished to live for as many years as there were grains of sand on the earth. It was done. With a single snap of his fingers, Apollo granted the girl her wish. As he began to woo the girl, she began to scream. A soldier – a hero we presume – came out of the woods to confront the girl's attacker. Apollo killed him but left the maiden alive. He never returned to her."

"Sounds like the typical myth." Elliot shifted to sit on my armchair. "What does this have to do with Eva?"

"Because this maiden was the first Sibyl." Cyrus gestured towards the mirror. "Apollo had been tricked by the beauty. She was granted her wish but denied him his own. The girl was granted beauty. Immortality, since the grains of sand covering the earth cannot be counted. As she lived, those who resided in Cumae became suspicious. Children not yet conceived on the day her wish was granted aged and died. The beauty was banished from the village by those frightened by her lack of aging. They called her a monster. Many believed her to be a witch in league with Hades himself."

"So what happened to her?" I tried to hide my yawn, but it was hard. "Where did she go?"

"The only place she could. The girl hid out in the forests of Cumae. She found solace in the nature around her. The years began to pass. When she felt it was safe, the girl would return to the lake where Apollo granted her wish with only her reflection for companionship. It was during one of these trips Persephone took notice of the maiden and pitied her. The Queen of the Underworld convinced Hades to give the girl the ability to speak with the dead. When the maiden returned, she began to see faces of her deceased relatives and friends in the water. They spoke with her about their memories. The girl was grateful. She returned daily to the lakeside to visit with her loved ones until she was spotted by a passing merchant who was taking a shortcut through her woods."

"Again, what does this have to do with me?" I curled my legs beneath me. "And at what part do you tell me why you've decided you're my - what did you call it? My keeper?"

"It was not my decision," Cyrus looked annoyed with my

interruption. "And yes. That is my official title. The Keeper of the Sibyl. But I will shorten my tale. I can see you are getting tired."

"We're all tired." Elliot patted my hand. "So if you can wrap this up, we'd appreciate it."

"Indeed." Cyrus moved across the room to look out the window. "Word got out about the mysterious prophetess inhabiting the woods in Cumae. Her story was floated through the highest circles and people began to flock to her in earnest. They believed she could contact their loved ones for them. The maiden could, and often did for a price. Her story became twisted as generations came and went. The girl began to truly give prophecies to those who visited her. Her wealth grew. But so too did those who dedicated themselves to the service of Apollo."

Cyrus turned back around to face us.

"Apollo was thrilled by his newfound resurgence with the people of Greece. He rewarded the girl in two ways. First, he gave her a golden mirror so she would not have to travel to the lake anymore. More importantly, he gave her a way to die. The girl had lived for centuries. Everyone she had ever loved had passed into the Underworld long before. Despite her wealth and visitors, the maiden longed to join her family in spirit. This was the chant you recited earlier this afternoon. It has been passed down from Sibyl to Sibyl since this time."

"So let me get this straight." I stood and crossed the room to stand in front of him. "You are telling me this Carter woman was a prophetess. She could speak with the dead. She could live forever. Yet she chose to pass it onto me? I don't get it."

"Forever is a very long time, Ms. McRayne." Cyrus smiled sadly. "I've been by Katherine Carter's side since she took the mirror from the fifth Sibyl during a Spiritualist session in 1832. The world she knew, and loved, had disappeared long ago. You too will discover the truth in my words someday."

I refused to believe I would be in this position tomorrow, much less a hundred years from now. "Which reminds me. You still haven't gone into your part in this little tale."

"I am assigned to the Sibyl. It is my duty to Apollo. My service, if you will." Cyrus stuffed his hands into the pockets of his jacket. "Where you go, so too do I. Power is a dangerous possession. You will be in danger from vengeful spirits who wish to return to the living world. You will need guidance to control them."

"Ok. I'm done." I stormed around Cyrus to the bathroom. "I'm going to show you once and for all I'm not the girl you think I am."

"I would advise against any impulsive actions." Cyrus was staring at me so hard, I could feel his eyes in the back of my head. "There are a great many precautions we must take for you."

"Precautions." I turned to face him. "What sort of precautions?"

"You must not look into any reflective surface until you have created your door to keep them out. The spirits of the Underworld are more than willing to use your powers against you. They can – and they will – pull you into their realm."

"Oh, now you're just being ridiculous." I opened the door and stepped inside, more than ready to make my point. "Glass is glass. It's solid. You can't be pulled through it."

The bathroom attached to my room wasn't massive, but it held a floor to ceiling mirror. I stopped in front of it and studied my reflection. Elliot was right. My eyes had become a bright gold color, which contrasted nicely with the dark rings underneath them.

"See?" I pointed to myself. "Just like I told you. All I see is myself."

I started to come up with some snide comment about how his mythology was mistaken. Until my hearing faded out. I could hear nothing except the whispering from my dreams. I turned to face the mirror just as my image faded and the scene before me changed.

A wild woman was sitting on a rock in the dark, muttering to the object in her hands. Even from here, I could see it was the mirror that now rested on my dresser. Her brown head jerked up the moment the fuzzy edges around the image became solid.

She was pretty, but nothing spectacular. Her nose was longer, and her cheekbones were gaunt. The woman looked as if she hadn't eaten in weeks.

"You must be the one. Apollo's newest victim." The woman smiled at me. "Eva, is it?"

Every fiber in my being was screaming to run away. I even tried to take a step backwards but ended up going closer instead. "Who are you?"

"Delphine, first Sibyl of Apollo. Messenger for the dead. Or at least, I was." The woman moved closer to the glass. "You are not afraid?"

I wanted to be afraid. I needed to be afraid. But I wasn't. I felt nothing but a sense of peace overwhelming any common sense I had left.

I shook my head.

The woman's grin widened. "Then take my hand, child. Join me here and all of your questions will be answered."

I reached for the glass when a loud commotion broke through my sense of peace. I felt someone wrap their arm around my waist then jerk me away from the glass. I stumbled and fell flat on my back for the second time that day.

My sense of peace was destroyed.

"Cover the mirror!"

I heard male voices over me, but I couldn't make out all that they were saying. Their words were muffled. Distant. It was as if I was underwater and they most definitely were not. The longer I stayed still, the more I could hear the commotion around me. Finally, when the sounds around me quieted, I opened my eyes.

I was surprised to find Cyrus on top of me. I looked to him then to the mirror, but it was too late. It was covered by the standard hotel comforter from my bed.

The woman and the peace she brought with her were gone.

"It would be in your best interest to get off of her." Elliot was standing by the door, his voice sounded colder than the tiles I was laying on. "Now."

Cyrus shifted his weight off of me while I tried to explain to Elliot how I'd pulled the man down with me. I couldn't speak. Instead, I sat up to reach for the mirror again.

"No, Ms. McRayne." Cyrus helped me to my feet. "Don't let Delphine take you so easily."

"They," I took a shaky breath as Elliot wrapped his arm around my waist. "Not 'they'. It was a woman. Not the scryer, though. Someone different."

"You asked before why you needed my assistance." Cyrus took his phone out of his pocket. "This is a perfect example. You are weak and unknowledgeable."

"Right." I drew a breath. "If I play along with this, does that mean you will be by my side indefinitely?"

"Yes." Cyrus smirked. "You won't even know I'm here. I'll be like a ghost to you. I've had centuries to perfect my line of work, after all."

"I doubt it." I barely managed to withhold the temptation to stomp my foot again. "So I'll never be alone? Or have any privacy?"

"You will. I will fade into the background and act as your shadow."

"Alright." I raised my hands in defeat. "You can help me, but only for as long as I deem necessary. Then you're out of here. Understood?"

Cyrus didn't answer. He tucked his phone back into his pocket and bowed his head in our direction before speaking.

"I will be just outside your door for the time being. I'm certain the two of you have much to discuss."

Cyrus slipped out of the bathroom before Elliot stormed out into my suite. I followed him only when I heard him pick up the phone by my bed. His voice was surprisingly normal given what had just happened.

"Front desk? Great. Can you send security up to Room 4632? There is a man outside my friend's door who is refusing to leave."

"Elliot," I hissed between my teeth. "What are you doing?"

"Yes. He's bulky, wearing a cheap suit. Black hair. Bad scar on his face. You can't miss him."

Elliot hung up the phone and smiled. "No worries, Eva. Security will have him out of here in no time."

I crossed my arms over my chest. "Did you just report Cyrus to security?"

"Yeah." Elliot stuffed his hands in his pockets. "I think you were right. He seems a little too crazy for me."

"This coming from the man who – not twelve hours ago – was touting up the best lightening and camera lenses to catch ghosts on film?"

"This is serious, Eva." Elliot closed the distance between us and took hold of my hands. "You didn't see how quick he jumped on you in the bathroom. That guy is trying to get something from you."

"What?" I frowned as I remembered the look on Elliot's face when Cyrus had fallen on me. "What could I possibly have that a man like that would want?"

"You're twenty-two years old. How in the hell are you so naïve?" Eli's blue eyes narrowed as he studied my face. "Men like that are dangerous, Eva. They prey on young women."

"Elliot," I spoke my words carefully. "You have nothing to worry about. Cyrus doesn't seem dangerous to me. I don't think he is going to hurt me. I think that he was telling the truth."

"Oh, come on." Elliot moved across the room and picked something up off my dresser. When he returned to me, he handed me my conference identification badge. "Have you looked at this?"

"Yeah. It has my name on it. So?"

"So it also says 'Theia Productions'." Elliot placed his hands on each one of my arms. "I think this Cyrus guy noticed that when you were out cold earlier. Even if he's not after you for your looks, he could be trying to use you to get into the entertainment industry."

"I can't believe I'm saying this." I looked up and waited for Elliot to make eye contact with me. "I trust him. I am convinced he wants to help me."

"You don't know how this works, Eva. I do." Elliot shook his head. "You can't trust people like Cyrus."

"I think I can." I shifted out of Elliot's grip. "He hasn't said anything about the show and neither have we. To be fair, the print on this badge is pretty small. It's possible he didn't even read it."

"Why?" Elliot threw up his hands in frustration. "Why are you so willing to believe him?"

"Because I've seen the ghosts in the mirrors," I paused at the sound of knocking at my door. "Listen, we'll talk about this later."

Elliot nodded as he moved across the room to open the door. "Yes?"

"Good evening, sir. Ms. McRayne, please."

I came up behind Elliot who stepped aside just enough for the security guard to see me. "I'm Eva McRayne."

"Ms. McRayne, I wanted to inform you we found no one out of the ordinary outside of your rooms."

"No one?" Elliot frowned. "But this guy swore he was going to stay outside of my friend's room. Have you checked the entire floor?"

"I've checked everywhere, sir." The stocky guard raised his hand to silence Elliot's protests. "There are only conference guests and employees on this floor."

"Thank you." I placed my hand on Elliot's chest to push him back into the room. "We appreciate your help."

The guard mumbled as he disappeared down the hallway. I started to close the door when I heard a soft laughter off to my right.

Cyrus was leaning against the doorframe. "I don't believe your companion cares for me very much."

"It's not you per say," I glanced over to see Elliot falling into the chair I'd vacated earlier. "He's very protective."

"Which is good." Cyrus nodded. "You will need all the help you can get, Ms. McRayne. If you listen to nothing else I tell you, please remember this. Do not get too close to anyone. It never ends well when they have to leave you."

"Why?" I felt stupid asking such a simple question, but I needed answers. And this was the only person who seemed interested in giving them to me. "Why me?"

"Fate? Destiny? You were in the wrong place at the wrong time? You've become intimately acquainted with death through two events in your life?" Cyrus shrugged. "There is no rhyme or reason to how the Fates work. It is best to just follow their plan without question. Otherwise, nothing but suffering will follow you for the rest of your days."

"Eva, who are you talking to?"

I was staring at the door across the hall when Elliot's voice broke through my thoughts. I whipped around to refute Cyrus, but he was nowhere to be seen.

August 27th

Something strange happened to me today. Something outside the realm of rational thought. Perhaps, I have actually lost my mind. Or more likely, it was already broken by the time we arrived at Paracon and I met a scryer who truly introduced me to the realm of the paranormal. A realm even more disturbing than the rituals my mother used to do.

You see, I am a believer in all things that go bump in the night, despite what I say aloud. I am frightened that my two week stay at UGA's psych ward would be extended indefinitely if I begin to speak with spirits or spout out that the polished and pristine Janet McRayne conducts dark magick in the attic of her Sullivan's Island mansion. Of course, rumors of her witchcraft were always prevalent around Halloween so maybe my revelations wouldn't be brushed aside so quickly.

I'm getting off topic. I wanted to use this entry to speak on my madness. Except, it wasn't madness. I saw two different spirits at two different times in two different mirrors. This was, of course, after I was told by one Cyrus Alexuis that I had been passed on the abilities of the Sibyl.

I can't put this on paper. It could be used against me. But there is no one else I can speak to. Even Elliot, who embraces all things strange and unusual, believes that Cyrus appeared with this story to get involved with Theia Productions. Elliot called me naive. He said Cyrus only wanted to use me.
But, if I'm honest, isn't Elliot using me as well for Grave Messages? And aren't I letting him use me in exchange for a career?

Or maybe, I am hoping that what I've seen is real. Maybe, I am hoping for something to validate my insanity. What better way to convince myself that I'm not crazy by having crazy things happen in reality?

SIX

"RISE AND SHINE, DOLL!"

I woke up confused until I realized where I was. We were still in New York. I was still sleeping in a strange bed. The drinks I'd shared with Elliot the night before to forget about Katherine Carter and Cyrus had done nothing to stop the whispers in my dreams. So I was surprised to see Elliot come into my room with a stack of thick folders in his hands as my alarm clock was starting to go off.

"No, it's too early." I smacked at the alarm then buried my face into my pillows. "Go away."

"It's just past seven." Elliot sat on the bed, swinging his legs up with the folders in his lap. "We have work to do."

"Elliot, you can't just burst into my room anytime you want to." I grumbled loud enough for him to hear me despite the pillows. "I could be naked."

"You don't have anything I haven't seen before." He was flipping through the folders until he stopped as if he was deep in thought. "Or do you?"

Elliot chose that exact moment to pounce on me, tickling my sides until I was gasping for air.

"Ok! Ok, I'm awake!"

When he stopped, I opened my eyes to see his face was inches away from my own. I was still trying to catch my breath as Elliot brushed his nose against mine.

Ok. That was weird. Maybe he was still drunk or something.

I heard a knock on the door as my friend sat up. He ignored the knocking.

"We don't have to go today. Let's take the day off. Be tourists for a while."

"Can we do that? I thought Connor wanted us to go to everything we could to spread the word."

I sat up when Cyrus appeared across the room. He bowed his head in greeting.

"Ok. I don't know why y'all think my room has an open-door policy, but this is ridiculous." I glowered at both men. "And Cyrus? The appearing out of nowhere trick? That's creepy. Don't do that."

The keeper shrugged. "You didn't answer your door. I wanted to make sure all was well."

"You gotta give me more than two seconds." I grumbled. "Next time you do that, I'm kicking you in the knee."

"We should begin your training this morning."

"No go, G.I. Joe." I shook my head as Elliot glowered beside me. "We are working this morning. I'll play with you later."

"Ms. McRayne..."

"Don't you 'Ms. McRayne' me." I snorted. "If you're going to be in here, fine. But I need to get stuff done."

I grabbed one of the folders Elliot had abandoned in his quest to tickle me breathless.

"What's all this?" I thumbed through the pages. There were pictures. Statements. I stopped when I came across what appeared to be a police report and whistled. "This is a lot of work."

"I know. David and the guys in Research have been scouting for locations for us to film the first season. I had them fax everything they had here for us to go through today."

I nodded. "And these are our choices?"

"Yeah."

We began shifting through the papers together, oblivious of the conference going on below us. I was sure Elliot planned this so I wouldn't have to go downstairs. He had room service deliver us breakfast. He talked non-stop about the abandoned places in the files spread out before us. When I glanced at the clock and realized I hadn't gotten out of bed after being awake for over three hours, I threw up my hands in surrender.

"Enough already." I interrupted him as he was chatting about the souls of mental patients. "I have to take a shower."

"There's no rush." Elliot tucked the papers he had in his hand back into the folder. "I was serious when I said we should be tourists for the day since you've never been to New York before."

"And I was serious when I asked if we should skip it. We can still make a majority of the sessions if we hurry."

"I called Connor this morning and told him what happened. Fortunately, he agreed with me when I said it was a bad idea for you to go." Elliot handed me another folder. "In fact, he gave me two choices. We can either return home for a few days or leave straight from here to head out to our first location."

"So we're not going back downstairs at all?"

I was skeptical. After all, Elliot loved to be surrounded by nut jobs. But my friend was serious.

"Not to the conference if that's what you mean." Elliot tossed the folder aside. "What would you like to do today?"

"I'll decide after my shower."

I was ecstatic over the opportunity to have my first free day since this whole mess started. I didn't give him a chance to respond. Instead, I rushed into the bathroom and shut the door behind me. I stopped only once to close my eyes as I passed the large mirror. It was still covered up by the huge comforter, so there was no way I could have seen anything, but I wasn't going to risk it.

I was in the shower longer than I needed to be, but without the worries of being late to one appointment or another, I used the time spent under the water to relax. Or at least, I tried to. Cyrus' words from last night kept creeping back into my thoughts like a bad dream. If what he said was true, I was immortal. I had been given a gift by the gods. I had powers no woman should possess. Granted, those powers were to talk to the dead, but still.

As I replayed the conversation from the night before, questions filtered through that I hadn't considered. Would I never see my own reflection again? Would I really outlive everyone I'd ever known, and would come to know? I laughed out loud at the thought of it. Impossible. Elliot was right about one thing. Cyrus knew how to pull me in. He was starting to make me believe things I would have dismissed as fantasy yesterday.

No, that's not right. I wanted to dismiss his words as fantasy, yet it was harder than I realized. I'd seen the images that made me believe I had another psychotic break down. I was still hearing the whispers and having strange dreams.

The only fact I could cling to right now was that the whole situation was spiraling out of control faster than I could get a handle on it.

I tried to go back to my original defense of hitting my head or being overwhelmed by all the changes which had occurred in my life over the past few weeks. I tried to talk myself out of believing what I saw in the mirrors yesterday were real. I even tried to convince myself that insanity was contagious. After being surrounded by the nuts dressed as aliens and zombies all day, Katherine Carter had pushed me over the edge.

Yet, even as I was telling myself to calm down and stop being stupid, I realized my thoughts were hollow. I knew what I saw. I knew what I felt when I looked into the mirror the night before. For the first time in my life, I had been at peace. I was happy.

That scared me. How easy would it be for me to be influenced by these things?

I stepped out of the shower and came face to face with the large, covered mirror when a new fear pierced through my heart.

How in the world was I going to make myself presentable without being able to see what I'm doing?

I jumped at the sound of a knock on the door. I snagged a thick white towel and wrapped it around me before I called out. "I'm nowhere near done, Elliot! You might as well get comfortable."

"Ms. McRayne, it is Cyrus."

I felt my heart sink at the sound of his voice. If he was going to be my shadow, it appeared we would have to set some boundaries. Ones I wasn't sure Cyrus would be too eager to agree to.

I didn't answer until I'd thrown on a bathrobe and wrapped my hair in the aforementioned towel. Then I opened the door to face the stranger who had forced himself into my life only yesterday. I was pleased to see a faint blush spread across his flawless face as he noted my attire. I was even more pleased when he had the graciousness to look away.

"What?" I wanted to sound stern, but my voice cracked. I swallowed and tried again. "What is it, Cyrus?"

"I need to speak with you immediately about this show you are doing." He reached in his pocket and pulled out his ever-present cell phone. "After all that has transpired, I feel it would be in your best interest if you dropped out of the production all together."

For once, I was at a loss for words. Elliot had mentioned something last night about how this guy might use me to get into the entertainment business. Instead, Cyrus was trying to pull me out of it. He opened his mouth to say more but stayed quiet when I raised my hand. I responded with the first words which came to mind. I couldn't stop myself.

I didn't even try.

"Are you insane?" I pushed my way past him to the closet. "You have some nerve, buddy."

"Ms. McRayne, it is far too dangerous. You must listen to me."

"No." I was snatching my clothes off the hangers so fast, the wooden bars clunked together. "You listen to me."

I stormed past him, tossing the jeans and t-shirt on the bed before I turned to face him. "Who do you think you are, Cyrus? We met less than twenty-four hours ago, and you are already trying to tell me what to do with my life?"

"It is for your own protection."

"I don't care what your reasoning is." I glared at him as I closed the distance between us and jabbed his chest with my finger. "You have no right to tell me who I am or what I am going to be. Sibyl or no. Are we clear on that?"

"As crystal." Cyrus' dark eyes flashed as he returned my glare. "You cannot seriously be considering putting yourself into situations where you will be forced to confront spirits on a regular basis. I told you last night you were inexperienced and unknowledgeable."

"I heard you last night, so you hear me now." I crossed my arms over my chest. "I am doing this show. I have to do it. I signed a very ironclad contract. I refuse to go back on my word."

I decided to return to the bathroom before he could respond. I grabbed up my clothes and headed in that direction when his next words stopped me in my tracks.

"What happens if you become someone else, Eva?" Cyrus' voice was soft. "Sibyls have been known to become possessed by the spirits they are surrounded by. Not all spirits are simple grandmothers wishing to contact their loved ones. Most are filled with hate. More than most are jealous of the living. You could very easily attack the ones you care for the most. Are you willing to take that chance?"

I could feel the heat rising in my cheeks as I faced him again. "I'm not a violent person. No matter how crazy I seem right now, talking to you about ghosts and all. I won't go around attacking people."

"But the spirits might. Some of them can be very violent." Cyrus gave me a sad smile as he clasped his hands behind his back. "You must make the time to train with me. Learn to control yourself if you insist on this nonsense."

"It's not nonsense." I could hear my own disbelief as I spoke the words. "It's important."

"To Mr. Lancaster, certainly. Not to you."

"Fine." I huffed. "Then I suggest you do your job and teach me what I need to know. When do you want to start this training of yours?"

"This afternoon. I'd prefer immediately, but you've made other plans."

"I have." I glanced at the clock on the bedside table. It was already after ten. "Let's meet tonight. I'm sure you'll be around."

"Indeed." He bowed his head towards me. "I'll be close by if you need anything. Please remember. No mirrors. No psychics. Nothing that could attract the spirits to you. Understood?"

"Not really." I looped my arms together beneath the pile of clothes I was still holding. "It doesn't matter. I'll behave. I don't want a repeat of what happened yesterday when I'm out on the streets of New York. I don't need the general public to know I'm crazy just yet. I'll let the show do it for me."

I earned a small smile from Cyrus with my words. One final bow and he was gone. I wondered where the hell Elliot had gotten off to before I started getting ready. Just when I finished brushing out my hair, I heard another knock on the door.

"Cyrus, I've already told you. I'm going to," I jerked open the door and felt the fire sizzle out of my voice when I saw Elliot's raised eyebrow. I finished anyway. "Behave."

"When have you ever behaved, doll?" My friend gave me a thin smile as he reached for my hand. "Ready?"

"As I'll ever be." I let Elliot take my hand. "Let's get out of here."

"Any ideas of what you want to do?" Elliot led me down the hallway towards the elevator. "General sightseeing or shopping?"

"I want to do exactly the opposite of everything we've been doing the past two weeks." I tightened my grip on his hand. "I want to forget everything that has happened, and not think about the things that could happen in the future. Can we handle it?"

Elliot chuckled as he pressed the button on the elevator. "We'll certainly try, Eva. We can try."

SEVEN

MY DAY with Elliot was a fantastic blur of all the cheesy things tourists do in NewYork City. We went to every skyscraper, rode on the ferry, and despite my adamant refusals to do anything I had been forced to do in L.A., Elliot talked me into a little shopping. We stayed on our feet until the sun began to set over the Hudson River and Elliot began to whine about dying of starvation. So I tagged along as he found a small restaurant close to the hotel.

I fell into the booth with a happy sigh as I tossed my bags aside. When Elliot settled in across the table, I couldn't wipe the grin off my face. "This has been amazing. Are you sure we can't just do a travel show instead?"

Elliot chuckled as the waitress approached our table. Two drink orders later, he responded. "We are doing a travel show, Eva. Our focus won't be on local landmarks though."

"Yeah, but I like going into places with modern conveniences." I snagged a breadstick from the basket the waitress had left behind. I stared at it then put it on my plate. I couldn't eat that. I knew better. My mother would have thrown a fit if she'd seen carbs in my hand. I shook my head then continued my original line of thought. "Lights and running water are huge bonuses for me."

"I'll bet they are." Elliot shook his head as he browsed the menu. "I thought we were on strict orders not to discuss the show though. Are you changing things up on me, McRayne?"

"I'm not talking about the show per say." I tore the breadstick into pieces then arranged them on the plate. "We've done very well at avoiding it all day. But there is something I need to tell you about."

"What?" Elliot became very interested in the menu before him. "Does this have anything to do with Cyrus being in your room earlier?"

"Yeah." I nodded to the waitress who placed our drinks in front of us. When she bounced away, I responded. "He was still there when I got out of the shower. I thought he had left when you did."

"I had forgotten he was there, to be honest." Elliot's features grew dark as he put the menu down. He clasped his hands over it. I couldn't help but notice how white his knuckles had become. "Are you alright?"

"I'm fine, Eli, really." I took a sip of my tea to clear my throat. "I told you Cyrus isn't out to hurt me. He just wanted to talk."

"I don't trust him, Eva. You shouldn't either." Elliot went back to his menu. After an awkward moment, he sighed. "What did he want?"

I shrugged. "Cyrus doesn't think it's a good idea if I do the show. He said I'd be putting myself in unnecessary danger by being exposed to the spirits in the places we'd be going."

"What did you tell him?"

"I told him to go to hell. I signed a contract. I'm not going to go back on my word because of some freaky woman and her suicide."

"You told him that? In those exact words?" Elliot grinned as the waitress returned. She took our orders and left us alone. "No wonder he told you to behave."

"Well, not those exact words." I admitted. "Pretty close, though. Elliot, I know perfectly well what I'm getting into by doing the show. Granted, I don't know how the whole Sibyl thing will affect it. Cyrus did say I can be trained to protect myself at our locations. In fact, I'm supposed to meet with him when we get back to start my first lesson."

"Tonight?" Elliot shook his head. "Not by yourself you're not. I'll come with you."

"You can if you want." I leaned forward to put my chin in my hand. "I'm probably going to skip it though. We haven't even started talking about how we are going to do the show. We need to figure out the layout. Are we going to write dialogue at all?"

"I am pretty eager to get started." Elliot admitted. "Eva, there's something else we need to talk about first. Something more important than *Grave*."

I felt my heart drop as I remembered how Elliot had questioned me last night. I knew he was curious. I knew he wanted to know what made me believe the Sibyl story.

I didn't want to talk about it yet. The waitress picked that precise moment to trounce on over, and I was grateful for the interruption. The delay wasn't long enough. As soon as Elliot's order was put down on the table, Elliot continued.

"What do you really think about this Sibyl story? Do you believe what Cyrus has been telling you?"

I remained silent. Elliot didn't rush me. He could be very patient when it meant the outcome would be just what he wanted it to be. In this case, he wanted me to talk. I'll admit it. I stalled by playing with the napkins and silverware.

When the silence between us became too much, I picked up my fork and started tapping it against the table.

"I don't think I have a choice in the matter. I have to believe him. I saw something yesterday. To be honest, I have experienced several things I cannot explain."

My words got stuck in my throat. I swallowed them down before starting over by telling him about the woman I'd seen the night before and how I wanted so desperately to join her. I told him not just about seeing Kathy Carter. I told him what she said to me as well. To his credit, Elliot just listened. He didn't interrupt me or ask me any stupid questions. Elliot's only response was to push his plate aside and lean forward.

"When we get home, you should see a doctor to make sure you really didn't hurt yourself when you fell." Elliot raised his hand to shush me. “Listen, I get it. You’re stubborn and hardheaded. I don’t care. You need to be checked out. Especially after-"

“It’ll only be a waste of time.” I interrupted him as I batted his hand down. “There’s no point in zigzagging back and forth across the country when we can just leave from here.”

I had no intentions of seeing a doctor. I could do just fine without them hearing my story then sneaking off to sign my commitment papers. Elliot looked as if he wanted to argue, but he nodded instead.

“Then I guess we need to decide on where we’re going.” Elliot pulled his plate back to its spot in front of him. “So what’ll it be? Battleground? Mental hospital? Creepy abandoned house with a gory background?”

“No battlegrounds. Not yet.” I ignored the food. It looked delicious. It smelled even better. “I don’t know much about ghosts, but common sense should tell you that being outside is going to contaminate any evidence we get.”

“Makes sense to me," Elliot was digging into his plate of food like a man deprived. I almost felt sorry for him. “You know more about ghost hunting than you think you do.”

“I know enough to make fun of you about it.” I wrinkled my nose at him. “And no mental wards either. Connor said we had to find a way to make ourselves stand out. A mental hospital is too stereotypical.”

Elliot gave me a huge grin for the first time since we’d sat down to dinner. “That’s my girl. Come on. Hurry up and eat that breadstick so we can get back to the hotel. Speaking of Connor, I have to call him. He will want to know what our plans are going to be. Then we’ll work on the show to figure out just where we want to end up.”

We walked back to the hotel and stopped to admire the street sights New York City had to offer. I found myself stalling. Cyrus would be waiting for me. As we approached my door, I stopped long enough to wonder about him. What was he? How did he do his little vanishing and reappearing act? And if he was immortal, did he have to sleep? Did I have to sleep?

Maybe those training sessions would come in handy after all.

"Let me throw my bags down and grab the folders. I'll be right there." I pulled out my keycard from my back pocket as Elliot stopped at the door next to mine. He offered me a small salute then disappeared inside. As I opened my door, I found myself listening for the strange whispers I'd heard in my dreams. I was greeted by a glorious silence.

Today had been exactly what I'd needed. Aside from our little chat over dinner, we had managed to keep our conversation light. I reached over to flip on the lamp sitting on the table by the door when a voice broke through the shadows.

"Have a nice time, Ms. McRayne?"

Cyrus. I knew he would be here. Yet why he was waiting in the dark was anyone's guess.

"Damn it." I threw my purse towards the sound of his voice. "Why are you so creepy?"

"Creepy?" My new companion flipped on the switch to the lamp for me. His handsome face was twisted into a smile of amusement. "I've been called many, many things over the centuries. I must admit, creepy isn't one of them."

"Yeah, well, it fits you." I huffed as I crossed the room to throw my bags in the closet. "You scared me to death."

"Hardly." Cyrus leaned back against the entrance door as he watched me gather my folders from the morning session. "Leaving so soon?"

"Yes. I have work to do." I went to the door he was blocking and waited for him to move. When he didn't, I gestured towards it with my folders. "Can you move? These things are really heavy."

"No. You are correct on one matter, Ms. McRayne. You have an astronomical amount of work to do." Cyrus pointed at the bundle in my hands. "But I'm afraid your little project is not on the itinerary. We need to start your training."

"If I'm now immortal, then I have the rest of my existence for your training." I shifted the weight of the folders to my arms.

"Besides, we've been over this. You do not get to tell me what to do."

"I am not telling you what to do, my dear." Cyrus took the stack from my hands. "I am telling you what you need to do to survive. The first thing is how to control the spirits so you can only contact them when you want to. This will cut down any threat your ghost hunting expeditions will cause."

"You can do that?" I shook out my arms. I wasn't kidding when I said those folders were heavy. "I mean, I can choose when and where these visions will occur?"

"Yes, as well as who you contact." Cyrus smiled. "But I will need your undivided attention. Tell Elliot you will discuss the locations tomorrow. I will take a look at them myself and aid you in choosing the safest one for you."

I started to tell this strange man to go to hell, but the words died in my throat. I knew I couldn't live my life the way I had today; avoiding every mirror or reflective surface. I needed to know how to control myself if I were ever to function in society again. I picked up the phone.

I was right. Elliot wasn't happy when I cancelled on him. I begged exhaustion and promised him we would catch everything up the next morning.

"There. My plans are officially cancelled. Are you happy now?" I flopped down on the edge of my bed as I disconnected the call. "You know, for someone who is supposed to only act like a shadow, you are killing my social life."

"What is this social life you speak of?" Cyrus teased as he pulled a chair up to sit across from me. "I'm assuming it is something important."

I scoffed before I noticed he had the hateful mirror in his hands. "What are you doing with that?"

"We are going to begin your training." Cyrus had the mirror face down. I could see the intricate carvings on the back of it. For the first time I noticed the lines formed the face of a woman. She was screaming.

"You must realize, Ms. McRayne, the veil works much like a

door. It can be opened and closed very easily." Cyrus wrapped my hand around the mirror's handle. "I want you to envision a mirror that is trapped behind a door. Imagine yourself being able to close this door at your whim. Three Sibyls before you added a lock to it for which only they had the key."

"I'm going to imagine a door." I spoke the words as if I were talking to a toddler. "That's it? Your extensive training, which you have been nagging me about for two days now, is to imagine a damn door?"

"No, this is not all. But this is the most important. You must realize the power your mind has over the paranormal. You – and you alone – must be able to use this power to block them out." Cyrus held up his hand to hush me as I started to speak. I closed my mouth as he continued. "Yet just as a door can be closed and locked, so too can you open it. When you are ready, you can call forth spirits from the veil."

"So if I close my eyes and wish for all of this to go away, will that work too?" I leaned forward. "After all, if I can create the doorway, then I should be able to stop this all together."

"I am afraid it is not that simple." Cyrus leaned back in his chair to create more distance between us. "Now do as I say. Close your eyes. Create your doorway."

I let out an exaggerated sigh as I closed my eyes.

"Now focus."

"I'm focusing." I grumbled. It wasn't long before a door appeared in my mind. Unfortunately, it wasn't some grand entrance like the Charleston houses I grew up around. The only door I could conjure up was the little wooden one from my studio apartment back in Georgia. I used this image as a base, adding not just a lock as Cyrus suggested. I added iron bars. I wrapped chains around it. By the time I was finished, my gateway to the afterlife could have protected the treasures at Fort Knox.

"You must be pleased." Cyrus spoke and I nodded, keeping my eyes closed. "Then look into the mirror. Apply your door to it."

I flipped the mirror over, confident enough in my own imagination to know this could work. I opened my eyes to see my reflection shimmering in the glass. I gasped as the face of the woman appeared once more. She smiled. I didn't.

"Hurry, Ms. McRayne." Cyrus' words were filled with caution. "Apply the door."

I returned my focus to the woman in the mirror as the whispers grew louder. This time, I didn't back away. I imagined my door slamming shut in the woman's face before me. I laughed out loud as the whispers ceased. I hurried to apply the iron bars and chains as I had done in my mind.

"It worked!" I laughed again as I looked into the mirror. The door was still there, but it was fading. Within moments, it was soon replaced by my own reflection. "Cyrus, it really worked!"

"Yes." The man nodded. "This has proven to be a very successful method for your predecessors."

"What else?" I stood and started pacing the room. "Should I go and do this with every mirror?"

"Yes. Practice this until your mind begins to subconsciously project the image you created on every reflective surface."

"I have to go tell Elliot." I crossed over to the door leading out into the hallway. "He is going to be so relieved."

"Not so soon, Ms. McRayne." Cyrus pressed the mirror back into my hands after I had put it down on the bed. "Keep this mirror with you at all times. Make sure this is the only one you use when making contact."

"Why?" I was confused. "If the door works, and I can shut it at will, why keep things contained to just one mirror?"

"Size." Cyrus shook his head. "If a mirror is large, it becomes a portal large enough for the dead to cross into this realm. When you open the door, you are inviting them to pass through."

"And they can't fit through this?" I waved the mirror at him. "I thought ghosts were wisps. Shadows. They would be able to fit through a keyhole."

"Many prefer to remain as they were in life, but their size can be adjusted as needed." Cyrus stared at me until I looked away. "Lesson two is simply this: keep this mirror on you at all times. Understand?"

"Yeah, okay." I didn't feel the need to tell him I would probably lose the mirror before the week was out. I had a tendency to leave things behind. "I'll do my best to remember."

Cyrus passed by me to stand by the small desk in my room. "Also, you need to learn about the god you now serve. You must study the written works about our history."

I hadn't noticed the pile of books placed on my desk when I had first come into the room, but I noticed them now. There were volumes thicker than my textbooks from UGA. I walked over to them and snagged the first one off the top. Of course, it was a book about crossing over to the other side. The one beneath it? A study on the role death has played in Greek mythology.

"Are you kidding me right now?" I stared at the pile then at the man beside me. "I am not going to read all of these. I don't have the time."

"Ms. McRayne, you are an immortal." Cyrus rewarded my exasperation with a half-smile. "You have nothing but time."

"Tell me more about the immortal part." I tossed the book down and leaned against the desk. "What does that mean exactly?"

"It means exactly what you think it means." Cyrus stuffed his hands in his pockets as he looked down on me. "You won't physically die as long as you are the Sibyl. Your body is now Apollo's vessel. You are considered valuable to him."

"How so?" I tilted my head to the side. "If I am not supposed to use my ability to talk to the dead in public, how does it benefit Apollo?"

"I never said you couldn't use your abilities in public. I simply suggested that you not go out and willingly seek opportunities to put yourself in danger. Ms. Carter would hold séances for her clients and speak at conferences. She used small venues to bring followers to our god."

"Perhaps I could try to make contact on the show." I spoke more to myself than to my protector. "This could be just what we need to stand out."

"My apologies, Ms. McRayne." Cyrus was glowering again. "I don't believe I heard you correctly."

"It's nothing." I waved his moodiness away. "Look, I'm really tired. Can we call it a night?"

"You are starting to look pale. Perhaps it is best if we say our goodbyes." Cyrus grabbed the folders I had forgotten about. "I'll take a look at these and let you know tomorrow morning which will be best."

"Alright."

I was only half paying attention as he left. My mind was racing as I thumbed through the pile of books Cyrus had left behind. Connor and Elliot both insisted we have a gimmick to attract viewers to the show. Could I use this whole Sibyl thing as a gimmick? Could Katherine Carter have given me the one thing needed to make sure the show was a success?

I needed to know more about the spirit world. The truth was, I had stayed away from anything even remotely related to the paranormal as I got older. My experience with Janet and the secrets she kept locked away were enough to make me want no part in the spiritual realm. But now? Now, it was different.

I needed to know the best ways to protect myself and Elliot. If I was going to be cursed, then I would be damned if I didn't use this newfound power to my advantage.

I plopped down in the desk chair with a new determination. I would learn everything I could about the veil and the myths. If the Sibyls were meant to pull in followers to Apollo, then I would be the best.

I always was when I put my mind to something. I had been trained from the cradle to never settle for anything less than perfection in myself.

I started with the thickest book in the lot and skimmed over most of the text. Especially when I came to the part about how the Sibyl was created. Since the story was a repeat of what Cyrus had already told me, I skipped it. I skipped over a lot of the text to be honest. I was having a hard time focusing. So much so that I almost missed the very section I had been looking for. It jumped out at me in the gray mass the sentences had become.

"*Contacting the Golden One.*" I murmured the words out loud, using my finger to underline each sentence as I read. Apparently, the keeper had direct communication with the god at all times in the event something catastrophic happened to the Sibyl. The keeper could request aid and keep Apollo informed on the activities of the Sibyl. There were brief prayers the Sibyl could chant in order to get Apollo's attention, but I wasn't sure if such small tokens would be enough. I needed his blessing to make sure the show was going to be a hit in the midst of all the other paranormal gurus out there.

I pushed the book aside and stood, searching the room. After all, I had been raised in South Carolina. We had our fair share of mystics who told fortunes and cast spells for a living. My own grandmother was a disciple to Hecate, the goddess of witchcraft. She had started teaching spell work to me by the age of three. Then there was my exposure to my mother-

No. I wouldn't think about her now or how close my actions were going to be to something she would have done without a second thought.

I found what I was looking for in the back of the television cabinet. The candle was white and stubby, but it would have to do. I snagged it along with a hotel matchbook and returned to the desk. Once I had cleared off enough room, I set the candle up on top of the golden mirror Cyrus had left behind and lit it.

"Apollo, keeper of the Sun, creator of the Sibyls, aide me in my quest."

I sat down in front of the candle then interlocked my fingers together as I closed my eyes.

"I know nothing about your powers, and only a little more about being your Sibyl. Golden One, grant me the strength to survive this life as your servant. Allow the show to be a success. In return, I promise you the attention you seek. Television is a voice heard throughout the world. Its images speak to millions of people. Let me do this for you. If I am to be your Sibyl, grant me my wish. Let our project be a success."

I closed my eyes then focused on everything which had led up to that very moment. Elliot's first proposal of the show, Katherine Carter thrusting the mirror in my hands; even the horrible spirits I had encountered so far. I saw myself being able to protect myself from them.

I opened my eyes to see the flames glowing brighter. The mirror itself shimmered, but no spirits were coming through. I began to wonder if Apollo had heard me or if I were a fool asking for help from the shadows around me. I couldn't be sure that everything I had experienced had been nothing more than tricks of the light. Perhaps Elliot was right. Perhaps I did need to see a doctor when we got home.

Maybe I needed another stint at the hospital. They could pump me with enough drugs to make me forget about all of this craziness.

I sniffed out the candle as quickly as I could. There was no doctor who could help me. I wasn't a fool. I believed in myself and what I had seen.

I couldn't afford not to.

I must have fallen asleep over the books on the desk because the next thing I knew, I felt myself being lifted up from my chair. Cyrus' whisper woke me up more than his disruption of picking me up.

"Spell work, Little One? You haven't done that in years. Now hush. Let the dead rest when you do."

"What?" I muttered, suddenly all too awake. My keeper was holding me close to his chest with my ear pressed against his shoulder. "What are you talking about?"

"You were talking to them." Cyrus laid me down on the bed. "A habit I am sure you will control in time."

"I don't talk in my sleep." I was going to say more. Refute him. But he simply smiled as he pulled the blankets over me. I felt like a kid being put to bed; safe and warm. I wasn't used to that feeling. Kindness at home had always been followed by something horrible.

Suddenly I was surprised at how much I wanted him to stay. As he nodded his farewell, I reached out to him.

"Stay. Tell me a story."

"A story?" Cyrus froze in mid-bow. "Haven't I told you enough for one night?"

He was joking with me. I could see his half smile in the faint light from the hotel's window. I nodded then snuggled further into my pillow with a yawn.

"Yes. Tell me more about you. If you are going to be by my side indefinitely, I may as well know who you are."

"Indeed." Cyrus pulled up the chair next to my bed and collapsed his long frame into it. "What would you like to know?"

"Anything. I don't care." I was getting sleepy again but I tried to fight it. "How did you come into this life of yours?'

"I was a soldier, Ms. McRayne." Cyrus leaned forward then linked his fingers together in front of him. "A man married to the service of Greece. I breathed the very battles which killed many of my comrades."

He paused as if deciding what he should say next. "I was meant to serve Artemis, goddess of war. I did, for a time. I wore her charms beneath my breastplate. My men chanted her name with every victory and begged her for forgiveness if we failed."

"What changed?" I yawned, harder this time. "I thought the Sibyls were Apollo's creation."

"They are." Cyrus smiled again. "I see you took my words to heart. You truly were reading the books I gave you. Did you learn anything useful?"

"Yeah, and you are changing the subject." I opened one eye to examine his shadow as the light from the window faded. "Go on."

"I told you of the hunter who doomed the first Sibyl of Cumae?"

I nodded.

"That man wasn't a hunter. He was me." Cyrus shook his head. "I was taking a short cut to the camp we had set up outside of town when I heard a woman scream. She was begging not to be harmed. When I came to the tree's edge, I saw them. Apollo is a master at taking the human form. This is how he appeared to me. I took up my sword. Yelled for him to release the poor girl at once or face the wrath of my blade."

"What happened? Did you have to fight a god?" I leaned up on a single elbow. "What was it like?"

He shifted in the chair as if uncomfortable. "Short. Apollo released the girl and turned on me as a lion would his prey. Before I could close half the distance between us, he fired a single arrow from his bow."

"Were you hurt?" I forgot all about my sleepiness as I listened. Cyrus was a master storyteller. "What happened to the girl?"

"Hurt?" Cyrus gestured to the scar which crossed over his face "I died, Little One, after taking an arrow through my eye. My soul had disconnected itself from my body. I was fading into the Underworld when he brought me back."

"Why would he kill you only to bring you back to life?"

"As punishment for interrupting his fun. Apollo cursed me then to always be by the girl's side. As I regained control of myself, he told me quite clearly that since I was so quick to protect the girl in life, then I would do so for all eternity."

"So this is how you became the Keeper to the Sibyl."

"Yes, but she wasn't the Sibyl just yet. When Apollo became pleased with her work, he changed her from the wild woman she had become into a figure who could rival the goddesses themselves."

"This is what I have become, then. A goddess on earth?" I tried to make light of my words, but the teasing in my voice faltered. "I'm going to need a crown or herald of trumpets to announce my presence whenever I walk into a room now."

"In a sense, yes. You are a goddess compared to other humans." Cyrus leaned closer, studying my face as he ignored my joke. "One look at your eyes would convince any man alive of your power."

"Will they ever change back?" I shifted beneath the covers. "Cyrus, will I ever change back?"

"No, I am afraid not." Cyrus shook his head as he stood. "You must rest. I am certain you have a full schedule lined up for tomorrow."

I remembered my promise to Elliot. If all went well, we were going to be leaving New York tomorrow night for parts unknown.

Parts filled to the brim with all the spooky ghosts he could get his hands on.

"Oh, alright." I sat up with a sigh. "I'll go to sleep. But you have got to stop calling me Ms. McRayne. It's going to get annoying in a hundred years or so. Call me Eva."

I was rewarded with another one of his crooked smiles as he faded into the shadows. I couldn't understand the emotion which came over me when I saw it, or why I felt so comforted by his presence, but I wanted Cyrus to stay with me.

I snuggled back into my pillow. How could I explain the connection I felt to Cyrus? As much as I detested the idea of having the strange man following me everywhere, I was starting to feel as if I needed him there. It wasn't because he was easy on the eyes, either. Cyrus knew things I did not. If I were to believe in the spirits I'd seen in the mirror, then I had to believe in what he was trying to teach me. I considered going over to the desk for only a minute before dismissing the idea. These stories had been around forever. They could wait a few more hours.

One thing I did know for certain was Elliot was not going to be happy about my decision. I could count on his displeasure. Arguments which would probably never happen filled my mind. Elliot would tell me I was being brainwashed by the keeper. Or that he had pushed me into too much too soon. I would snap back. It would be an argument for the ages.

Cyrus was right. I needed my sleep if I were going to get through tomorrow.

I woke with the sun the next morning, surprised to find myself alone in my room. I ordered coffee through room service then pulled my journal from my luggage. I snagged a pen from the nightstand next to an abandoned copy of the King James Bible just as my coffee arrived.

I ignored the fruit and toast that had come with my first dose of caffeine for the day. Instead, I doctored my drink with enough sugar and creamer to kill a horse and carried it over to the bed.

I flipped open the journal to a new page and considered what I wanted to focus on. Finally, I decided just to write whatever came to mind.

August 29-

I couldn't have been more than three years old when my mother sat me down in front of a piano for the first time. I had to sit on pillows to reach the keys. And my piano teacher worked the foot pedals. Mrs. Joanna Taylor. Her name still makes me freeze up in terror. Not because of anything she did to me, but because she held a power that she didn't know she possessed.

She would tell my mother if I made a mistake. She would tell my mother everything I did wrong in my lessons with her then give Janet a list of things I needed to work on throughout the week.

"You are the daughter of Olympus," She would snap at me on the trip home. "You will be as perfect as your blood."

I didn't see anything divine about myself. I didn't see anything except a gangly girl who was never good enough. But I knew that I needed my mother. I needed her acceptance. Her pride in me.

I needed her to love me.

So I played the piano until my fingers were bruised. I repeated and perfected the classical pieces under the scathing gaze of Janet McRayne. If I failed to live up to her expectations, she would make my life...difficult. I feared her punishments more than I hated playing piano, so I became the best. I was called a prodigy and played recitals for the social elite. Then, as I grew older, the venues became more elaborate. Concert halls filled with a faceless audience who all clamored backstage to meet me. I was called the Ivory Angel thanks to the piano keys. And I began to wish I was invisible.

The crowds scared me. They smothered and grabbed at me. Janet, of course, adored the attention. She heaped on the praise for her beautiful daughter. A girl who would go far in life.

It's funny, thinking back on this now. I quit playing piano when I turned fifteen. I won't go into the details of Janet's wrath, but in the end, I won. I was determined to run as far away from her vision as I possibly could. And yet? Here I am. About to film my first episode of a television show.

Perhaps, I didn't run fast enough. Perhaps, I never could.

EIGHT

I WAS RIGHT. Elliot was not happy with me. In fact, he seemed downright furious as he stomped around my perch on his bed.

"Eva, you can't be serious. You can't keep Cyrus. He's not a stray dog who needs a home." Elliot threw an armful of clothes into the open suitcase beside me. "Though it might be better if he was."

"But I'll feed him and pet him and call him George." My fragile attempt at humor was lost as Elliot turned around to glare at me. "Fine. I won't pet him. But I need guidance, Elliot. You have to understand how complicated my life has become over the past two days. Cyrus is helping me figure out how to deal with those changes."

"No, I don't have to understand. You didn't listen to a single thing I told you yesterday." Elliot picked up a mass of black t-shirts and they joined the pile. "He is just trying to use you. That man is trying…"

"To what?" I returned his sour look with one of my own. "What exactly is Cyrus trying to do? From what I've seen, he has done nothing but help me since this whole mess started."

"That's my point." Elliot stopped what he was doing and put his hands on each one of my shoulders. "Eva, you don't need him. You have me. We can figure this out together."

"Can we?" I searched his face for the answers I wanted so badly. "I want to believe that, Elliot, but I think that this Sibyl business is too much for us to handle alone."

My confidence was shaken. The visions, the whispers – these things were so much more than I'd ever imagined. If Cyrus was right, then they could take over. I could lose myself in the past and never come back.

"Of course, we can." Elliot's tone of voice seemed to be laced with honey. "Eva, we can do anything together. You know that."

"That was before I started seeing dead people. Cyrus can help me with controlling them. Last night, he taught me how to shut the mirrors down."

"Last night?" Elliot released me. "I thought you were too exhausted to do anything last night."

"I was." I searched for a way to get out of the lie I'd been caught in. "But Cyrus dropped by. Since I want to be able to look at myself getting ready in the morning, I asked him to teach me how to make the visions stop every time I look into a mirror. And he did."

"Strange men in your hotel room at night for a lesson, huh?" Elliot had a snide tone in his voice I didn't appreciate. "Is that all he happened to teach you?"

"Is that..." I snapped, unable to finish my sentence as I realized what Elliot was implying. "Yes, that is all! How can you even suggest such a thing? By god, how long have you known me? Do you really think I would sleep with a man I've only known for two days? Give me a little credit, Elliot. I think I've earned it."

I jumped up to head for the door when he grabbed my arm.

"Eva, wait. Look," Elliot's shoulders were slumped in defeat as he turned me to face him. "I'm sorry, ok? I didn't mean what I said. You gotta understand how worried I am about you. Don't shut me out. Please."

"Then don't go and make accusations about things you don't know anything about." I tried to pull away, but his grip tightened. "Let me go."

"No."

Elliot started to say more before two short knocks broke through the tension between us.

"Let me go."

I repeated my words again. This time, Elliot listened. He lifted his hands up in a motion of surrender before I stormed over to the door. I knew who it was before I turned the knob though because the same sense of security which had filled me in the darkness last night was surrounding me now.

"Cyrus is here." I opened the door to see the man brooding over the stack of folders he had taken from me. "And in such a chipper mood! I don't know if I can stand so much happiness this early in the morning."

"Good morning to you too." Cyrus ignored my sarcasm as I stepped aside. He crossed over the threshold just enough for me to shut the door before he started. "You can't be serious about going to these hovels."

"Hovels?" Elliot stood and crossed his arms over his chest. "Those aren't hovels. They are locations where people need our help."

"Hovels." Cyrus stressed the word. "Had you taken the time to actually read the information I did last night, you will see why I would come to such a conclusion."

"No, I didn't get to read them because you took them from me." I pointed out the obvious since he wasn't going to. "Remember? You insisted on having a say in where we were going to be filming."

"Did he now?" Elliot shook his head as he resumed the packing he had abandoned earlier. "I told you so."

"Told you what?" Cyrus refused to look at Elliot, so he focused on me. The tension between those two were so thick, it covered the room like a blanket. "It doesn't matter. You are too inexperienced to expose yourself to such places."

"Give me those." I reached for the folders but Cyrus was much quicker than I was. He stepped back, flipping through them as if they were a deck of cards.

"Great Falls Insane Asylum. Fort Smith Hospital. Green Lawn

Mortuary. Abandoned Pennsylvania coal mine. Ah, this one is my personal favorite." Cyrus stopped at a folder in the middle. "The Black Hollow Murder House."

"Sounds like quite the tourist attraction." I snatched the folder away before Cyrus could stop me. "But a murder house? Really?"

"Would you like to tell her, or should I?" Cyrus turned towards Elliot who had come up beside me. "I'm afraid my memory fails me when it comes to all the gory details you have highlighted."

"You're exaggerating." Elliot rolled his eyes as he reached over my shoulder to pull out the single photograph buried in a mound of papers in my hands. "It's nothing more than an old farmhouse in Kansas."

"A haunted old farmhouse in Kansas, I presume." I raised a single eyebrow as I took the picture from him. "That could be anywhere, Elliot. What's so special about this one?"

"It wasn't just a murder. There was a suicide, too."

"Oh, ok. That's much better."

"Alright, fine." Elliot glared at Cyrus as he pulled me down into the overstuffed chair in the lounge area of his room. "This house has been kept in pristine condition since the time of the murder. The family who remained turned it into a shrine of sorts. As a result, the spirits stayed behind. Joanna Whitaker, our contact and descendant of the victim, said the ghosts of her great-great grandparents appear to her or to anyone who will come to the house."

"Alright." I looked down at the photograph in my hands. It looked simple enough. A two story, middle class home found anywhere in the United States. The only difference between this place and a normal home was the history behind it. "It's just an old house. How many spirits are supposed to be there?"

"Two." Elliot shifted through the papers. "Samuel and Elizabeth Tillotson."

"Two ghosts, as opposed to the hundreds inhabiting a hospital or an asylum." I nodded. "Let's go there."

"Eva." Cyrus said my name as if it were a warning. "You don't understand."

"Oh, come on. It's two people, if they are even there at all. I can handle two spirits. And you can teach me more on the flight."

"What do you mean, handle?" Cyrus glared at me much like Elliot had done earlier when I told him Cyrus was sticking around. After a moment of silence, he scoffed. "No. It is far too dangerous."

"It is not." I shook the picture in my hand then tapped it against my knee. "I think this could work."

"Are you going to let me in on this conversation, or do I need to leave the room?" Elliot had stuffed his hands in his pockets as he stood between the two of us. "I'd hate to be an interruption."

"There is no conversation." Cyrus sat the other folders down on the small table by my chair. "Eva has decided she is going to use the powers of the Sibyl to pull in ratings for your little project. She is putting herself in more danger than you could ever imagine."

"You are so dramatic, Cyrus." I grinned at the man so obviously a soldier, it hurt. "I am simply using the gift granted to me to get the messages from the dead out into the open. Isn't that the point?"

"No, it is most certainly not. The gift of the Sibyl is not meant to be used in such trivial manners."

"Yes, it is. That's exactly what Katherine Carter did every day." I shrugged. "Don't worry. I'll make sure Apollo gets the credit he is after. I think that was the original point, was it not? To pull followers into Apollo's temple?"

My keeper looked stunned for a second before he quickly recovered the stoic look he wore so well. "You surprise me, Little One. Apollo will be pleased."

"I told you I did some of the reading you gave me last night." I ignored Elliot's obvious displeasure at the nickname Cyrus had assigned to me. I had also decided it was for the best not to mention my own attempts at contacting the god himself. "Then it's settled. Elliot, call Connor and have him book us a flight to Kansas. We've got a show to do."

NINE

THERE WAS no easy way to get to Black Hollow, Kansas. We took the first flight out to Wichita, landing well after midnight then drove another two hours before we passed the town sign welcoming us to the heartlands of America. Even in the dark, I could tell this wasn't much of a heartland. The two-lane road Elliot was driving us down was lined on both sides by flat pastures, broken up only by the occasional silo or billboard. Most of the signs were pointing us back to Wichita, where there were actual things to attract people to the good state of Kansas.

"Turn right in two miles."

The mechanical voice of the rental car's GPS broke the silence that filled the car. Cyrus was in the back seat, flipping through his phone and muttering to himself. Elliot kept his eyes on the road, still refusing to speak to me after I demanded he get Cyrus a ticket on the plane with us. And me?

I was lost in my own thoughts of what Cyrus had taught me. I kept imagining my door to the otherworld, adding chains to it then taking them away. The only way I could ever be helpful was to learn how to open the door and let the spirits speak for themselves. I had to learn how to call specific ones forward while pushing the others away.

"Cyrus, I can call forth specific spirits, right? Isn't that what the other Sibyls could do?"

"Yes. It took them years of practice to accomplish such a feat."

I took his words for what they were; a deterrence. I ignored them.

"That's what I want to learn next." I shifted in my seat to face him. "If this is going to work, I need to know how to ask for the specific souls in the underworld."

"Do you really think it could be so easy? Elliot was making the right turn onto Main Street when he interrupted me. "Besides, I'm not convinced of this whole Sibyl thing. Sure, your eyes have changed. And you've claimed to see two spirits. But I've been around you this whole time and nothing has happened to me directly. Seems like I would have experienced something too."

"I know it sounds ridiculous." I chose my words carefully. "I don't know how to explain what I've seen, Elliot. You've told me at least a hundred times that there are things in this world we cannot explain. I hate to say this, but I believe I am now one of those things."

"And I hate to say this, but maybe you should listen to Cyrus. You are too new at this life."

"Indeed, she is." Cyrus tucked his phone into his jacket pocket. "Perhaps you can convince Eva not to put herself into unnecessary danger as it seems I have failed. She listens to you."

"Last time I checked, I am an adult." I frowned. "One who is capable of making her own decisions."

"You are." Elliot glanced over at me as he came to a stop at a red light. "Just promise me you'll be careful."

"Hey, I heard what Cyrus said about being possessed. I happen to like who I am. I'm not looking to become anyone else."

I tried to make light of my fake self-confidence. It was hard to do so. I hated myself. I hated the memories that popped in and out of my mind so easily. Memories that led to me missing my own college graduation.

I was determined to see this through. I was also afraid. Images of the wild woman in my hotel mirror returned to the forefront of my mind along with how much I wanted to join her on the other side of the glass. I chased the memory away with a quick shake of my head. "I'll be careful, I promise."

"We're here." Elliot pulled into a small parking spot right in front of the town's only hotel. It blended in so well with the other storefronts, I had a hard time figuring out just which door we were supposed to go into. As we got out of the car, Elliot spoke up once more.

"The rest of the crew will be flying in tomorrow. We'll call Joanna and set up a time to meet with her. Find out exactly what is going on before we go to the location."

"Alright," I took a breath as Cyrus climbed out from the backseat. "We have to come up with a backstory for Cyrus, too. I'm not ready to announce to your production team just why I need a bodyguard."

"It's just as good a cover as any." Cyrus leaned against the car as he took in the quiet street. "Elliot has already told them you were attacked at the conference, correct?"

I nodded.

"Then tell them I was hired on from a security firm in New York for your protection."

"You know," I paused for only a moment as I snagged my purse out of the floorboard and went to join Elliot on the sidewalk. "That makes perfect sense."

"Come on." Elliot reached for my hand, intertwining our fingers. "Let's get inside. It's been a very long night and tomorrow isn't going to be any better."

I resisted the urge to get back in the car and tell Elliot to get us the hell out of Kansas. As much as the move to California was a new start for me, tomorrow would be the start of what we were here to do. I was nervous, but I wouldn't be chased away from the contract I had signed.

Spirits and possessions be damned.

I couldn't sleep.

Maybe it was because of jetlag. Maybe it was the fear of making a complete fool out of myself. More than likely, it was because I couldn't shut the damn whispers up. I had left the mirror packed up in my overnight bag and even after I moved it into the armoire that served as my closet, I could still hear them. I tried to block them out. I tried to imagine my mental door. Nothing was working. I finally gave up after burying my head underneath every pillow and blanket I could find. I climbed out of bed, threw on my clothes from the trip to Kansas before heading downstairs.

There was a small lounge area by the front door decked out in big fluffy couches and chairs. Since the nights were getting colder out here on the plains, someone had been kind enough to light a fire in the fireplace against the far wall. I curled up on one side of the biggest couch. The whispers were silent down here. There were no mirrors decorating the walls; only cheap paintings in even cheaper frames. It was peaceful.

Quiet.

I stared at the flames jumping around in front of me and waited for them to ease my troubled mind. I decided to go over everything Cyrus had taught me so far. He was so worried about what could happen when we went to the farmhouse tomorrow. Me? I was more worried about what had already occurred. I wanted nothing more than to forget about the past few days.

"Can't sleep?" Cyrus stepped out of the shadows to hand me a silver flask. "This should help."

"Liquor?" I looked up to him in surprise as I accepted the container he pressed into my hand. "I would never have suspected you were a drinker."

"It's not just any liquor." Cyrus gave me a look of horror that made me laugh. "You are holding the ambrosia of the gods in your hands."

I took the top off and sniffed. "Whiskey?"

Cyrus grinned as he perched on the armrest of the chair by my head. "Any strong liquor will do. They don't call them spirits for nothing. I happen to like whiskey. Go on. Try it."

I gestured for him to sit next to me and took a swig. The whiskey burned like hell as it went down. I choked then passed it back to him as quickly as I could.

"How in the world do you drink that?" I managed as I caught my breath between coughs. "It's disgusting."

"Perhaps so. Or perhaps you haven't given it a proper chance." Cyrus smiled before he took a sip. "We all need something to quiet our ghosts, Little One. I am no different."

He passed the flask back to me. "Now tell me what troubles you. The spirits?"

"Yes. No. I don't know." I swallowed another gulp as our drinking session officially began. The fire in my throat went down easier this time. "If I'm honest, I'm trying to make sense of this Sibyl business."

"There is no point in trying to find logic where it doesn't exist." Cyrus accepted the flask. "And believe me, there is no logic where the gods are concerned."

"I thought that I had put the occult behind me. I thought that once I moved to Georgia, I was done." I took my turn to drink, turning the flask in my hands. "Now, I'm getting hit in the face by ghosts and insanity."

"Your grandmother was a disciple of Hecate. Why do you hold doubt? And why are you involved in this television show?" Cyrus was studying me in the firelight as if I were a puzzle he needed to solve. "That is what I can't make sense of."

"Money." I answered before I could stop myself. "Pride. The need to carve out my place in the world."

"And so, you have found it." Cyrus smiled at me. "You will realize this in time. You will see."

"What do the dead have to say?" I decided to change the subject. "I mean, once you die, your worldly troubles should fall away, right? What's the point of coming back?"

Cyrus was right. The more I drank, the easier it became to swallow the whiskey. I was drinking too much and I knew I would pay the price tomorrow. I didn't care. We continued to pass the flask between us until it was empty, alternating between staring at the flames and each other. Cyrus finally responded once the whiskey was gone.

"Life is a difficult thing to let go of, but the memories of that life are even harder to relinquish. No one can truly determine what the spirits will say. The most tortured souls often hold their secrets close, but once they share them, they are able to find peace. You will learn some horrible things, Eva. I want to warn you so you can be prepared."

"It can't all be bad. Do you have anything funny to go with all your melancholy?"

"During the time of the second Sibyl, one spirit wished for her to find the gold he had hidden from his family. He wanted to make sure it was still there so he could reclaim it if he were ever reborn. Believe me when I say that I spent two weeks trying to find his damn treasure. It wasn't there."

I raised an eyebrow as I asked the only thing I could think of. "How many Sibyls have there been, Cyrus?"

"You are the seventh Sibyl."

There had been six Sibyls before me. I wanted to ask him questions about these women. How did they survive their role without going insane? Did any of them actually want to talk to the dead? I wanted to know, but the whiskey was making it difficult to concentrate.

I decided to focus on what he said about finding peace instead of my questions. I could understand the need for peace. I curled up against Cyrus' side then laid my head on his knee. He stiffened, but I ignored his reaction. I was sure it was the liquor making me so friendly, but I couldn't stop myself.

"I am glad you are here with me, Cyrus. I think we can be good friends despite your creepiness."

"I am still creepy?" Cyrus relaxed. I could hear the amusement in his voice. "Perhaps creepy is a part of my charm."

"You never did finish telling me your story." I smiled to myself. There was something about Cyrus I found comforting. He was so solid; so focused on his position as my keeper. Suddenly, I wanted to know everything I could about him. "Are you drunk enough to finish telling me your secrets?"

"I don't get drunk. It's not possible." Cyrus shifted beneath me. I couldn't help but move too. I moved just enough to look up at him without removing my head from the spot I'd claimed. After a few moments, he continued. "You are the strange one, Eva. None of the others have been as curious about my past as you are."

"I told you, we're going to be friends." I frowned. "Unless there is some rule you haven't shared with me about Sibyls and Keepers can't get to know each other."

"No." Cyrus shook his head. I felt his hand brush against my hair before he pulled back. "I don't believe such a rule exists. I will share my past with you, Sibyl. Just as the rest of the dead do."

"You're being creepy again, bringing up the dead and all."

Cyrus chuckled. "Do you want to hear this or not?"

"I do. I'm infinitely curious. You left off where you were first cursed by Apollo."

"Yes, I remember." Cyrus fell silent for a moment before he began. "As I said, I became tied to Delphine. As the weeks passed, men from my regiment came to Cumae searching for me. Despite my newfound status as her guard, Delphine didn't trust me. She barricaded herself into her rooms. My men passed me by without ever learning of my fate."

"Did they consider you a traitor? A deserter?" I didn't mean to interrupt him, but I wanted to understand. "Were you ever able to speak with them again?"

"No, they never found me." Cyrus' features looked twisted in the shadows. "I was given up for dead. As the years passed, I grew to hate the role thrust upon me. How could I not? I had no freedoms whatsoever. Delphine did not leave her father's house unless forced to. She despised the looks she received from the townspeople. I was always behind her. I had become her shadow. Yet, her life was peaceful. Boring. It was torture for a man who had strived in the fires of war."

"Didn't you say she was ran out of town?" I studied the flames lighting the room around us. I tried to imagine what his world had been like. Cyrus was ancient. You didn't have to be a psychic to see the age in his eyes.

"Indeed, she was. Delphine had seen her hundredth birthday pass when the fear became too much for those who knew of her. It was in the spring when the mobs gathered to put an end to her life. She had survived in the comfort of her home for so long, she became convinced the world had forgotten about her. It hadn't. As the mob crashed down her gates, I did the only thing I knew to do."

"You fought them, didn't you?" I turned just enough to see his face. "You must have, being her guard and all."

"I wish I could say I had been so brave, Little One." Cyrus smiled down at me. "But alas, no. A true warrior knows which battles to fight, and which to avoid. I pulled Delphine down into the servants' quarters. The men who had come for her head looted the wealth her parents had left behind as they searched for us. They called out horrible things. Many promised to send her down to the Underworld before the night was through."

"If the two of you were truly immortal, why didn't you fight them? I don't understand."

"I would have fought them – Delphine as well. But it would have been for naught. Our days in Cumae were over. We both realized it. Killing the men who had attacked her house that night would have been a waste of Greek life. Since we had a method to escape, I saw no reason to send them to their deaths."

"So you're a big softie after all." I had returned to my original position of resting on his knee. "How did you escape?"

"A servant passage." Cyrus chuckled as if the memories he was recalling were funny to him. Perhaps they were. "It was the easiest thing in the world. Delphine dressed in the clothes of a male servant. We slipped out into the night, using the light from the fires set in her house to find our way out of town. We returned to the forest where we had been damned. Though I hated her, I came to respect her. Here was a woman who had known nothing but luxury during her existence, yet she discarded it with such ease. Delphine accepted her banishment to the forests and adapted as I did to life in the wild."

We fell into a comfortable silence then. Every once in a while, he would stroke my hair and I was sure he was just as wrapped up in his own memories of his life as I was in the story he had told me. I found it to be very sad.

I don't know how long we stayed on the couch, but soon, Cyrus shifted beneath me. "You must return to your room, Eva. Whiskey can be wicked if you don't sleep it off."

I let Cyrus lead me up the stairs since my own steps were unsteady. He was right. I needed sleep if I was going to survive my first day as a ghost hunter. As we crossed the threshold into my room, I found the whispers had gone silent.

I was asleep the moment my head hit the pillow.

"Eva, you have got to sit still."

Jonathan Ford was two seconds away from smacking the back of my head with his hairbrush as I adjusted in my chair for the umpteenth time. Not that I could blame him. He had been sent by Theia Productions to make sure I fit the role I was determined to play. Connor had sent in a small army along with him. There were three people from Wardrobe along with countless people to set up the old farmhouse. I swear, he sent the entire Hair and Makeup department to make me more presentable. That is where Jonathan fit into the picture. The man was a perfectionist with a vision. No wonder he was getting so frustrated with me.

I wasn't being very helpful.

"Fine." I groaned as I slumped down into the chair. "I'll behave."

"Sit up." Jonathan pulled at my shoulders until I complied. "There's a good girl."

He made small talk about his life in L.A. as he danced around my chair with scissors and potions meant to make my blonde hair even lighter. Thirty minutes of my life I would never get back passed as he worked. To be fair, I was taking the time to read up on the history surrounding the old farmhouse. It wouldn't look very professional for me to be meeting with the family of the victims and not know the first thing about them.

I was struck by the tragedy of the story. Samuel Tillotson had been a farmer. A good man who simply snapped after being confined in his small house for months after a blizzard hit Black Hollow in January of 1876. The newspaper clippings sensationalized the story. Journalists at the time claimed Samuel found his wife in bed with another man. Or that he had gotten drunk in town then killed his wife in a fit of rage. Neither of these claims had any sources nor did they make any sense.

If you are trapped in a small house during one of the worst snowstorms in history, how could people get to you? How could a lover trek through the snow undetected? And as far as the possession, well. I'd seen the nightlife Black Hollow had to offer when we pulled into town yesterday. There wasn't any. I'm sure there was even less in 1876.

I switched my focus to the police report the guys in Research had managed to get a hold of. The handwriting was tiny and it was extremely difficult to read. I could make out how Samuel's body was found with a knife buried in his chest. Catherine's bones were piled up next to him. They couldn't determine how long they had been there due to the frozen temperatures. The police were quick to note it was an apparent suicide, although no note was found. It was unclear whether Catherine had been murdered or died from natural causes during the blizzard.

The researchers had found us a good story. One filled with the promise of vengeance or, at the very least, madness. I chalked one up for them as Jonathan continued his assault on my poor hair. I must have made a face because the man's chatter was interrupted by Cyrus chuckling from his perch by the door.

"You look miserable, Little One."

"That's because I am." I grumbled as I blew at the strands covering my right eye. "You would be too if you were in my position."

"Indeed, I would." Cyrus smirked. "Then again, I know better than to put myself in such a situation."

"Just be quiet." I pouted as he continued laughing at me. Jonathan huffed despite the fact my words weren't meant for him. He fell silent as well as he tugged my newly bleached hair into thick pink rollers.

"There. It's not much, but it is all I can do for now."

Jonathan clapped his hands as a group of women began to swarm around me armed with crap meant to highlight my natural beauty.

I hated each and every one of them.

"Cyrus, go find Elliot." I managed as a perky assistant brushed a thick paste across my forehead. "Tell him I want to see him right this instant."

"I can't." Cyrus shrugged. "Bound to you, remember? I'm not allowed to leave my post."

"You can't or you won't because you're enjoying this too much?"

Cyrus gave me a lopsided grin. "Both?"

"Just go. No one could get past this group if they wanted to."

"Very well." Cyrus stood with a sigh of annoyance before he vanished into the shadows. He would have to learn how to use the door like normal people if he was going to act like a bodyguard. Well, a human one at least.

"Eva, what's wrong?"

Elliot came through the door with his own face covered in the goop. "Cyrus said you needed to see me. It was important."

"It is important." I huffed, brushing aside the pair of hands tilting my chin upward. I was not rewarded for my efforts because those hands returned. I could have sworn the woman muttered something about difficult divas with dark circles as she continued her work. "Can you explain to me why I'm getting assaulted with hairspray and foundation? I thought we were just doing interviews today."

"We are." Elliot's tone was full of the laughter he was trying so hard to contain. "Joey is going to be filming them though. Without the makeup, you'd look like a corpse underneath the lights."

"Poor choice of words, Ellioti." I forced my head straight despite the woman's attempts to keep me in place. "We are starting filming? Today?"

"Yeah. The sooner the better. Joanna is meeting us over at the house in two hours. You've got to be ready."

The more I thought about what Elliot said, the bigger the knot grew as it formed in my throat. We were filming. As in television.

What in the world was I doing?

"What you were meant to do." Cyrus spoke up as if I had spoken my concerns out loud. "You were right. He was extremely pleased with your decision."

Cyrus didn't have to go into any further details. He could only mean Apollo. I made a note to ask him about how his contacts with a god worked.

"I'll be just a minute longer then I'll come to keep you company."

Elliot started to come towards me but stopped when I shook my head. The woman almost stabbed me in the eye with an eyeliner pencil.

"No, take your time. I'm not going anywhere."

"They are almost done with me anyway." Elliot waved my words away. "Are you really ok? I'm sure we can put this off for a little longer if you need to."

"Elliot, I have been in this chair for a good hour now, and from the looks I keep getting from your appearance people, I might be here for another one. I do not want to repeat this process if I don't have to."

Elliot laughed. "Then we'll do it. See you in a little while, Eva."

"See you." I muttered as he left the room. Cyrus took the papers from my lap as the women continued their work. I think I dozed off because one of them tugged at my arm.

"Ta da!" She cried out as I opened my eyes to the mirror she held in front of me. "What do you think?"

I couldn't respond. The whispers I had been so successful at holding back were rushing forward. There was no time to prepare myself as there had been in the hotel room when Cyrus and I were practicing. I stared at the mirror with an expression of horror as the woman who I recognized from the newspaper drawings in my lap formed in the glass. Her eyes were hardened with a look of hatred. I tried to look away, but I couldn't. She held my gaze and began to speak.

"You have come to free me."

"What..." I knew Cyrus was by my side. I could feel him there. He was speaking, but I couldn't hear him over the woman. She continued, clutching at her throat as if trying to hide the wound stretched across it.

"I'll see you soon enough, Sibyl. We have much to discuss."

"The door, Little One. Close it. Now."

Cyrus. He managed to refocus my thoughts. I imagined my door, watched it appear across the image, then slammed it shut. Cyrus had wrestled the hand mirror away from the woman. He sat it aside face down on the table.

"Out, all of you." Cyrus didn't yell, but he didn't need to. His voice was one they dared not disobey. I used the time it took for them to leave to try to gather up my thoughts. I felt disoriented and nauseous. When they were all gone, Cyrus knelt down by my feet. He took my chin in his hand to better examine my face.

"Are you alright?"

I threw my arms around his neck and buried my face into his shoulder. Cyrus held me until my body stopped trembling. He said nothing as I told him of the woman I'd seen. What she had said. He was good to me. Cyrus didn't try his usual tactic of telling me I didn't have to go. Or offer me a chance to run away from Black Hollow as fast as possible. Instead, he let me work through the fear until I was well enough to pull away on my own. I wanted to go back to my little room to cry, but a promise is a promise. Besides, I wasn't kidding when I told Elliot this beauty routine was too much to handle.

"Sorry." I mumbled, reaching up to wipe my eyes then stopping before I smeared anything. "They are going to think I am insane."

"They already do." Cyrus offered me a small smile. "I believe the exact phrase the women were using was 'difficult diva'?"

I wanted to smile but couldn't manage it. Instead, I shuddered. "Cyrus, if this can happen here, in a safe place, what happens when we get to the house?"

"Remember your door, Eva." Cyrus took my hands and squeezed

them. "I will teach you more as time passes, but for now, believe each mirror in that house is covered by the very image you created. Allow the spirit to speak with you only through Apollo's mirror."

"How do I keep them quiet?" I leaned forward. "The whispers. She was talking to me. I could hear her."

"Block them out. You have to; otherwise, you can truly go insane from it." Cyrus glanced around the empty room. "If it becomes too much, ask Apollo for assistance. Guidance. He has always aided his Sibyls. You are no different."

"Is there a prayer, a chant?" I stood up to pace the room. "I've never talked to a god before. Do I give him an offering?"

I didn't count my little spell back in New York. I wasn't so sure it had qualified as actual contact with a deity since I never heard anything back from him.

"You already have by promising to showcase him on this project of yours." Cyrus stood along with me then tucked his hands in his pockets. "Talk to him as you would to me. Well, not exactly like you talk to me. Be respectful."

"Hey, I can be respectful when I need to be."

It was Jonathan who knocked on the door to interrupt us. He gasped at the sight of me and clamored with excitement over my new face as he pulled me over to the chair. He was back to the chatter when he began to pull the rollers from my hair. I looked at Cyrus. Apollo would be able to guide me, but it was Cyrus who would protect me.

I was sure about that.

TEN

THE BLACK HOLLOW MURDER HOUSE looked exactly like it did in the picture. In fact, without its horrible nickname or history, it was a house I could see myself settling down in one day. Bay windows gleamed in the sun. The black shutters contrasted nicely against the outside's white paint. It was far enough from the road to block out any noise from passing cars. Not that there were many cars driving past it. This place was out in the middle of nowhere.

"Welcome to Black Hollow!" A chubby woman decked out in full Victorian regalia stepped off the front porch. She grabbed for Elliot's hand to shake it with a warm smile. "You must be Elliot and Eva. I'm Joanna. So nice to be able to put a face with the voice I've been talking to on the phone."

"It's nice to meet you, too." Elliot returned her shake. "Is Joey Lawson here already? Has he talked to you about the interview?"

"Yes. I believe I've talked to him. Your people have been here since nine this morning, setting everything up. Several of them made sure to tell me what I needed to say."

"We need you to tell us the truth." I moved away from the car to stand by Elliot. "Otherwise, this is never going to work."

"The truth?" Joanna smiled. "Well, now. What fun is that?"

"We don't need fun." I glanced at Elliot. "In order for our evidence to speak for itself, we have got to know the whole story. This is where you come in."

"I was teasing, my dear." Joanna's friendly smile had turned cold. She must have decided that Elliot was more to her liking because she took him by the arm and led him inside. I was left outside alone with Cyrus.

"Hey, McRayne!"

The man I recognized as Joey Lawson had opened the front door with a large black camera slung over his shoulder. "You coming?"

"Yeah." I allowed myself one last moment of peace before I climbed up the stairs after him. "I'm coming."

"It was a horrible tragedy. Black Hollow had never seen such violence before and hasn't since that fateful day in 1876."

I had to make an effort not to roll my eyes at Joanna's theatrics. We were seated on an overstuffed Victorian couch better suited for a parlor in Charleston than this small house in Kansas. In fact, the whole place seemed to be made up in the most garish Victorian fashions imaginable.

Much like Joanna herself. She was simpering now, overcome by the deaths of two people she had never met. I caught Joey standing off to the side. He was struggling to open a piece of gum while holding the camera steady and tried not to laugh. I wondered if he knew this was what he was signing up for when he agreed to join our little show.

I doubted it.

"How are you related to the Tillotsons, Ms. Whitaker?"

Elliot had leaned forward, resting his elbows on his knees as he listened to her explain how she was the daughter of Samuel's great uncle. Not direct granddaughter as we had been led to believe. I made a mental strike in my head of the first lie she had been caught in, promising to look up her history as soon as I could.

"I was raised here, you see. These very walls speak of the murder which happened here. Poor Catherine."

Joanna was on the verge of tears again, so I stepped in. "Tell us about them."

"What?" She paused, either for the effect or because she was surprised I had finally spoken. Either way, the woman had the decency to stop her ridiculous dramatics.

"The murders. What happened that night?"

"Oh, well. It is told that Samuel flew into a rage after he discovered Catherine had a lover. He had adored her, you see. He even had built this house for them to raise a family in."

"But tax records show Samuel bought the house in 1872." I had no problems interrupting her second lie. "It was already here when they came to Kansas from Tennessee. He didn't build anything."

Joanna glared at me. "Well, perhaps I have my facts wrong. But he did, at least, buy this house for her. And they were madly in love."

"How did he find out about this lover?" I mirrored Elliot, leaning forward as if I were engrossed by her tale.

"It was such a scandal!" Joanna threw a gloved hand to her forehead. "He walked in on them in the midst of a passionate embrace. Her lover got away, but poor Catherine! She met the edge of her husband's blade that very night."

"I don't understand." I gestured to Cyrus who brought my folder to me. I thumbed through the paperwork and found what I was looking for. "According to the Wichita papers, there was a blizzard during the week of the murder. And it had been snowing for weeks prior to that. How could a lover get to this house – which is out in the middle of nowhere – then get away without freezing to death? Besides, we don't know if Catherine was stabbed or not. Even the police reports are unclear on how she actually died."

"Can we take a break please?" Joanna was positively furious as she pulled a fan out from her elegant costume and slapped herself on the knee. Joey made moves to cut the camera off. She made sure he sat the equipment down before she turned on me.

"What are you trying to do?" Our client snapped at me. "You ask me questions but refuse to believe my answers. How dare you!"

"I told you outside and I'm telling you now, we are here for the truth." I returned her glare as I gestured to the papers in my lap. "There is this new thing called the internet. I'm sure you've heard of it. The people who watch television also utilize those services. They can easily pull up the information you give to us. If it is wrong, it will do more harm than good. Your theatrics are fantastic, I'm sure. But I did not travel all the way here to be lied to."

"Lied to?" Joanna was huffing. "Why, I never! You understand, don't you?" She turned on Elliot like a cat. "You understand how important the legend is around these parts. It is what keeps our town on the map because tourists want to believe the tragedy."

"Yes, I do." Elliot disentangled himself from the grip the woman had on him. "But Eva is right, ma'm. We are doing an investigation, not a travel show. We need to know what really happened so it can support what the spirits are telling us."

"There are no facts!" Joanna stood up in a swirl of skirts and spit. "We don't know what happened."

I caught sight of Joey finally getting into that piece of gum. I noticed the small red light on the camera was blinking. God bless him, our cameraman had turned the camera back on when she wasn't looking.

"Alright, alright." I stepped in, trying to act as a mediator. "Let's start over, shall we? Joey, grab your camera. Let's start with what we do know. Two people died here, right?"

As Joey raised the camera up, Joanna's anger fell away to the genteel facade she had when we arrived. She sank back into her chair with a nod. "Yes."

"Catherine Tillotson was believed to be murdered by her husband, Samuel Tillotson, who then killed himself in the backyard?"

"Yes. It was," She looked up to me and the tone in her voice fell a notch. "That is where they found him with the knife buried in his chest."

"Ok." I started to pace, but there wasn't enough room with all the knickknacks and tables cluttering the room. I settled on tapping my fingers against my chin instead. "And it is believed this place is haunted."

"Yes." Joanna's face lit up as she saw an opportunity for the theatrics to continue. "We see them, you know. Catherine and Samuel. They appear before us in the shape of wisps and shadows."

"What else?" Elliot shifted in his seat and I could see the interest in his eyes.

"Well, things move on their own accord. The knickknacks and such. I believe Catherine loves to have them in her home. She always loved such delicate things."

"Ms. Whitaker," I made sure the underlying warning was clear in my words. "The facts and nothing more."

"Oh, very well. Come see the rest of the house. I'll show you the diary Samuel kept when they first moved here."

Joanna led us up a thin staircase and into an even smaller hallway. When she reached the final room to her left, she opened the door. "This was their bedroom. We had it restored to fit the time period, just as every other room in the Tillotson home."

Elliot stepped inside, but before he could utter a single word of warning, I followed in behind him to be faced with a large oval mirror. There were no whispers in my head this time; only the loud screams of the woman in the glass. She was covered in the blood which ran from her neck. The moment I stepped into the room, I felt a sharp pain rip across my throat as her anger overwhelmed my mind. I screamed along with her. She reached out and her arms slipped through the glass.

My scream became silent. I could feel myself trying to get it out, but there was nothing. No sound. No echo. Nothing.

"Eva!" Elliot pulled me from the room so quickly I crumpled into a heap on the carpet. He then turned to a bewildered Joanna. "Close the door. Now!"

I heard the door slam shut as Elliot helped me to my feet. I couldn't shake the fear surrounding me. I knew the woman I'd seen was Catherine. I had been blindsided by the mirror itself and she took advantage of it to scare the daylights out of me. Elliot sat me back down on the sofa with Cyrus crouching down beside me.

"Eva," Cyrus reached up and brushed his hand over my neck. "You are bleeding."

"No, I'm not." I was trying to get a hold of myself as my voice came back. I sounded like I had swallowed a bucket of glass. "She didn't touch me."

"She didn't have to." Cyrus lifted up his hand to show me his fingers were streaked with blood. "Catherine Tillotson shared more than her presence with you, it seems. She shared her wound."

"How?" I stared at him in shock. "How is this possible? Why can't I feel it?"

"What is going on here?" Joanna was off to the side, upset she was no longer the center of our camera's attention. "I thought you didn't want dramatic."

"Take care of her." Cyrus gestured to Elliot from his position by my feet. "She will only be in the way."

"Damn you, no." Elliot looked as if he were going to knock Cyrus clear across the room as he put his cell phone to his ear. "Let me get a doctor in here to take a look at Eva. She needs help. That cut looks pretty serious."

"It will heal on its own before any physician can get here." Cyrus stood then faced Elliot. "If my words weren't true, if she wasn't what she is, then Eva would be dead by now. There is nothing to worry about. Now go. Take care of the spectator. I will ensure Eva's safety."

"Spectator? Why, I never! And in my very own house!" Joanna was so upset by Cyrus, her lily-white complexion became red with anger. "I have every right to be here if any of this footage is going to be shown on television."

"Ma'am, Eva has had an injury. It is best if we give her some room."

Elliot sounded tired when he took the woman's elbow to lead her outside. I could hear him from out on the porch. He reassured her I would be fine and that Theia Productions was not going to sue her. I could tell he had his hands full, but I didn't have the strength to go outside to save him. I reached to my throat and traced the jagged line stretching across my skin. I took a brief moment to wonder if I would end up with a scar before I pulled my hand away. A quick glance down at my shirt told me it was ruined. After I finished my brief examination, I turned to my keeper for answers.

"I didn't die because of the immortality clause in this whole Sybil contract, right?"

Cyrus didn't answer. He didn't have to. I could see the affirmation in his dark blue eyes as he busied himself with examining me.

"How could she harm me, Cyrus? Catherine wasn't contained by the glass. She reached through it."

Cyrus lifted himself up to sit on the couch beside me when he was satisfied the wound had indeed closed on its own. I was sure he did it to buy time to find his answer. I wasn't mistaken. When Cyrus spoke, his words were slow and careful.

"As I told you many times before, Eva, you have much training to do in the event something like what just happened does indeed occur. The spirit world is one of power. Certain souls have more than others. You must be prepared."

"So they can physically hurt me now?" I hissed in an attempt to keep my voice down. It was hard enough to sit here as if nothing had happened. "I thought my powers were limited to just seeing and speaking with them. Messenger of the dead remember?"

"I do." Cyrus kept his hands together in his lap. "Messenger of the dead, Daughter of Apollo. Those are your titles, Little One. I thought you did the readings I gave you. Did you skip the ones regarding Hades?"

"I don't know. I read a lot, mind you. It seems like I missed the most important parts though." I sighed. "How can I keep them from harming me? Or at the very least, from being so scared I need to change my jeans after an encounter."

He chuckled. "Time? Practice? Exposure? There are no certain methods to protect yourself. I can only tell you what the others before you found to be useful. Expect to see them. Learn to listen to the sounds of the dead long before you are faced with a portal they can get through."

"Like the mirror upstairs."

"Yes. I told you before, use only Apollo's mirror to make contact. The glass is too small for them to reach through." Cyrus tapped the side of my head gently. "Stop and listen before you walk into any space. If you start to hear the whispers, put up the door in your mind. This will hold them off until you can actively do so when faced by them in the glass itself. If they come through, form a shield much like your door around you. This too will be easier with practice. I will be able to pull you free if I must, but I prefer for that not to be necessary."

"My new role has become extraordinarily tedious." I grumbled as I stood up to go outside. I could feel the hate in this place now. It was so much more than I could have believed possible. He'll, even the walls seemed to vibrate with the scream that still echoed in my mind. "Let's go. I think we are done here for now."

"Yes, I believe so as well." Cyrus nodded as he followed me. "For now."

ELEVEN

"I KNOW this might be a bad time to bring up the blood and all, but do either of you care to explain what happened back there?"

Joey took in a mouthful of pizza after his question. I handed him a napkin from the basket in front of me with a sigh. We had left the farmhouse on the pretense of getting ready for our investigation tonight. Not that it was much of a pretense. We really did need to get our equipment together. Truth be told though, I needed to get out of there and the boys needed to eat. After a quick stop so I could change clothes, we found a pizza joint then collapsed into the most secluded booth we could find.

"I'm not sure if you want to know, Joey." I pushed my own plate aside. Having your throat slit by an angry spirit did wonders for killing your appetite. "It's quite the long story."

"Hey, I'm on the clock. I got nothing but time since you're paying me to be here." Joey turned his attention to Elliot as if he would give him the answers I wasn't willing to give up so easily. "So what gives, Lancaster? Our girl some sort of psychic or something?"

"Or something." Elliot took my hand from across the table. "It's up to you, Eva. Your story. Your choice."

"If Joey is going to be with us for a while, he will need to know."

I sighed. "Ok. Just promise you won't call me crazy when I'm done, ok?"

"I won't call you crazy. I can make no promises, however, of not making fun of you."

I smiled despite myself. "Fair enough. You know about our trip to Paracon, right?"

"Yeah. I got out of it since I'm just the equipment guy."

"Well, I walked away with a bigger souvenir than the classic swag bag."

I started from the beginning. How could I not? I told him about the scrying session, how Kathy Carter tricked me into taking the mirror. How I had chanted the words which changed me. Cyrus lurked in the shadows next to our table. He only nodded when I introduced him to Joey for what he really was. I told our poor camera man everything I knew. When I finally fell silent, Joey whistled.

"That's one hell of a hook, McRayne. You gonna use it?"

I laughed. I couldn't help myself. With all the blood and screaming spirits, I had to find something amusing. Joey taking this so well? That was my something. "Yeah, I guess it is."

I had already made the promise to Apollo to use television to bring attention to him. I just had no idea how to do it yet.

"So this is it. You found the one thing to make yourself stand out from all the other paranormal gigs out there."

"You really think that this is going to work?"

"Hell yeah, I do." Joey rubbed his hands together before taking another slice of pizza from the pan in between us. "You've already promised Connor you'd find a way to make the show stand out, right? This is how you do it. We won't have to change much in the way of formatting, either. We go in, get the history. Then, bring out the fancy mirror. Let Eva talk to the spirits while we film the whole encounter in the dark. Hell, you gave me enough footage this afternoon to get started. No wonder you're going to call it *Grave Messages*."

"I do love that title" I took a sip of my water as I considered what he said. "Cyrus is teaching me how to keep the voices quiet. And I'm working on how to shut the mirrors down before I can be attacked. We can cover the mirrors in our locations until we are ready to film the part where I contact them."

Elliot pulled a notebook out of his jeans and gestured to me for a pen. I handed him the first one out of my purse. He began to jot down the ideas now flying between the three of us. This was a meeting that should have happened back in L.A. when the contracts were first signed. But the timing never seemed right. Now, we had ideas. We had formatting.

We had a show.

After our impromptu meeting, the four of us had gone back to the hotel to grab the equipment; packing it up in the back of the crew's rented SUV. Elliot had pulled me aside once we finished, tugging me into a dark corner of the hotel lobby.

"Eva, are you sure about this?" Elliot was holding my hands between us, searching my face for any signs of doubt. "We can find some other way for this to work."

"I'm sure." I squeezed his hands. "I believe this is going to work. I believe Cyrus will protect me if need be."

"I will be there, too." Elliot reminded me. "Cyrus isn't the only one who can help you."

"I know." I smiled as he tugged on the hand he still held to pull me into a hug. "Just stay safe yourself, ok? I've seen Catherine twice now. She is extraordinarily strong."

"Twice?" Elliot rested his chin on the top of my head. "I didn't realize."

"Yeah. She hit me up in the midst of my beauty routine this morning." I pulled back. "Besides, neither of us can get hurt. You never did take me out for coffee in New York, Eli. I'm holding you to your promise."

"And you have been a really good sport about all this."

"Exactly." I hit his chest lightly. "So forget the cheap corner stuff. We're talking Starbucks quality now, mister."

"We going or what?" Joey bounded past us and held the door open. "I didn't lug all those cases down those stairs for nothing, you know."

"Fine." I muttered as Elliot returned his grip on my hand. "I guess we shouldn't keep the others waiting."

"Guess not. Joey might just go off and leave us here."

"Do you really think he would?"

"Don't sound so hopeful." Elliot smirked as we walked outside. "It'll ruin your reputation as a good ghost hunter if people find out you don't want to go into spooky old houses."

"Ah, yes. My ghost hunting reputation. Whatever would I do without it?" I got in the front seat and buckled my seat belt. "Whatever would I be?"

———

I was more than just a little disappointed to find the house still standing as we pulled into the driveway leading up to it. Wasn't Kansas known for its wicked tornadoes? I was even more disappointed to find Joanna standing on the porch with her gloved hands crossed over the front of her skirt.

"What is she still doing here?" I turned to Joey whose eyes widen into the very picture of innocence.

"Don't ask me. The setup crew told her to clear out before the sun went down."

"Well, it's not night yet." I muttered as I pressed the button to release the seat belt. "Maybe she is hoping for one more monologue on camera."

"Oh, wonderful!" Joanna bounded down the front stairs with a dexterity I found surprising given the layer of skirts she was wearing. "You're back."

Elliot stepped out just as she came to a halt in front of the car. I didn't miss the disappointment in her voice when she continued.

"You're all back."

"Of course, we are." I slammed the car door as Joey began to unload our equipment. "We are supposed to start filming tonight, right?"

"Yes, well," Joanna's disappointment turned into a sickening sweetness. "I just thought, since you were hurt, Elliot here might need someone to stand in as co-host."

"So you wanted to take my place." I tilted my head in her direction before I turned towards Elliot. "I don't think she realizes what we are here to do."

"You are here to document my darling Catherine and Samuel." Joanna's eyes flashed. "I wanted to make sure the show was still going to happen despite your breakdown earlier."

"Breakdown. How nice." I had a sharp retort ready but swallowed it down when I remembered the ironclad contracts and flight across the country. "Ok. Let's start over, shall we? Ms. Whitaker, I am fine. I did not have a breakdown. I saw Catherine."

"You saw her?" Joanna gasped, placing her hands over her heart. "Why didn't you say so?"

"I am not going to say anything more. You will see our evidence when we are finished. I believe this was in your contract to Theia Productions which allows us to film here in the first place. Now if you will excuse us, we need to make sure this location is secure."

I gestured for Cyrus to follow behind me as Joey took Ms. Whitaker by the arm to escort her to her own vehicle. When we got to the porch, I turned to him.

"Are you sure I can do this?" Even outside in the fading afternoon sunlight, the darkness of this place was starting to surround me. "Because I'm starting to think this was a very bad idea."

"You can always leave." Cyrus shrugged. "I will do what I can to explain to Apollo why you decided against being a part of this horrible television show. Perhaps you can attend conferences much like Ms. Carter did."

"No," I sighed then watched Elliot and Joey. I decided to ignore what he said about conferences. I'd had enough of those for a lifetime. "Those two are depending on me. I won't let them down. But Cyrus, you have got to tell me how you are able to talk to Apollo someday. I am curious about it. Do you go somewhere sacred? Does the room shake when he speaks?"

Cyrus gave me his lopsided grin and waved his ever-present cell phone in the air next to his head. "Text messages. The golden one loves human technology. He uses it every chance he gets."

Well that explained why Cyrus was so attached to his smart phone. I snatched it from him. "Let me see."

"Actually," Cyrus pulled out a flat phone much like his own, except this one was encased in a shiny gold case.

"Apollo asked me to give you this."

"A gift?" I took the phone with more than just a little hesitation. "Why?"

"So you won't burn candles on his ancient mirror anymore." Cyrus smiled at my surprise. "Yeah, he told me all about your little spell back in New York."

"You found out about that?" I grimaced. "Did I cross a line or something?"

"No. There are no rules saying you can't contact him directly. In fact, Apollo found it amusing. Hence, the cell phone. He thinks you are quite the entertaining creature."

Cyrus leaned over my shoulder then touched the sun symbol on the screen and a blank square popped up. "Here. This is how you contact him."

"So no more candles?"

"Pray, no. It took me two hours to scrub the wax from the glass. I do not wish to do that again anytime soon."

I had been so busy teasing my keeper I failed to notice the other two had finished moving all the cases inside. Elliot came over to wrap his arm around my shoulders.

"Ready?"

"Yeah." I handed Cyrus back his own cell phone. "I want to see what you've been saying about me later."

I let Elliot lead me inside as I sent my first message on my new phone to Apollo.

Protect us, Golden One. I believe we are all going to need it.

The old farmhouse was quiet. Almost peaceful. Elliot whistled when he stepped around the power cords taped across the floor to connect with large boom microphones placed next to the walls. The tacky furniture remained, but it had been rearranged to give us some breathing room. I joined Joey next to the cases then pulled out the tape recorders we would need to pick up any audible noises made by Catherine or Samuel. We decided to use some of the more basic equipment to substantiate my communication with the spirits. Spirit boxes, digital recorders, motion sensors – all could be used to track the movements of the dead.

"It feels like a thunderstorm is brewing in here." Elliot joined us. "The energies in this room are amazing."

"If you say so." I checked the batteries of the recorder in my hand then made sure to tuck a few extra ones in my pocket. Just in case. I may not have been a paranormal expert, but I'd seen enough television to know spirits liked to drain battery sources. A few extra couldn't hurt in case we were stuck upstairs. "I don't feel anything."

"Really?" Elliot took the recorder I handed him. "Joey, let's get some dialogue on film before we turn the lights off."

"Sounds good to me." Joey lifted his camera onto his shoulder. He focused it onto me. "Just act natural. Be normal."

Natural? Normal? In a house known for its tragedy? Where I knew there was a really big mirror with a really angry spirit inside of it?

Yeah, ok.

I nodded then moved to stand by the staircase. We were going to improvise our lines when we talked about the history of the house. It was decided I should be the one to start since I was officially coming out to the public as the Sibyl. Elliot shifted around the sofa then stood behind Joey to watch me in action.

"Welcome to the very first episode of *Grave Messages*." I didn't know what to do with my hands, so I tucked them into my back pockets. "My name is Eva McRayne. I am joined by Elliot Lancaster and Joey Lawson. Tonight, we are showcasing the Tillotson farmhouse which is located in the heart of the middle of nowhere. A town known as Black Hollow in Kansas.

Joanna was not going to be pleased that I refused to use the term 'murder house' on television. It sounded too cheesy. Thankfully, the guys had agreed with me. I locked eyes with Elliot as I continued. "The local papers documented the deaths of two people –Catherine and Samuel Tillotson- at this house during the blizzard of January 1876. Their bodies were found weeks later after the ice had thawed. Catherine was nothing more than a pile of bones while her husband had stabbed himself to death. Since then, there have been numerous reports of paranormal activity within these walls."

"Cut." Joey grinned as he flipped the camera up towards the ceiling. "I've always wanted to say that. Anyway, so far, so good. Let's get Elliot in there."

Elliot moved over to stand next to me then introduced himself to the camera much as I had. But where I had gone into a brief history of the house, he focused on the paranormal activity.

"Locals claim to see shadow figures walking through the rooms. Objects move around the rooms; sometimes thrown at unlucky visitors. Voices call out from the walls. In fact, we have had our own experience here earlier today."

Joey held up his hand and counted down to five. I knew that meant he needed a break in what we were saying without actually turning the camera off.

"Shall we?" I picked up the recorder from the table next to the stairs. "We will start with the classic EVPs. Electronic voice phenomena. This will be our initial method for contacting the spirits. Then I will use my own gift which will be featured later on during the show."

Elliot took a second recorder and walked the length of the first floor. Joey was following behind him at first. But he stopped then swung the camera back around to focus on the front room. He moved so quickly he almost knocked me over.

"What was that?"

"What?" I turned to see a shadow sweep across the room towards the stairs. I could see its outline against the windows. I beckoned for Joey to follow me as I approached the front. "Who's there?"

Strange noises began to fill the air around us. Moans and creaks I could have caulked up to the age of the house. Elliot moved past us to stand in the center of the room. He began to fire off questions then pausing.

"Who are you?"

"Is anyone there?"

"What's your name?"

He stopped only to allow the spirits a chance to answer. I went to stand beside him when he rewound the tape. His voice came through loud and clear. There were no answers to the first two questions. Yet on the third, a thin whisper could be heard beneath the white noise.

"Sibyl. I'm waiting."

"Oh, wow." Elliot grinned like a kid at Christmas as he replayed the message. "As you can see, folks, none of us were talking or moving when this was captured."

I wanted to be happy with him, but I was shaken. I found Cyrus in the shadows and he gestured down to the equipment cases. I knew what he was referring to. I had hidden the mirror in my duffle bag. He was saying I needed it. I shook my head.

I wasn't ready to contact Catherine. Even if I was, I'm sure the large mirror upstairs would be a much better conduit for the communications.

"Sibyl. Sibyl, come to me."

I spun around to face the direction the voice was coming from. Joey had followed my lead then whistled when he spoke. "Did you hear that?"

"Yeah." I swallowed. "Catherine wants us to come upstairs."

"So let's go." Elliot had his recorder ready as he leaned over the bannister to look up the staircase. "Eva, you stay here."

"Are you kidding me?" I was hit with an anger I couldn't explain. "Do you think I can't handle her? Do you really think I can't face this thing?"

I don't know where the anger came from. I didn't even question where the flare came from. I cursed, snatched the recorder from Elliot's hand, and shoved him aside.

"Get out of my way."

"What the hell, Eva?" Elliot went to grab my arm but froze when the voice from above could be heard again.

"Sibyl, oh, Sibyl." Catherine was singing the title I'd been given as sweetly as a lullaby. "Come. See me. I've got a message for you."

I bounded up the stairs two at a time. I didn't stop running until I was in the bedroom. Catherine had fallen silent, yet I could feel her presence. I could feel the anger radiating from the mirror showcased in this wretched place. I wanted to be afraid, but I didn't hesitate as I entered the room.

The door slammed closed behind me.

I paid no attention to it. Or to the sounds made by the guys as they tried to get inside.

"What do you want from me, Catherine? What is your message?"

Her image was just as terrifying now as it had been that afternoon. Yet she made no moves to harm me. Catherine Tillotson laughed then caressed the line across her throat.

"My message is more of a request. A demand if you will."

"Well what is it?" I stomped my foot in frustration. "I don't have all day."

"You are immortal, are you not? I am well versed in your history, creature. We all are." Catherine's dark eyes flashed. "What I want is simple enough. I wish for you to free me from this purgatory Samuel cast me into."

"Samuel." The second spirit who was supposed to haunt this place had yet to make an appearance. I didn't see anyone else in the mirror nor had we had any interaction with him since this whole thing started. "Where is Samuel, Catherine?"

"Down below." She turned her head toward. the darkness behind her. "So far down below."

"Let me speak to him."

"Samuel is gone. A hopeless cause." Catherine returned her focus onto me. "Do come closer, Sibyl."

"Yeah, I don't think so." I planted my feet in the carpet then crossed my arms over my chest. "I still have a mark where you cut me earlier. I am not going through that again."

"It was a test. Nothing more. I had to make sure you were truly who I thought you were."

I felt the anger that had propelled me to the bedroom evaporate. It was replaced with an exhaustion which caused my eyes to burn.

"I am a messenger, Catherine. I will tell your story to the world. This is all I can offer you."

"Ah, but it is what I can offer you that will " Catherine pressed her hands against the other side of the glass. "I can offer you the peace you crave so badly."

The image on the surface of the glass shifted. Catherine was no longer there, but I was. I watched as the reflection changed from the bedroom around me to the small bathroom of my studio apartment back in Athens. I watched myself as I staggered into the room. Tears streamed down my face as I grabbed the razor blade I'd used earlier that morning to shave with. I knew I had to get the metal out. I knew it was my only chance to escape the memories that flashed through my mind.

Memories of my mother. The knowledge that I was so hated - so wretched - that she herself had tried to kill me first through starvation then, with poison. She wasn't successful, but I would be.

I slammed the razor against the sink until the cheap plastic broke around it. I worked the metal blade free then stumbled backwards as I pressed it against my wrist. What had Janet told me before? Always cut vertical? Follow the veins to hit an artery?

I choked back a sob as I watched my reflection dig the blade into my skin. I had been shaking when I sliced at my right wrist, so the cut wasn't as deep as the one on the left. The doctor who had treated my wounds told me that my lack of precision was the reason I was still alive.

I moved across the bedroom towards the mirror and reached out to myself. I wanted to tell that girl that it was going to be alright, but I didn't believe those words. I wanted to tell her that everything would change after she tried to end her life, but I knew better. It was easy to lie to my parents and to Elliot, but I couldn't lie to myself.

I was distracted only when the old door finally gave way. I turned at the sound of the crash to see Elliot, Joey, and Cyrus rush into the room.

Their distraction proved to be my damnation. Catherine shrieked and broke the image that had captivated me.

"I will live again, damn you!" The spirit screamed as she lashed out. I felt the blood I had seen in the mirror rushing down my wrists. "I want my life back!"

I heard Cyrus screaming. I heard Elliot before I collapsed to my knees. He clasped my wrists and stared with widened eyes as he recognized the wounds.

He had seen them before, after all. My friend jerked off his jacket and began to wrap them around the cuts that had appeared out of nowhere. He had done that when he found me back in Athens. He had whispered to me then as he was whispering to me now.

"Hold on, Eva," Elliot gasped. "You're going to be ok. You're going to be ok."

"Don't let her get too weak, Lancaster!" Cyrus yelled from his spot by the mirror. "The spirit wishes to use her-"

I didn't hear the rest of Cyrus' words as I lost the ability to think. I lost the ability to breathe.

I lost the ability to fight. Catherine's memories began to flash behind my eyes and I knew. I could see the farmhouse as it had been before. The windows were white from the piles of snow that had drifted up around them. The blizzard had been worse than anything we'd read about in the historical reports. Snow had fallen for weeks to barricade the Tillotsons inside. I could see Catherine, her body weakened by the starvation which had set in when their food supplies had run out two weeks before. She was laying in the bed since she had become too weak to stand.

A man appeared in my vision at the side of the bed. Samuel Tillotson was staring at her. He had been waiting on her to die. She knew this just as I did. But Catherine was too strong. She reached for her husband until he sat on the bed by her side. Samuel was as hungry as she was. But he was too stubborn to join her deathbed. His family had been pioneers. They learned to survive despite the death surrounding them when the first settlements had appeared in the mountains of Tennessee. She knew he would find a way to survive this. So when he pulled his knife free from the belt he wore it on, she wasn't surprised. She was angry.

"What is this?" Catherine swallowed. "Are you planning on ending my suffering here? Tonight?"

"Yes." Samuel grasped her hand. "And mine."

These were the last words he ever spoke to her. Samuel Tillotson had slit her throat as easily as he had the remaining animals they had slaughtered weeks before. I watched in horror when Catherine's body went limp. I whimpered when I saw her soul release itself from her body.

Then, it was her turn to watch.

Catherine's spirit formed in the corner as her husband stripped off her plain shift and carried her body downstairs. He had lit a fire in the fireplace. There was a single pot above the flames. She watched in horror as he worked. She knew all too well what her fate had become.

"Oh my god." I wanted to throw up at the images assaulting my mind. "Oh my god."

I felt myself falling backwards. I collapsed onto the floor as Catherine's hold on my mind began to slip.. I forced my head up to see that she was coming out of the glass. She chanted words I couldn't understand as my vision began to blur. I wanted to sleep. I needed to sleep.

Elliot's grasp on my wrists made sure that I didn't.

"Release her." Cyrus stood between me and the spirit. In his right hand, a transparent sword glowed with a golden light I'd never seen before.

"Where does he keep that thing? In his coat pocket?" Joey whistled when he inched forward to stand behind me.

Elliot had knelt down to pull me back as Cyrus thrust his weapon forward. Catherine shrieked when he found his target, her arm fading into the shadows. She tried once more. She lunged towards me as Cyrus did his best to keep her back.

"Eva, the door. Do it now!"

The door. My door. My protection against the hell filling my mind. I stared at the woman still struggling to free herself from the glass.

I don't know how I managed to focus. Maybe it was the fire that was now rushing through my veins. I felt stronger despite my desire to sleep. I allowed the wooden door I had created only a few days to form next to my own reflection as I pushed Elliot away from me. I stood up with a strength I shouldn't have possessed then shoved my arms outward as if to slam it close. The glass shifted. It rippled when the door moved in my mind's eye. Catherine screamed when the weight of the wood shoved her back into the mirror. I rushed forward then pressed my palms against the glass and said the first words which appeared in my mind.

"By Apollo's light, leave this realm never to return."

The door in the mirror glowed as the screams coming from the other side fell silent. I didn't move until the door faded beneath my hands. I stared at the mirror in shock as Elliot stumbled over to my side. I didn't sound like myself when I spoke. My voice was hoarse. Thick with emotion as I dropped back down to my knees. I examined my wrists to see that the wounds Catherine had created had returned to their previous state as pale white scars across my skin.

No, not wounds that Catherine had created. Wounds that I myself had created back when I was broken. But I wouldn't be broken for long. I couldn't afford to be if I planned on living this life. I forced myself to breathe before I looked up to Elliot. He took the invitation for what it was and knelt beside me.

"She's gone, Elliot," I whispered. "She's gone."

TWELVE

"THE MYSTERY behind what occurred in the Tillotson household was one of desperation. Samuel Tillotson killed his wife in order to survive. I believe he killed himself in the weeks that followed not out of guilt, but because he didn't have any other choice. Catherine's spirit drove him mad."

I leaned back in the plush theatre seat and stared at my lap so I didn't have to face my image on the screen. I had been sitting on the porch steps, Elliot beside me, as we talked about what happened during filming.

Now, three weeks later, we were screening the first episode with a small group of handpicked staffers to gauge their reactions. If they didn't like it, we would have to go back to work. Joey could cut or add the scenes we had taken out back in. Joseph Lancaster was famous for the quality of his television shows. Ours would be held to the same standard.

My voice on screen melded into the music Elliot had chosen for the ending credits. He decided to have text close out the show which detailed the aftermath of our investigation. These last three lines talked about Joanna's shock in finding out just how wrong

Catherine's legend had been. They also said that all paranormal activity had ceased since our visit there.

This much was true. Joanna had been furious when we called for a follow up interview last week. She screamed at Elliot for chasing Catherine away. There hadn't been a single footstep since we left. Cyrus had explained to me why that was. Catherine's soul had been banished thanks to my little chant. Then Joanna screamed at me for making up lies about her ancestor murdering his wife just to eat her.

I wish it had been a lie. My encounter with Catherine's memories had given me enough nightmares to last a lifetime.

The film ended and there was silence while the lights came back on. Elliot took my hand and squeezed it as we waited.

We didn't have to wait for long. The applause and cheers that broke the silence was the first thing to tell us we had a hit.

Connor was the second. He stood up from his seat on the front row then gestured for the three of us to stand.

"Eva, Elliot, and Joey, everyone!" He raised a champagne flute in our direction. "Congratulations on *Grave Messages*."

Elliot pulled me to the front then turned and addressed the small group. He answered all the questions he could, but unfortunately, the focus was on me. Questions were thrown at me like knives.

"Have you always been able to talk to the dead?" A fat woman decked out in diamonds called out from the back row. "Were you born with this gift?"

"What was it like to go through the mirror?" This one came from a man who could have stepped out of an issue of *Hipster's Quarterly*. "What can you tell us about the afterlife?"

I answered what I could before turning to Elliot for an escape. He picked up on my distress immediately.

"Thank you all for coming out tonight. Connor has all the information you will need about the show. Thank you again."

The questions continued until we were out of the room. Only then did Joseph Lancaster step forward to extend his hand out to his son.

"Congratulations, Elliot. Eva."

"Thanks, Dad." Elliot shifted in place as he shook Joseph's hand. "We appreciate it."

"Kathy was right about you, Eva." Joseph smiled as he released Elliot's hand and clasped my own. "She said you would be strong enough for her line of work. I was not disappointed."

"Wait," I tightened my grip on Joseph's hand. "Kathy, as in Kathy Carter?"

"Yes. She was," Joseph paused for a moment before he continued. "She was an old friend."

"I don't understand." I thought back to New York and the session which changed me. "She picked me out of a crowd after I had disrupted her presentation. How could she have talked to you about me?"

"Kathy saw you here through her mirror. She asked that I send you to New York to ensure that you two met up." Joseph released my hands. "It all worked out for the best, don't you see? You have your hit show. Kathy was able to go to her death."

I was too stunned to be angry. I had been set up. Joseph bid us his farewells and disappeared back into the screening room. I turned on Elliot like an angry cat.

"Did you know about this?" I was so mad I could have spit. I think I did a little. "Were you in on setting me up, too?"

"Eva, whoa." Elliot stepped back with his hands up in the air. "Of course not! How could you even think such a thing?"

"You were the one who wanted to go to that stupid conference. You were the one who picked out that particular session and, might I add, the front row seat. Did you know her, too?"

"I'd heard of Kathy Carter." Elliot crossed his arms over his chest. "But I care about you, Eva. Give me some credit. Dad's right about one thing though. Things did turn out pretty well for you. After all, without the mirror, you wouldn't have your precious Cyrus by your side."

"What does he have to do with anything?" I glared at him. "Cyrus is a friend, Elliot."

"A friend you happen to get cozy with in Kansas." Elliot's eyes flashed with his own anger. "Don't deny it. I just happened to come downstairs when I didn't find you in your room. As I recall, you two were drinking away and snuggling up pretty close on the couch."

"What in the hell do you care about me and Cyrus for?" I lashed back.. "As long as you got what you wanted?"

"This was a mistake, Eva."

I felt the anger temper down as I willed for him to tell me how wrong I was. I wanted him to tell me that he had nothing to do with his dad's scheme to set me up. But Elliot was stubborn as I was. His face became unreadable as he studied me.

"We signed the contracts, so we are stuck with each other for another year. I will do my best to stay out of your way at home until I can find a new place to live."

My heart broke as I realized what he was saying. Our friendship was broken. Shattered by cracks that I didn't even know were there. I felt my tears burning in the corners of my eyes, but I refused to let them fall.

It was the hardest thing I'd ever done.

"Come on, Eva. Let's go." Cyrus appeared to take my arm. "There is nothing more to be done here."

"He's right." Elliot watched me. I knew he was waiting on me to break down and apologize to him. When I didn't, he turned his back on me. "Go home. Get some rest. I'll see you at work on Monday."

"Elliot, wait."

"No." He went back towards the room we had just left. "There is nothing more we need to say."

I didn't have the strength to follow him. I held back my tears until I sunk down into seat of a cab which pulled up out of nowhere. Cyrus shut my door for me and joined me moments later.

"Hush, Little One. Things will right themselves. Just give it some time."

I lowered my face into my hand and sobbed. Cyrus was still for only a moment before he wrapped his arm around my shoulder to pull me against him. Cyrus was my rock. He was here for me.

Cyrus had no choice. He had to stay by my side whether he wanted to be or not.

"Do you wish to talk about it?" Cyrus shifted beneath me, then handed me the silver flask. "Drink some whiskey. It will calm your nerves."

I shook my head, not ready to drown my sorrows yet. Instead, I pulled out the golden cell phone he had given me. I hadn't used it since the night we filmed in Kansas. I turned it on, unlocked the screen, and pressed the icon to pull up the text screen I needed. I started typing, stopping only to wipe the tears away when they began to blur my vision. I needed to get my mind off Elliot, even if it were only for few minutes. I turned my focus towards Apollo.

The screening audience loved the episode. I will have premiere details next week. I hope it's all worth it in the end.

October 1st -

We are on a plane heading to Iowa. Some prison that Elliot found for our second episode of Grave. Since he's barely speaking to me outside of work, he threw my concerns right out the window. Actually, no. That's not right. He didn't throw them out the window. He damn near ignored them. Just as he has been ignoring me since our fight at the premiere.

I don't understand how he could have changed so quickly. Granted, Elliot has always been one who was quick to anger and slow to forgive. I thought that if we just took a few days apart from each other, things would go back to normal between us. Isn't that why he wanted me to do the show with him in the first place? To ensure that we could work together - and stay friends? Or was I delusional when I began to believe that?

Pretty sure I was just being delusional because how he views me became crystal clear when he moved out of the condo the day after the premiere. I didn't even know he was gone until I walked into his bedroom with the intentions of smoothing things over to see that it was empty. There was no evidence that he had ever been there at all.

Perhaps, he never was. Perhaps, Elliot only saw me as a means to an end despite our friendship. I'm still convinced that he had a hand in setting me up at Paracon. He wanted his hit show and he was willing to do anything to get it.

Even if that meant saving my life back in Georgia. There's no telling how long this little scheme has been in the works, after all. Maybe he knew as far back as freshman year. Maybe that's the only reason he became friends with me in the first place.

My mind is a mess once more. I am looking for clues and excuses to explain away the pain I feel at Elliot's coldness. But as my mother would say, it is only what I deserve. I should be more grateful. I should be more appreciative of Elliot's offer.

I'm trying. God knows, I'm trying.

THIRTEEN

SEASON 1, EPISODE 2: IOWA STATE PENITENTIARY

"Look, I stole it, alright?" Gordon Morrow leaned forward on his elbows to gesture at me with his hands. "You. You're a smart girl. I can see it. You gotta believe me."

"Believe what?" I leaned back against the cold metal chair. "You haven't said anything except that you stole something. And we knew that already."

I glanced over to Elliot, who was doing a damn good job at ignoring me. He tapped his pen against his notepad as he stared at our client. Not that there was much to look at. The man had been in prison for two years and was slated to be here for another three before he was eligible for parole. Late forties, balding. The classic look of a white-collar crook.

"Ok." I smacked my hand down on Elliot's pen to stop the annoying noise. "Start from the beginning. How did you end up here in Iowa State Penitentiary?"

"I was the best." The man rubbed his hand over his mouth. "Especially with the cards. I could become anyone I wanted to be as long as they were dead. But the devil caught up with me."

"Don't you mean the police?" I scoffed. "The devil doesn't exist outside of Sunday School."

"Yes, he does. Look, I'm not crazy. I graduated at the top of my class at Cornell. Ran a successful accounting firm..."

"And yet, here you are. Sitting at Iowa State Penitentiary. Talking to the hosts of a ghost hunting show." I rolled my eyes to the ceiling. "Elliot, why are we here again?"

"The devil." Gordon hissed at me. "I keep telling you, and telling you..."

"Nothing." I pushed the chair back to stand. "Great interview. Really."

"I stole identities." Gordon clutched his hands together so hard, the handcuffs around his wrists clanked. "It was damn simple once the government started putting social security numbers online."

I glanced over to Joey, who gave me a small shrug so he didn't jostle his camera too hard. I rolled my eyes at him before turning my attention back to the man who had finally started talking.

"I got the information off them little stickers." He gestured into the empty air with two fingers. "You know. The memorial ones? I'd drive around for hours and snap pictures of everyone that I spotted. They had all I needed, you know? A name, a birthday. I'd go, plug in the information into the government's death database. The information would pop right up."

"And you started applying for credit cards, right?" Elliot was back to tapping his damn pen against his pad. "When did you run across the devil?"

The man rubbed his hands over his mouth. "Six months before I turned myself in. Did my thing. But this time, I got the wrong man's information. Luke Belzer. Born July 9, 1945. Died May 3, 2014. I used his information and got loans. Credit cards. It was the biggest haul I'd ever done."

"The devil's real name is Luke?" I chuckled. "Cute."

"He chased me. Haunted me in my dreams. The stuff I bought with his money? Cursed. The money I had obtained through my crimes? Dried up. Hundreds of thousands of dollars gone within months."

The man lowered his head and coughed against his hands. When he composed himself, he continued.

"The cops had no idea. I confessed everything. Got locked up. I thought the bars would protect me. I thought if I served my sentence, it would be enough."

"Let me guess. It wasn't." I raised an eyebrow. "What happened, Gordon?"

"The nightmares kept comin'." The man grimaced. "Dark. Twisted dreams of voices and fire. I dismissed them until I started hearing the voices during the day. They'd hit me out of nowhere."

"What would the Devil tell a man like you, Gordon?" I raised my eyebrow at him. "Good job for stealing? Atta boy?"

"Eva." Elliot hissed my name. "Stop it."

"What?" I shot back. "If you haven't noticed, we're in a prison, Elliot. This isn't your average Sunday School crowd."

"He said he would release me if I paid the right price." Our client shifted in his chair. "And that price was you."

"The price was to get publicity through the show?" I narrowed my eyes at him. "I don't understand."

"No. You. The Sibyl." Gordon grinned. "The devil's coming for you, girl. You will pay the price for my sin and I'll be free."

I started laughing before I could stop myself. I gestured to Joey so that he would stop filming, but he was way ahead of me. My friend lowered his camera and gave me a look of concern.

"Ok. Time to go, Gordon." I pushed away from the table. "Thanks for the interview. It was the most amusing thing I've heard in awhile."

"He's here." Gordon stood up as a guard approached us. "Tonight. He says he will be with you tonight."

"You can see him?" I turned around to take in the standard room we were in. It was empty save for those of us gathered around the table. "Is he really red? Does he have big, pointy horns?"

I gave our client the sweetest smile I could manage then waved as the guard led him away. When the heavy door closed behind them, I turned onto Elliot like an angry cat.

"Elliot, the devil? Seriously?"

He decided to ignore me, but I wasn't giving up that easy. Elliot glanced down at his notepad. When he started to speak, I could barely hear him.

"Luke Belzer wasn't the devil, Eva. But he was high up in the Satanist church. It's completely possible that he is haunting the man who victimized him after his death."

I started to refute him but closed my mouth before I could get the words out. Less than a month before, I was attacked by a spirit who was pissed off because her husband ate her. I knew I should have been more open to Gordon Morrow's story. But the devil? Really?

I didn't think so.

"Elliot, the man is a crook and a liar." I crossed my arms over my chest. "I get that prisons tend to be haunted. How can they not? But come on."

"Gordon Morrow's house burned down three weeks after he started using Luke Balzer's information. He got into a bad car wreck the next day. Almost killed him." Elliot held up his notebook. "His bank records show that his money was stolen while he was recovering in the hospital. That's a lot of bad luck in a very short amount of time."

"So the money he stole from other people got stolen from him? That doesn't sound like bad luck. That sounds like karma."

"What about his threat?" Joey must have decided to join our little conversation. He sat his camera down on the table between us. "The devil is coming for Eva."

"A move to make his interview more entertaining." I countered. "Remember how dramatic Joanna Whitaker was? Same thing."

"We will be careful."

I spun around to see Cyrus step out of the shadows. He had been there the entire time, but he faded in and out so well I had forgotten he was there. My keeper stepped forward with a nod in my direction.

"Creepy."

I breathed the word so that only he could hear me. My keeper chuckled before he spoke again.

"It is almost dark. Gordon Morrow's cell block has been evacuated. The prisoners moved to another area of the prison. You should have no problems if you want to go ahead and get this over with."

"Good."

Elliot glared at Cyrus so I glared back at him. Don't get me wrong. It hurt like hell to work with my old friend after our fight. And I was bitter.

I shook my head to clear my thoughts. I was still new to this life. This craziness. I didn't have a full grasp on it yet, and I didn't think I ever would. I had to take things one at a time and right now?

I had to focus on filming the second episode. I didn't have time for Elliot or his unnecessary drama. I had to find out just what this devil was that threatened me.

I looped my arm through Cyrus', ignored Elliot, and turned towards the door. "Let's go."

" I don't like this, Little One." Cyrus whispered when we followed Elliot and Joey through a hall lined with bars. "The essence of this place is vile."

"You don't like anything associated with *Grave Messages*." I gave him a sad smile. "But I think you're right this time. I don't like this either."

Cyrus must have noticed my sadness because he squeezed my hand against his arm. He had witnessed my fight with Elliot. And he had spent the past few weeks holding my hand as I cried myself to sleep. My keeper was becoming more than just a necessary staple by my side. He was becoming a friend as well.

A concerned friend. Cyrus gave me a stern look when we approached Gordon's cell that told me more than his words ever could.

Be careful. Use Apollo's mirror. And by god, don't do anything stupid.

"Yeah, yeah." I muttered. "I got it. I'll stay safe."

"If you two are done over there, I'd like to get started."

Elliot snapped. He was standing in front of a cell identical to the ones we had passed. I bit back my own smart response when he opened the door. I stepped inside with a whistle. The cell was basic. Bed. Sink. Toilet. It was dark. Tiny.

Totally uninhabitable. I couldn't understand how a human being could survive in a space so small. I swallowed down the claustrophobia that threatened to overwhelm me as I straightened my hair. I turned to see Cyrus nod at me before he faded back into the shadows. At least he was here. At least he would help me get through this.

Of that, I was certain.

"In three, two..."

Joey lifted his camera to his shoulder and pointed at me. That was my cue. I forced a smile onto my face and began to speak.

"Welcome to the second episode of *Grave Messages*. Tonight, we come to you from cell D29 here at Iowa State Penitentiary. Built in 1839 before Iowa was even a state, these walls have the capacity to hold some five hundred and fifty of the state's worst offenders."

I stepped forward. Joey stepped back.

"Like most prisons, this one has a dark past. Riots, murders, suicides. Death reigns in a place such as this. But we aren't here to explore the past. We are here to examine the claims of a man who says he is being haunted by the devil himself."

Elliot slipped past Joey to stand behind me. I couldn't explain it, but the room grew cold. The walls seemed darker. Closer. My co-host clasped his hand on my shoulder as he began his monologue.

"Gordon Morrow invited *Grave Messages* here with the hope that we could contact the spirit haunting him. You see, our client's crime was fraud, pure and simple. He used the personal information of the dead to steal hundreds of thousands of dollars. This time, he got more than what he was bargaining for."

Joey held up three fingers and Elliot went silent. I knew what he was doing. The pause would mark the video so that our cameraman could splice in our interview with Gordon. When he lowered his hand, Elliot continued speaking.

"Gordon has suffered misfortune after misfortune since he stole the identity of Luke Belzer, a Satanist who died under mysterious circumstances. A fire. A car wreck. Voices."

I heard a strange scratching noise in the wall closest to my head. Joey must have heard it too because he swung his camera to focus on me. I turned to see three long scratches forming across the pale green paint.

"Hey! Too close!" I cried out as I jumped back. Elliot caught me against him as a low rumble filled the tiny space. No, not a rumble. Laughter. Something was laughing at us.

"Joey, did you get that?" Elliot released my shoulders. "Tell me you got that."

"Yeah." Our cameraman's voice was thick. "I got it."

"Explain that one, Eva." Elliot tried to sound stern, but there was no mistaking the excitement in his voice. "Joey, give me the recorder."

"What is the point of ESPs?" I studied the scratches. "Give me Apollo's mirror."

"Eva, I don't think that's such a great idea right now."

"Why not?" I frowned. "That's the whole reason why we are here, right? To use my abilities to talk to the dead? We'll just see what this Luke has to say for himself."

I moved past Joey and knelt to the equipment cases we'd left outside the cell. I pushed aside the crap Joey insisted we needed until I found the mirror. I freed it from the velvet cloth it had been wrapped in. The effect on me was immediate. Frenzied whispers filled my ears but I forced myself to ignore them.

"As you know, I'm still learning how to do this whole Sibyl thing." I lifted the mirror up so that Joey could see it. "What you see is a single mirror. But to me? It's an ancient relic used to speak with the dead."

I flipped the mirror around. Faces shifted in a blur as the dead scrambled to get through. It was the same thing that happened every time I looked into a reflective surface. I didn't think I'd ever get used to it. The faces. The whispers. It was frightening. Maddening.

But I had to do it. There was only one way out of the hell I'd been put in and I wasn't ready to commit suicide just yet.

"Show me Luke Belzer." I tightened my grip on the mirror's handle. "As the Sibyl of Apollo, I demand..."

"Nothing. You cannot command me."

The faces stopped and a single man appeared in the glass. He was young. Gaunt. His dark hair fell over his eyes

"I can't believe Gordon thought you were the devil." I laughed as Joey shifted behind me to capture the mirror I was talking to on film. "You look like you work for a goth store in the mall."

I heard a thick growl just before a force shoved me so hard, I smacked into Joey. He managed to keep his grip on the camera, but I couldn't keep mine on the mirror. It clattered against the tile floor.

"Dammit."

I disentangled myself from Joey and bent down to pick up the mirror. Or at least, I tried to. The golden handle was so hot, it scalded my fingers. I hissed as I dropped it.

"Why are you here?" I demanded. "And what the hell is your problem? That hurt!"

"I've come to collect what my master has demanded." The spirit leered at me. "Come closer, Sibyl."

"Who is your master?" I refused to get any closer to the glass. "What do you want from me?"

"The Dark One." Luke shimmered. I wondered if I was losing contact with him. "He has demanded your head for the blood that runs through your veins."

"I," I laughed. I couldn't help it. "I don't know what to say to that. I didn't realize I was so popular with Satan. Is he a fan of the show?"

"Stupid girl."

The spirit hissed. I saw his hand appear in the corner of the glass just before a wicked burning spread across my back. I cried out as I fell forward.

Too bad I fell closer to the mirror. Just where he wanted me. Luke's hand slipped through the glass to grab my hair. He jerked me down and laughed in triumph.

"Hades will be pleased! I have ended the reign of the Sun!"

Luke Belzer screamed when a thick golden blade sliced through his wrist. Cyrus wrapped his arm around my waist to pull me back.

"Send Hades my regards." Cyrus turned to me. "The door, Little One."

"But, I still don't know..."

"The door. Now."

Cyrus looked at me as the spirit began to hiss. He struck out again, this time aiming for my keeper. Cyrus blocked the thing with his sword.

"Eva!"

I closed my eyes and envisioned the mirror lying on the ground by my feet. Even through my mind's eye, I could see the spirit of Luke Belzer struggling with Cyrus. I heard a crash against the bars, but I didn't look to see what caused the noise. I saw the door I had created appear. I shoved it closed when the spirit reared back once he lost his grip on my Keeper.

The crazy whispers began so strong, I slammed my hands over my ears to block them out. It was no use. Cyrus swept up the mirror with one quick move. He tossed it back into the equipment case, but it wasn't until he slammed the lid closed that the voices in my head stopped.

"Eva, are you hurt?"

My keeper approached me while Joey focused on me again. Even Elliot joined us. I shook my head until Elliot clapped me on the back. I whimpered as the burning resumed.

"He did something to my back." I winced. "It burns."

"Turn around." Cyrus' tone left no room for argument. I shifted around and the other two went behind me as my keeper lifted my shirt.

"Good lord." Joey broke the silence. "Hold still, Evie. I have to get this one on film."

"What is it?" I twisted my head around, but there was no way I was going to be able to see anything. "What did he do?"

"He scratched you." Cyrus brushed his fingers across my exposed skin. "Minor wounds, Little One. You should be healed within the hour."

I couldn't stop myself when I whirled around to press my face into Cyrus' chest. I ignored Elliot when he stomped out of the cell. I even ignored Joey as I willed my body to quit shaking. Once I had control over myself, I looked up at my keeper. My guardian.

My mentor. One I was sure would have the answers I needed so badly.

"Belzer said Hades. Does that mean he is a threat? Why would he want my head on the proverbial platter?"

"Hades' reasoning is as unstable as his reputation." Cyrus shook his head. "I told you before, Eva. This is not a life for the weak. You will gain many more enemies than friends."

I swallowed down my fear at his words. I hadn't been the Sibyl for a good month yet, and I'd already been attacked by two spirits. Could I do this? Was I strong enough to live this life?

There was only one way to find out. I squared my shoulders then faced Joey as I relished in a newfound determination.

"Joey, set up the perimeter cameras. Mr. Morrow's devil wasn't as strong as he thought he was. We need more to make a full episode. Let's explore the other spirits that may roam these halls."

"Sounds like a plan, Evie."

Joey grinned as he took off. He was ruffling through the equipment cases when I caught sight of Cyrus grinning down at me.

"What?" I placed my hands on my hips. "Did you think a few scratches were going to scare me into suicide?"

"No. There was never a doubt in my mind that you were meant to be the Sibyl, Eva." Cyrus took my hand and put it in the crook of his arm. "Never a doubt in my mind."

October 2nd -

So Iowa turned out to be interesting. I encountered the spirit of a Satanist and I think I figured out what the hell is up with Elliot. He's jealous of Cyrus. If he would talk to me, I'd tell him that he had nothing to worry about. I'd tell him that Cyrus wasn't going to replace him as my friend. But at the rate we're going right now? I don't know how much longer I can even classify Elliot in the friendship category.

I will admit, his sudden change has scared me a little. Elliot has always been moody. He's always wanted to be the center of my attention when I was around him. How could I not have realized that before now? Have I been so wrapped up in my own misery all this time that I completely ignored the signs that maybe - just maybe - Elliot Lancaster has his own problems?
Probably. My mother was always quick to call me selfish. Self-absorbed. That was her response to my suicide attempt. How dare I ruin her chance to attend my graduation? Couldn't I have waited another week before I did something so selfish?
She didn't understand. Janet McRayne would never understand. The concept of suicide was only beneficial if it got someone out of her way. Someone like me.

At any rate, we're heading to Detroit, Michigan to some photography studio. I have no idea where Elliot found this location and truth be told? I probably didn't want to know.

FOURTEEN

SEASON 1, EPISODE 3: DETROIT, MICHIGAN

HERE WE GO AGAIN.

I watched the rain-soaked skyscrapers pass by in a blur. We had been on the road for over a month now if you counted our trip to New York. We'd bounced between airports and hotels so much, I was starting to question where I was at any given moment. I frowned at the back of Elliot's head as he pulled down a side street.

"Elliot, how in the ever lovin' hell do you find these places?"

I groaned when I caught sight of the decaying Victorian he had parked in front of. The house was located just south of downtown Detroit and its gray exterior matched the late October sky to perfection.

"HauntedPlaces.com." Elliot teased. "Google it. I guarantee you'll spend hours reading the stories on there, Evie."

I jerked my head away from the depressing scenery at his use of my nickname. Elliot and I had a very torrid history. Right now, we were working together under a fragile truce that threatened to break each time I made Elliot mad.

And I was exceptional when it came to pissing my co-host off.

"Because you should believe everything you read online, right?" I scoffed. "Next time I get to pick the location. This one is way too cliché."

"How so?" Elliot unbuckled his seat belt. "Just look at this place! It's the perfect image of a haunted house."

"Exactly my point." I called after him as he exited the vehicle. I kept talking when he opened the back hatch. "We need to stand out from the other ghost shows, Elliot. Haunted Victorian is not going to do that for us."

"No but having a Sibyl who can talk to the dead can."

"You wouldn't happen to know anything about this house, would you, Cyrus?" I let my keeper help me out onto the sidewalk. "Elliot hasn't said a word about the history of this place. It'd be nice to know if I'm going to be attacked again."

"Always be ready for an attack, Little One." Cyrus gave me a small smile. "But no, I am afraid I cannot help you with the details."

"Great." I muttered. "I thought you knew everything. Thanks for ruining that delusion."

Cyrus chuckled before he took my arm. "Just know that I will be here when you need me."

"Anything else?" I raised an eyebrow at him. "Any helpful tips for contacting the dead?"

"Nothing that I haven't been trying to drill into your head over the past month." Cyrus shifted so that we could start up the narrow walkway. "But I do not sense any danger for you inside those walls."

"Just lots of cobwebs and crazy people." I frowned up at him. "You don't seem right today. You're more philosophical than normal. You ok?"

Cyrus didn't get the chance to answer me. Joey bounded over to loop my free arm through his.

"We can't get started without our star player. Hurry up, Evie. It's freezing out here."

"Really?" I shrugged before I glanced back at Cyrus. "Tell me later?"

"Perhaps."

My keeper gave me a nod when he took a step back towards the car. Within seconds, he had faded away into the shadows lining the street.

Elliot was already on the porch. From the glare he threw me, I knew he had overheard my conversation with Cyrus. I started to snap at him. Tell him to mind his own damn business when the front door flew open.

A thin woman looked up from the book she carried in one hand. She stared at us for a moment before calling out behind her.

"Taylor, your ghost people are here!"

Ghost people?

I mouthed the words to Joey who just shrugged at me. I suppose there are worse things to be called, but really?

I didn't get a chance to introduce myself. The woman snapped her book closed then beckoned us inside.

"Taylor was so excited when you called." Our client flipped her long dark hair over her shoulder. "I keep telling her she's reading too many damn paranormal books. But what do I know?"

"I'm Elliot." My co-host gave the dark beauty a grin. "And you are Michelle, I presume?"

"Yes. Michelle Morales. Nice to meet you."

"I'm Eva. Eva McRayne." I stepped forward to interrupt the sudden silence. "And this is Joey Lawson. He's our camera guy and tech guru. He'll be setting you up with microphones."

Michelle was staring at Elliot with obvious interest. My co-host stared right back. So, I cleared my throat to break up their little moment.

"So, listen." I stuffed my hands in the pockets of my jacket. "We need to scout this place out for good spots to set up perimeter cameras. And since I've been in makeup all day, I'd like to get the interviews over with as soon as possible. Where can we set up?"

"The parlor." Michelle answered automatically. "I know you asked for full access to the house, but there is one place you can't go. Taylor's darkroom. If you open the door, you risk ruining her photographs."

"Alright." I glanced over to Elliot, who was still standing by the door like an idiot. "You said Taylor contacted us. She's here, right?"

"Of course. She wouldn't miss a chance to talk about her ghosts for the world." Michelle sat her book down on a hall table. "Stay here in the parlor. I'll go get her. I don't think she heard me call out before."

The parlor was a room not far from the front door. I watched Elliot shake his head before he decided to join us. I crossed my arms over my chest and resisted the urge to smack him out of his daze when Joey piped up.

"You said she has a darkroom?" My friend's excitement lined his words. "Is she a photographer?"

"Yes." Michelle stopped in the open doorway with a look of confusion. "Taylor Forester. She runs Still Life Photography. I thought she explained all that when your people called."

"We haven't had a chance to read over your file yet." I threw Elliot a scathing look. "Elliot told us we were taking a detour to Detroit when we got to the airport this morning."

"Oh." Michelle shrugged. "Doesn't matter. Let me get Taylor. She'll tell you all you need to know about her ghosts."

Our client left us alone in a room decked out in rich reds. I could hear Joey practically drooling as he started to open his equipment cases.

"Ok. First off," I took the opportunity to smack Elliot's arm. "We are not filming a dating show. You need to stop staring at our client that way. And second, when are you going to let us in on the history of this house? I feel like I need to know something if I'm going to hold an interview."

"What?" Elliot asked, never taking his eyes off the door Michelle had gone through. "Did you say something?"

"No. Of course not." I narrowed my eyes at him. "I'm just talking to the walls over here. What is wrong with you?"

"Nothing." Elliot cleared his throat when he looked over at Joey. "Why don't you take a look around, Evie? I'm going to help with the set up."

"Fine." I rolled my eyes. "We'll have the two girls sit on the couch. Pull those two wing back chairs closer to it. That way we can have an actual conversation."

While the two of them did what I asked, I started to meander around the room. The style was a strange mix of Gilded Age and Victorian antiques. It would have been an impressive collection except the beauty was coated. Hidden by a thick layer of dust that made me sneeze if I got too close to anything.

The most fascinating aspect of the entire room were the pictures. Each one was hung in such a way that they tilted away from the wall. Old tin types of men and women who stared out into nothingness. I stopped long enough to study the one closest to me. Two women dressed in their finest were draped over a small couch. But the picture was damaged. Three jagged lines cut downward across the figures.

"They were sisters."

I spun around to see a wispy blonde dressed in black from head to two standing behind me. She gestured at the picture.

"It's true. You can still see the resemblance a hundred years later. Not even death could take that away from them."

Ok. Creepy. I took a breath and stuck out my hand.

"Eva McRayne. You're Taylor?"

"Yes." She gave me a small smile. "I was surprised when Theia Productions contacted me back. I was sure it was a mistake. After all, why would you be interested in my little ghost story?"

"Why not?" I shrugged. "I'm sure it's the same as all the others."

"I wouldn't say that, Sibyl." She chuckled. "Perhaps we should get started. It will be night soon."

"Sure."

I watched the women approach Elliot and Joey, both throwing their heads back with laughter at something Joey said. I sighed before I moved over to one of the chairs.

"Joey, you ready?"

I glanced up when he didn't respond. My friend was staring at Taylor with a fascination I couldn't explain. I looked between them with a frown before I snapped my fingers in front of Joey's eyes.

"Joey, earth to Joey. You ready?"

"Yeah."

He cleared his throat and lifted his camera. I clipped my

microphone on the collar of my shirt then checked to make sure Taylor and Michelle had been equipped as well.

I was surprised to see that they were with the way Joey and Elliot were acting. Maybe they were tired. Maybe they needed a night off.

Or maybe, just maybe, I was being paranoid. This was only our third location. But after the first two?

I was expecting the worst. I was expecting the boogieman to jump out from any corner any minute now.

I waited until Joey pointed at us before I spoke. Elliot didn't seem to mind. He was too busy staring at Michelle to be of any use at the moment.

"Taylor Forester and Michelle Morales, everyone." I gestured towards the two on the couch. "Taylor, Michelle says that you are convinced your home is haunted."

"I'm not convinced." The woman lifted her chin up in defiance. "I know it is."

"How so?" I pulled a pen out of my pocket under the pretense of taking notes. "What have you experienced?"

"Knocks." She glanced over at Michelle. "Every night at nine o'clock, we hear a series of loud knocks over our beds. It never fails."

"Could it be a train? Noises from passing cars?" I jotted a word down on my pad. It wasn't a nice one. "The plumbing?"

Michelle shook her head. "No. We thought about that. We used to laugh it off until we started seeing scratches appear on Taylor's collection."

"Collection?" I turned towards the blonde. "The antiques?"

"No." She shook her head. "The tin types. I adore them and the stories they tell."

"Tell me about those." I gestured around the room, but Joey didn't take my cue. Nor did he take the camera off the four of us. I rolled my eyes and let my arm drop. "The walls are all covered in Victorian photographs for our viewers at home."

Joey jerked but he stayed focused. I turned back to the women when Taylor spoke up.

"I have collected them for years. They are each the product of post-mortem photography."

"Post-mortem?" I interrupted. "Your house is covered with pictures of dead people?"

"Well, not all of them are dead." Michelle broke in. "Family members would often pose with their deceased loved ones. It was the only photograph they would have of the one they lost."

"The only remembrance." Taylor nodded. "So, no, I don't see my house as covered with pictures of dead people, as you put it. But filled with remembrances."

I felt the hairs on the back of my neck stand up as she was speaking. Her dark eyes flashed when she stared back at me. For the first time in a very long time, I was rendered speechless.

"Do you think your haunting is connected to your photographs?" Elliot finally decided to play a part in this episode. "I mean, did the paranormal activity start after you brought a particular tintype home?"

Michelle and Taylor looked at each other. I didn't miss the small grins that passed between them. I cleared my throat and decided to ask another question when they didn't answer.

"Ok. Tell us about the house itself. Any deaths that you know of?"

"Oh, lots!" Michelle turned towards me. "This house was built in 1902 by the Guillard family. They all died here."

"Natural deaths? Murders? What?"

Me again. The boys were still standing stock still. Still staring. I would have been freaked out if I wasn't so annoyed. Maybe they were more tired than what I thought.

"Natural." Taylor responded as she picked at the sleeve of her dress. "We looked up the history of the house when we bought it. Heart problems, I believe."

"Well, at least there's that." I jotted a single line down on my notepad. "I couldn't help but notice the lack of mirrors here. There's none in the hall. None here in the parlor. Do you have any in the house that I should be aware of?"

"No."

The two of them snapped in unison. I raised an eyebrow when Michelle recovered enough to give me a reason.

"We believe in the old ways. Spiritualists believed that mirrors were portals for the dead. Since we are having issues with ghosts, we decided not to give them another door to come through."

"Alright. So you two are Spiritualists? I thought that fad died out with corsets and big hats."

"Yes." Taylor smiled. "Now you will have free reign in the house. But promise me you won't go into my darkroom. If the light hits the pictures I have drying, they will be destroyed."

I started to tell her that I had no interest in going into her precious darkroom when I felt the sweet security that meant Cyrus had joined us. Most people couldn't see him unless he stepped out into the light, but I could have sworn I saw the two women turn in his direction.

Michelle gave me a smile before she stood. "It is getting dark outside. Perhaps it is time for your investigation to begin."

"I suppose so." I closed my notebook. "Where will the two of you be staying?" "A hotel in town. Care to escort us outside?"

When Taylor walked past Joey, she winked as she ran her fingers under his jaw. I saw Michelle take Elliot's arm. The four of them walked out of the room without another word.

"What in the hell is going on here?" I crossed my arms as Cyrus approached me. "Cyrus, that was not normal."

"Eva..."

I didn't give him a chance to finish. I went to the equipment cases set up in the hallway. I dug through them until I found one of the personal video cameras Joey had tried to force on me when we first started the show. I was snapping the battery in place when Cyrus spoke up again.

"Little One, what are you doing?"

"Taking advantage of the distraction that the Barbie twins are creating." I stood up then pressed two buttons on the side. "Let's go exploring, Cy."

"Are you certain?" Cyrus raised a dark eyebrow at me. "Perhaps it would be best if you wait for the others."

"Are you kidding me?" I scoffed. "You saw how infatuated Joey and Elliot were. They weren't any help during the interview. I seriously doubt if that's going to change."

I turned the camera towards me and made sure the night vision was on. It had gotten dark in the room much sooner than I expected.

"Welcome to the Guillard house in Detroit, Michigan." I panned the camera away from me to cover the room we were standing in. When I was finished, I focused it back on myself. "So, this is going to be a first one for me. I'm filming by myself. Where's Joey? Elliot? Yeah. They are preoccupied at the moment."

I gestured to Cyrus to follow me up the stairs. The boards creaked so loud, I was convinced I was going to fall through them. I grinned when I reached the top.

"This house is owned by Taylor Forester and Michelle Morales. The truth is, I am absolutely clueless about what we are going to find. I'm learning about this place along with you."

I pushed open the first door and held the camera as still as possible. The room was large. Dark. I jerked away from the doorway when I walked into a massive set of cobwebs.

"Ew." I breathed. "Check this out, Cyrus."

My keeper stepped in behind me. I didn't have to turn around to know that he had stiffened behind me.

"The room's empty." I spoke to the camera, but I was thinking out loud too. "There's nothing here."

I whipped around and went to the next room in the hallway. Then the next. Each room held the same story. All empty. All barren except for faded wallpaper that had seen its best days decades before. I whistled as I faced Cyrus in the last room.

"Strange, don't you think?"

"Very." Cyrus pressed his lips together in a hard line. "But perhaps there is an explanation."

"Like what?" I frowned. "Come on, Cyrus. Ask yourself the most important question here. Where's their stuff?"

"What do you mean?"

"Clothes. Makeup. Piles of crap collected after each mall trip." I shrugged. "There's nothing personal in these rooms."

"Perhaps they stay downstairs." My keeper shoved his hands in his pockets. "It was not uncommon for families who lived in large houses to shut off sections of it in order to cut back costs."

"Maybe." I bit my lip. "Let's go downstairs. I'm sure the guys have finished drooling by now."

I was out in the hallway when a low moan filled my ears. I stopped so quick, Cyrus had to grab my shoulders to keep from bumping into my back.

"Careful, Little One." He whispered. "Even I have issues seeing in the dark."

I ignored the shiver that ran my spine. I glanced at him over my shoulder with a small smile, squeezed his hand, and put my finger to my lips. I wanted to see if I could hear the sound again.

I wasn't disappointed. Seconds later, I heard the moan coming from the room I'd first entered upstairs. I grabbed Cyrus' hand and used the screen on the camera to find my way back to the room. I stepped past the nasty cobweb then scanned the room with the camera. It was still empty. No movements. Nothing until I caught sight of the window in my small screen. I lifted my head to see words written in the thick layer of dust against the glass.

"Help me." I read the words out loud. "What the hell?"

I turned to Cyrus, my eyes wide. "Do you have Apollo's mirror?"

"Of course." My keeper started to reach into his front pocket when we heard a crash downstairs. We met each other's eyes before I took off towards this newest interruption.

"Elliot? Joey?" I called. "Where are you?"

Nothing. I checked the parlor. The rooms set off to the side. There was no one here. But that wasn't the strangest part of this little tale. The parlor was the only room that had furniture in it. Like the rooms upstairs, the rest of the house was empty. I reached a final door that had a small sign on it.

"Taylor's dark room." I tilted my head towards Cyrus. "Hmm...I wonder if Theia will pay for any damage if I'm wrong."

Not like I cared. I had a sinking suspicion that I was going to find something horrible behind that door. I saw the tip of Cyrus' golden broadsword enter my line of vision. I took a deep breath then shoved the door open.

If I thought the rest of the house was dark, it was nothing compared to this room. The walls had been covered with a black material. Black and white photographs hung from a clothes line across the ceiling. I held my hand over my mouth when a strong chemical smell filled my nostrils. I shut the door behind Cyrus and held up my hand when I heard a female giggling.

"You deserve eternal life, darling Elliot, for your beauty alone."

I tried to be quiet, I really did. I peeked around a thick black cloth to see Taylor and Michelle standing over a small couch that looked strangely familiar. I couldn't see Elliot, but I could see Joey. He was barely sitting up. His dark head flopped back against the cushions with a stupid grin on his face.

Every fiber in my being screamed for me to run, but I stayed put. I lifted the camera up and focused on the women. I watched Taylor lean over Joey to whisper in his ear. Michelle disentangled her arms from around Elliot's neck to stand. I forced myself to stay still until I saw the woman return with two glasses in her hands. She passed one to Elliot and the other to Joey.

"Join us, won't you?" She purred. "Live forever with us here in the land of the dead."

Ok. That was enough.

"Hey!" I put the camera down on the bookshelf on my right. "What in the hell is going on here?"

Neither woman appeared surprised that I had found them. Nor did they seem to care in the slightest.

"Jealous?" Taylor giggled. "Come now, Sibyl. Surely you wouldn't deny your friends the same offer you were given."

"Jealous?" I repeated her word, but my version had much more venom in it. "I'm not jealous. What did you do to them?"

"Ah, don't be such a square, Evie." Joey slurred. He sounded worse than a drunk. "Sit down. Have your picture taken."

"No." I snapped. "Come on. We're leaving."

I started towards the couch when the two women appeared right in front of me.

Michelle clicked her tongue against the back of her throat while Taylor shook her head.

"You can't have them." Taylor sounded almost apologetic when she spoke. "Their souls belong to us now."

"Souls?" I narrowed my eyes. "What are you talking about?"

Our clients shifted. Their bodies changed before my very eyes. Their torsos became longer. Their hands? Claws. I took a step back when Michelle threw me a wicked grin.

"Men, dear Sibyl, are the most vulnerable of creatures, don't you think? They fall into traps so simple. A pretty face. A happy smile."

I glanced up at the ceiling as I remembered the moan upstairs. The words written in dust on the second story window. I felt Cyrus grab my arm to push me behind him. I realized this was not their first time.

"Who are you?" I whispered. "What are you?"

"Did Tom pay you a visit?" Michelle's grin widened. "He was a favorite of mine until he wasted away. That happens, you know, when you become too arrogant for your own good."

"Tom?" I blinked. "Who is Tom?"

"Oh! And Foster!" Taylor twisted her long fingers in front of her face. "He was just as bad until we put him in the pictures!"

The pictures that lined the walls in the parlor. I held onto Cyrus and took in the couch. It was the very same one I had seen in the photographs. Except this time, it had two people on it that were still very much alive.

I hoped.

"You killed men to take pictures of their corpses?" I couldn't hide the disgust in my voice. "I thought you said you collected the post-mortem shots as remembrances."

"They are!" Taylor stomped her foot. "They are our memories. Men think they can come and go as they please. But a little wine and a drop of poison was all it took to keep them where we wanted them."

"Ok." I squeezed Cyrus' arm to tell him that we needed to get Joey and Elliot. I felt him tense up in front of me. "That explains the why of your horror story. But not the what."

"You don't know what we are? Truly?" Michelle blinked. "Why, it's true then! The spirits told us you were ignorant."

"Yeah? Well, I don't." I snapped. "I know you're not human. I know you're not sane. The only thing I don't know is what you are."

"Banshee." Taylor sang the word. "That's my favorite title."

"Women who are harbingers of dark omens." Cyrus decided that now was the perfect time to fill me in. "Often seen in houses where death is imminent."

"And you wanted us to film your little murder spree for what reason?" I was inching further behind Cyrus. "I don't get that either."

"To pull in more visitors." Michelle sighed as if it should have been obvious. "We get lonesome. Our walls haven't had a new picture on them in months. We were hoping your little show could bring us the company we so crave."

I grabbed the camera off the shelf and smacked the buttons on the top. The light on it was small, but it would have to do. I said a small prayer of thanks when a warm yellow glow filled the darkroom.

"Cyrus, get Elliot! I've got Joey!"

I cried out, but there was no way he could have heard me. The second the light broke against the shadows, the banshees in front of us began to scream. Taylor covered her eyes as she groped for her pictures. Michelle? She groped for my head.

"Damn you!"

She shrieked. The creature wrapped her hand around my shoulder, but I had the advantage of momentum. I shoved myself away from her to see Cyrus had lifted Elliot over his shoulder.

"I'll get him outside." My keeper shouted over the noise. "I'll be back in a few seconds for Joey."

"Evie, what's going on?" Joey muttered before he grinned at me. "You know you like it when I'm helpless."

"I'd like it if you were doing your damn job." I had to lean into him to hear what he had said, so I had no problems with yelling in his ear. "And how the hell do you weigh so much, Lawson? All you eat is sushi and McDonalds."

"No!" Taylor's cold arm snaked around my waist to jerk me back. "You can't have him!"

I saw Cyrus reappear, his broadsword in hand. He pressed the tip of his sword against Taylor's throat. The wretched screams went silent so fast, I could hear ringing in my ears. I could see Cyrus talking. I felt the banshee release me. But I had no idea what was going on.

I snatched the camera off the floor where it had fallen, wrapped my arm around Joey's waist and got him out the door. It felt like forever, but I was halfway to the front door when Cyrus appeared beside me. He grabbed Joey, threw my friend over his shoulder, and yelled at me when another round of shrieking filled the house.

"Run!"

I didn't stop to argue as the walls around us began to shake. The glass windows shattered around us when we pushed past the stairs. I slammed my hands over my ears as I made it to the front lawn to see Elliot sprawled out in the grass by the sidewalk. I fell to my knees beside him when I heard the unmistakable sound of wood cracking. Even over the screams, I could see the house was falling in on itself.

"Eva, are you alright?"

Cyrus asked me his inevitable question, but I couldn't respond. I watched the house implode. The roof began to crumble downward when I looked down at the camera I had dropped in my lap when I fell.

"Yeah." I choked. "I'm fine. And I've got the footage to prove it."

"Welcome to Detroit, Michigan and to the latest episode of *Grave Messages*."

I was sitting on the steps that led up to the rubble once known as the Guillard house. Joey gave me a sheepish smile as he filmed my monologue. Elliot sat behind him pouting since he'd spent the entire time with banshees in a stupor. I winked at my cameraman before I continued.

"Tonight, we bring you footage we shot two days ago inside this very house." I gestured to the pile behind me. "And believe me when I say it was quite the ride. This house was built by Sir Albert Guillard in 1902. Old money. New power. He expanded his wealth with investments. And he had a family. So far, so boring?"

I smiled as I stepped over to the remains of a sign. I picked it up so that Joey could focus on it.

"Not quite. You see, his daughters allowed us to film them here. You will meet them in a moment. Taylor and Michelle Guillard who married to become Taylor Forester and Michelle Morales. Independent women who, when love failed them, decided to take action into their own hands."

Joey held up his fingers, counted to three, then gestured for me to continue.

"They became obsessed with spiritualism to the point where they combined Taylor's love of photography with Michelle's obsession with the soul. The two women did horrible things and became something else. Something unworldly."

I went silent and waited for Elliot to join me. When he didn't, I dropped the sign back into the grass.

"Fear may be able to twist the mind, but loneliness is strong enough to break it. The creatures you will meet tonight fell into a darkness they couldn't understand. And all that was left?"

I turned back towards the house and tucked my hands in my pockets.

"Each other. They shared memories of a time long forgotten so they created pictures of the dead. The love they held for each other? It was their one last remembrance."

Joey raised his hand in a fist then counted to five with his fingers before he lowered his hand. I snapped off the microphone before I whirled around on Elliot.

"So are you embarrassed? Or are you just going to start being an asshole to me onscreen as well as off?"

"How am I being an asshole?" Elliot stood and approached me. He stopped when he was inches away from my face. "You made the entire episode about you. About how you 'saved' us. And you expect me to be happy about that?"

"What did you want me to do? Let you become banshee food?"

Before Elliot could respond, my phone started to ring. I pulled it out of my back pocket, chiding myself for not putting it on silence before the camera started rolling. I saw my mother's number on the screen and groaned.

"I have to take this."

I headed back to the car and got in the backseat before I answered. I didn't want to risk Elliot leaving me behind. Given the mood he was in, that was definitely a possibility.

"McRayne."

"Evangelina," My mother's clipped voice was as welcome as the banshee screams. "I am very disappointed in you."

Of course, she was. Not a day went by during my childhood that she hadn't been disappointed in something I had done. But I knew better than to say such a snarky thing out loud.

"You must have seen the premiere last night."

"I did. An unfortunate travesty. I won't be able to go outside for a month now."

"I didn't follow the press on it, but Elliot did mention this morning that the critics loved it." I tried to defend my work against *my* harshest critic. "And the ratings went through the roof."

"You showed your...your...scandal!" She sounded more disgusted than concerned. "Do you know how hard I have worked to keep that quiet? And you paraded your madness with pride! You should be ashamed of yourself! Not to mention your wardrobe. You looked huge on my screen! I was mortified, Evangelina. Mortified!"

I winced as she continued to rail on me about the Black Hollow episode. I waited until the others joined me inside the vehicle before I dared to interrupt her. "Mom? Listen, I have to go."

"How dare you?" Janet sounded indignant. "I am your mother! You can't hang up on me!"

"I'm not hanging up on you." I lied. "I have to catch a plane and I'm about to miss the boarding call."

"Where are you going now?"

"Back to California. We're planning a live Halloween show." I shifted the phone in my hand. "I'll call you later, Mom."

"No, you won't. You're a horrible, disrespectful girl."

She hung up on me and I released a sigh of relief. Joey popped up from the third seat behind me and rested his elbows on the top of my seat. "So...that sounded awful."

"My mom," I gestured to him with my phone. "She's not too happy with me."

"She's never been too happy with you." Elliot snorted as he pulled into traffic. "Don't sugarcoat it, Eva. We could all hear her."

"Just drive, please," I tucked my phone in my bag. "I want to go home."

"Your wish is my command, your highness," Elliot sneered at me through the rear view mirror. "Whatever you say."

FIFTEEN

SEASON 1, EPISODE 4: LOS ANGELES, CALIFORNIA

"Evie! You made it!"

Joey bounded down the hallway of Theia Productions with such enthusiasm, I paused just to watch him. My cameraman stopped less than two feet away from me to hand me a Starbucks cup. I knitted my eyebrows together when he leaned over to catch his breath. He gestured for my messenger bag.

"Let me carry that for you."

"Ok, no." I glanced over at Cyrus then back to him. "Joey, what do you want?"

"Nothing!" He straightened up before flashing me a bright grin. "Just a friendly welcome back to the office."

"A short-lived welcome." I tilted my head this time. Something was going on and I was sure I wasn't going to like it. "Aren't we about to get on another plane tomorrow?"

"That's the good news!" Joey looped his arm through mine. "We're going to be staying in L.A. for another couple of days. We've got an episode right here in the office."

"Wait." I stopped then held up my hand. "Free coffee? You offering to carry my bag? Now you're saying we get to stay home for a few extra days? Where's the catch?"

Joey didn't answer. Instead, he threw open our office door and extended his arms towards my desk. Sitting in the very center of the wooden surface was a filthy rag doll.

"Eva, meet Sally. Sally, Eva."

I glanced up at Joey when Elliot shoved his chair away from his desk to roll into my line of sight.

"Evie!" He grinned. "Welcome to work."

"Details. Now." I clutched at the strap of my bag. "Or I'm working from the coffee shop today."

"Here goes." Joey gave me a little nudge towards the doll. "Sally here is a bona fide haunted doll."

I felt my jaw drop. My mouth actually dropped open before I started laughing. "You're serious?"

It was all that I could manage. I was laughing too hard to say anything else. When I finally finished, I wiped the tears at the corners of my eyes to see Joey and Elliot staring at me.

"Ok." I waved my hand. "Let's be serious here for a second. You said this thing is haunted. With what? Dirt mites?"

"According to the story," Elliot leaned back in his chair. "This doll is haunted by the spirit of the woman who made her."

"Standard." I nodded. "And let me guess, she made the doll for her granddaughter?"

"No." Joey grinned. "That's the best part, Evie! She was made by Sally Adelaide."

"That name means nothing to me."

"Sally Adelaide was a voodoo priestess in Mississippi. She died in 1982 at the age of a hundred and five."

"Ok." I breathed out the word. "So what? She cursed the doll to hold her spirit?"

"You got the curse part right." Elliot grinned at me while he intertwined his fingers across his stomach. "The doll was her instrument to harm her enemies."

My co-host jumped up and grabbed the doll by the back of the neck. He held it up to finish his grim demonstration.

"Those in possession of the doll have been known to have grisly nightmares." Elliot waved the thing two inches away from my nose.

"They hear strange voices. See visions. And they are cursed with a string of bad luck."

Cyrus shoved the doll away from my face before I had the chance to do it myself. I cut my eyes over at him before I turned back to Elliot.

"Yeah. Right." I smirked. "And let me guess. You and Joey are going to be filming this thing for the next few days? I thought we were supposed to be filming a live Halloween special. This does not scream ratings to me, Elliot."

Elliot glanced over at Joey before he plopped the doll down on top of my bag. I had to grab it to keep it from falling to the floor.

"Nope. Not us. You." He grinned again. This time, it wasn't a nice one. "We're pairing the great Sibyl with a haunted doll. No mirrors. No danger. But Joey here is going to document your every move on Halloween night."

"Tell me you're joking." I stared at my former friend as if he'd gone crazy after the banshees last week. Maybe he had. "Elliot, every other paranormal show on the air is going to locations famous for their hauntings. You know. For the excitement? History? A nasty doll that you got off of E-Bay does not fit that description."

"How do you know we got it off of E-Bay?"

Joey started before Elliot broke in. My co-host bounded over to his desk to toss a small camera in my direction. Somehow, I managed to catch it against my chest without dropping the damned doll.

"Joey is going to film you while you figure out all the gory details." Elliot snagged his wallet and tucked it in his back pocket. "I don't care how you do it. Just make it good."

"Where in the hell are you going?" I frowned at him. "Why aren't you in this boat with me?"

"Can't." Elliot grinned. "I've been invited to go ghost hunting with the big boys over on the Journey Channel. Plane leaves tonight."

"You're ditching us." I narrowed my eyes at him. "On Halloween. The biggest holiday for ghost hunting shows."

"Not ditching." Elliot ruffled my hair when he passed me.

"Expanding our audience by tapping into a whole new legion of ghost fanatics."

I didn't say another word until Elliot shut the door behind him. Then I dropped the camera and my bag on the desk with a huff.

"Can you believe this?" I whirled around to face Joey. "He's sabotaging his own show!"

"What do you mean?" Joey moved to stand next to Cyrus. "Evie, it could be a great opportunity to get the word out about *Grave*."

"It could be, but it's not." I crossed my arms over my chest. "Think about it, Joey. He's headed off to greener pastures while we're stuck here in L.A. filming a show about a doll."

"Well," My cameraman took a deep breath. "I'll admit this doesn't look good on Elliot's part, but..."

"But nothing." I turned the doll to face me with a grim smile. "Voodoo, huh?"

"Little One," Cyrus spoke up. My keeper had become damn good at reading me over the past few months. So I wasn't surprised that he knew the gears in my head were spinning. "No. It is unwise to take on the spirits in such a manner."

"Oh, come on." I gave him my sweetest smile. Cyrus narrowed his eyes at me in return. "We're going to have a little fun, that's all. We're going to beat Elliot at his own game."

"And I feel like the third wheel for what reason?" Joey leaned back against the desk Elliot had abandoned. "What do you have in mind, Evie?"

"Oh, a little of this. A little of that." I grinned. "Get the camera, Joe. It's time to get to work."

"You managed to get commercial slots for every break? That's great, Connor." I tapped my pen against the notepad in front of me. I had been trying to ignore the doll which had stared at me for the past two days from its perch on my desk, but it was hard. The damned thing was creepy. "Ok. We'll start the camera rolling as soon as Joey gets here."

I listened to Connor drone into the phone about the details of the theme song for a few minutes, but I wasn't worried about that. I was too busy studying the doll that would make or break my episode. It was dirty with black markings drawn all over it. One eye had been crossed out. And the hair?

Knotted string had a better chance of getting smoothed out.

"Ok." I interrupted Connor's monologue about making sure I had everything set up. "I gotta go. Just send the crew over to the condo by three. That should give us plenty of time."

I hung up the phone before he could say another word to hear Cyrus chuckling in the background. I raised an eyebrow when he pushed himself away from the wall.

"What?" I watched him approach the desk. "Are you laughing at me?"

"A little." He gave me a crooked smile that made my stomach flip. "I find it amusing that the Daughter of Apollo has decided to align herself with such a simple form of magic."

"What do you mean, simple?" I leaned back in my chair to look up at him. "Do you know about voodoo?"

"Of course, I do." Cyrus shook his head. "Such magic deals with the spirits, dear girl. A practitioner can do immense damage with the power they hold over those in the Underworld."

"It's so weird to hear you talk about something that's not Greek." I rested my chin in my hand. "What else do you know about Voodoo?"

"You like that, do you?" My keeper chuckled. "Very well. Though I believe you are using my knowledge to supplement the research you should be doing."

"I've been studying up on voodoo and rituals for the past two days." I shrugged. "Listening to you is much better than anything I could find on Google."

"At least there's that." Cyrus chuckled. "Voodoo is a monolithic religion. It started out as a form of healing magic. Those who believed would call upon the spirit world to influence their workings."

"How?" I frowned. "Why on earth would the dead be interested in the living?"

"You don't understand, Eva." Cyrus tilted his head towards me. "Those who have entered into the Underworld will do anything to be acknowledged. That is why you are so crucial to them. They use you as a vessel to speak to those they left behind. The Sibyl is their reassurance that the dead have not been forgotten."

I reached out to stroke the cheek of the doll. I couldn't explain it, but I was drawn to the thing. I knew that Cyrus was right. As the Sibyl, I had been granted the ability to speak to the dead through mirrors. It was the whole basis of *Grave Messages* in the first place.

"I want to talk to Sally Adelaide." I dropped my hand. "I want to call her forth on the show."

"You are not strong enough to bring forth specific spirits, Little One." Cyrus pointed out. "There is no guarantee that she will speak to you."

"Yes, she will." I lifted my chin in defiance. "I can feel it. I think she wants to talk to me."

"How do you know?" Cyrus raised an eyebrow at me. "Surely you do not believe in the nonsense of her spirit being in that doll."

"Maybe." I frowned as I studied our object of discussion. "The truth is, I don't know what to believe in anymore."

"Our lord Apollo." He placed his hand over mine. "Me. We will do all in our power to make sure you succeed in this life, Eva."

"I know." I gave him a small smile. "But right now? I need this show to succeed. We're four shows in and my co-host has already abandoned me. It's not looking good, Cyrus."

Joey came through the door before my keeper could respond. He glanced at our hands but didn't say anything. Instead, my friend lifted his camera to his shoulder.

"You ready for this, Evie?"

"Always." I grinned. "Let's show Elliot what we've got, eh?"

"Yeah, yeah." Joey hoisted up the camera. I waited until he gave me his three-finger countdown before I smiled.

"Welcome to *Grave Messages*. Now I know what you're thinking.

What the hell, Eva? Why aren't you at some cool location waiting to get the crap scared out of you?"

I stood up and moved around my desk. "Because we've got something very special in store for you tonight. It's just me, Joey, and Cyrus. Flip over to the Journey Channel if you want to see Elliot, but I promise you, you'll be missing out."

I reached behind me to pick up the doll. I rested it in my arms before I turned back to the camera.

"You see, I've brought you into my home. This is my condo here in Los Angeles. And the doll in my arms? It is believed to hold the spirit of Sally Adelaide. Sally was a voodoo priestess who used this very doll to heal or curse those around her. Legend has it that she was so attached to this particular token that her spirit entered the doll after she died. The reports I've found say that those who possess this doll experience everything from shadow forms to bad luck. Yeah. So far, so standard, right?"

I smirked. "I thought so too. And I have to say, so far? I haven't experienced anything out of the ordinary. But tonight, we are going to film the doll and just before I have to let you go? We're going to perform a voodoo ritual to see if Sally will speak with us."

I paused long enough to be dramatic before I started up again.

"Now, onto the good stuff. We're going to find out if this doll is, in fact, haunted." I glanced over at Cyrus. "If you've seen the show before, you should be familiar with Cyrus. For those of you tuning in for the first time, meet Cyrus of Crete. He is better known as my Keeper. My bodyguard. And infinitely more interesting to listen to than doing a Google search."

We shared a smile between us at my little joke before he hit the lights. The room went pitch black for me, but I knew Joey had switched on the night vision.

"Sally grew up in a time we can only imagine today. While we tend to see spirits as entertainment, they were a means to an end for a select few in Tipton, Mississippi. Born in May of 1878, Sally lived a privileged life thanks to the money her family made during the Reconstruction. But that doesn't mean she lived a happy one. Ignored by her parents, Sally was raised by her nursemaid

Frances. A nursemaid who taught her charge the power of voodoo."

I picked up the thermal camera with my free hand.

"I can hear you now. Eva, you have no proof of that. You're just making this up. The truth is? I'm not. Sally wrote volumes of diaries throughout her one hundred and five years on this earth. She detailed everything from her childhood to her rituals. One of which we will be conducting here tonight."

I pushed away from the desk. "Joey, let's put Sally in the living room. We should have more room in there. I want to give the thermal imaging camera a try."

"Sure thing, Evie."

I turned on my heel and headed into the living room. I was almost to the couch when I heard a bang behind me. I whirled around with a sense of dread as Joey cursed under his breath.

"Coffee table." He stood up straight. "I'm not hurt, only my pride. Thanks for asking."

I stuck my tongue out at him when I sat the doll down on the sofa. I felt around the edges of the camera in my hands until I found the switch I was looking for. The tiny screen flickered to life after a moment. My couch and the coffee table Joey was still muttering about were a mixture of blues and purples. I panned out as my cameraman focused on my little screen. It was dark and boring until I noticed a small orange dot begin to glow.

I snapped my head up to see what I could have caught, but there was no one on the couch. Just the doll. Cyrus had moved to stand behind it, and I frowned when I realized he didn't show up on my screen.

"See that orange light? The one that's getting brighter? That color indicates that heat is coming off of the doll. I'm not even picking up Cyrus, who is standing right behind her. I'm surprised about Sally's doll, but not Cyrus. He's an episode all on his own."

I chuckled when I heard Cyrus snort. He despised *Grave Messages*, but our patron deity did not. Apollo was sure the show would help lead to his resurgence in power. Maybe. Maybe not. But there was only one way to find out.

Keep filming.

"Could the heat be residual from your hands?" Joey broke through my thoughts. "The glow is coming from its center."

"No." I frowned. "The heat is spreading through the doll, Joey, not cooling off."

Cyrus started to add to our little dialogue when a loud knock resounded through the room. I jumped away from the doll and whirled around to study the darkness.

"Sally, is that you?" I called out to a spirit I wasn't even sure existed. I remembered a method of contact that Elliot had taught me before I became the Sibyl. "If that was you, knock once for yes, twice for no."

Imagine my surprise when a single knock surrounded us. The hair on my arms stood on end when the air in the room seemed to change. It seemed charged. Vibrant.

Weird.

I resisted the urge to grab Apollo's mirror from my bedroom. I had to fill an entire hour, after all. I couldn't take the easy way out this time. So I gestured to Joey, who followed me over to the wall in my foyer. I felt like an idiot standing there, talking to the wall, but I did it anyway.

"Sally Adelaide, will you speak with the Sibyl tonight? Do you have a message for me?"

Another single knock. I glanced over at Joey when he tapped me on the shoulder. "Ask a question that you know will get a 'no' response." He shook his head. "We need to show this isn't the pipes expanding or your neighbors."

"Look at you being all professional." I teased. "Fine. Sally, do I have dark hair?"

Two quick knocks in quick succession. I raised an eyebrow at Joey two seconds before something flew between us to smash against the wall.

"What the hell?"

I threw myself back as Joey turned the camera towards the couch. Cyrus caught my shoulders when he appeared behind me. I ducked this time when another picture flew in our direction.

"Stop that!" I snapped. "I will drop you in a bottle of bleach if you don't."

I glared at the doll that had fallen over on the coffee table before I realized why that was so strange.

"Cyrus," I grabbed his hand to hold it to my shoulder. "Did you move the doll?"

"I'm sorry, what?"

"Did you move the damn doll?" I scrambled to my feet. "Because she was on the couch when the knocking started."

"No."

Cyrus dropped his hands from my shoulders. But for some reason, I didn't want him to. I shuddered as I approached the doll. It seemed so broken. So little since it was flopped over the stack of books I had used for decorations. I could relate.

The damn doll mirrored how I had felt after Elliot had turned his back on me. And how I felt now that I was doing this stupid special without him.

I took a deep breath. I was on live television, dammit. I wasn't going to lose it here. Not now.

Not ever.

"Ok. So, there are only three of us here." I turned back to face Joey's camera. "And we all can attest to the fact that we weren't near the doll. So how did it get on the coffee table?"

"How did two pictures get thrown at our heads?" Joey piped up. Even in the dark, I could tell he was grinning. "I told you Sally was a good buy, Evie."

"Yeah, yeah." I muttered. "Let's go ahead and get the ritual started, shall we? I don't want the rest of my pictures broken if I can help it."

I bent down to pick up the frame as I walked back to Joey. Inside was one of my favorite photographs of me and Elliot. We had spent three weeks of our last summer break hanging out in my studio apartment before the fall semester started. The picture had been taken of the two of us as we sat in the window overlooking the street. As I brushed the broken glass away from Elliot's face in the picture, I felt a sharp pain as it sliced my thumb.

"Ow." I muttered. "Dammit. I got blood on my picture."

"The boy will betray you."

I dropped the broken frame to see a woman step out of the shadows behind the couch. She lowered her hands down on the back of my sofa before the doll floated up from its resting place on the table. Cyrus stepped in front of me, but I shifted to the side enough so that I could see the figure that had made such an entrance. She was tall. Wispy. Her long dark dress faded into the nothing before it reached the ground.

"What boy?" I kept my eyes trained on her. "I don't understand."

"No, I suppose you don't." She folded her hands over the doll then clutched it to her chest. "Yet, you will. In time."

"Ok. Why can't one spirit give me one clear answer?" I glared at the woman. "Is that your message, then? A warning?"

"Yes." Sally seemed to be fading in and out. Her form shimmered against the shadows. "Release him before it is too late."

"Why?" I pinched the bridge of my nose between two fingers. "Why are you using your last message to warn me?"

"Who says this is my last message?" The woman smiled when I looked at her. "Perhaps I wish to thank you for taking such care of my heart."

The doll. She had to be talking about the doll. I tilted my head to the side.

"Your heart? Did you truly use this doll in your rituals?"

"Yes." She chuckled. "And you did well to care for her. You have earned the reward she holds inside."

Again with the cryptic words. I rolled my eyes and caught a glimpse of Joey. He had his camera glued on the spirit. I had no idea if he could get her on film as well as we could see her, but I let the worry pass.

"Is there anything else you wish to say?"

"Only this." The woman released the doll. I watched as it fell back against the books. "Do not do the ritual, child. Your connection to the gods and the dead is strong enough already. It will only bring forth unwanted attention."

I nodded as she disappeared. The strange aura that had filled the room earlier was gone. I waited until Joey lowered the camera before I went over to the wall to hit the light switch. When I approached him, my cameraman lifted his contraption once more.

"And that is what I call a successful ghost hunt, people." I forced a smile on my face. "No ritual required."

"What about the doll?" Joey broke in. "We have to open the doll now."

"Why?" I frowned. "Joey, there's no guarantee that there is really anything of value inside that thing."

"But what if there is?" He shifted on his feet. "Come on, Evie. It'll help prove that who we really captured was Sally Adelaide."

"Fine." I groaned. "Cyrus, I know you have a knife on you somewhere."

My keeper chuckled as he pulled out a small dagger. He picked up the doll and flipped it over. When he handed it over to me, I noticed a small slit down its back. I bit my lip as I reached inside.

"Well?" Joey again. "What have you got?"

"Not a spider bite," I muttered. "Which is what I was expecting."

I wrapped my fingers around a very solid piece of stone and pulled it out. It was a thick chunk of yellow topaz that had been cut into the shape of a heart. I held it out for Joey to catch on his camera.

"Sally's heart." I brushed my thumb over its smooth surface. "It was just as she said it would be."

I handed the stone to Cyrus before I held the doll against my chest. I couldn't explain the sudden sadness that filled me when I realized I would have to let her go. Despite her history, despite the lore that had followed her for decades, the item so prized for being haunted would be discarded. Tossed out. Abandoned.

I couldn't let that happen.

"I hate you."

Elliot slammed the door before he stormed across the room. He stopped just short of my desk to glare at me.

"What?" I widened my eyes with mock innocence. "I thought you'd be pleased. *Grave Messages* hit the top of the viewer polls."

"And shut my guest appearance out. Nobody watched us!" Elliot pounded his fist against my desk. "Dammit, Eva. That was my chance..."

"To what?" I snapped back. Cyrus placed his hand on my shoulder to keep me from rising in my anger. "To explore the other side? To broaden *Grave's* audience? Or to get a taste of greener pastures where *you* are the star?"

"That damn doll..."

"Was a hit." I shrugged. "Leave it at that, Elliot. Connor's happy. Your dad's happy. *Grave* is finally starting to get some attention."

Elliot didn't respond. He threw his hands up in the air before he stormed back out of the room. I watched him go before I shook my head.

"I want you to be careful with him, Little One." Cyrus squeezed my shoulder. "He does not seem stable."

"Elliot's fine. He's an ass, but he's fine." I studied the doll that had caused my co-host's anger. I had put her back in the spot she had occupied on my desk over the past few days. "But I won't forget Sally's warning, Cyrus. I don't know how much I trust Elliot now."

"Promise?" Cyrus dropped his hand from my shoulder. "I do not want you to make any unnecessary enemies, Eva. You face enough dangers as is."

"I'll be careful." I offered him a small smile before I went back to work. Our next episode was going to be in Mississippi, and it held all the wretched soap opera drama that the audience seemed to love. "Promise."

SIXTEEN

SEASON 1, EPISODE 5: BILOXI, MISSISSIPPI

I WANTED to look away from the skeleton of a man sitting in front of me. I *needed* to look away before his image was seared into my brain for eternity. But as I examined his gaunt cheeks, his hands waved in front of my face to pull my attention back to the point he was trying to make.

"I don't need your help." Stephen Williams swung those bony fingers so close to my nose, I had to lean back to keep from getting swatted by them. "We're in love. We're made for each other. Nancy just doesn't understand."

"Nancy…as in your wife, Nancy?" I raised a single eyebrow in his direction before I focused on the woman who had contacted us. "Mrs. Williams, would you care to tell us why you called *Grave Messages* into your home?"

The woman was glaring at her husband. She crossed her arms over her chest with a sniffle. I glanced over to see Joey attempting to hide his own astonished look behind his camera. It wasn't working. I gave my head a quick shake to tell him to cut it out when the woman began to speak.

"This all started two months ago." Nancy Williams released her arms to rest her elbows on her knees. "We moved to Mississippi so that Stephen could go to graduate school. Not go crazy."

"Perhaps he isn't crazy, m'am." Elliot spoke up from his seat beside me. "We have experienced several spirits over the past few weeks..."

I snorted. I couldn't help myself. Elliot may have 'experienced' the spirits, but that was nothing compared to what I'd been through over the past three months. The whispers that haunted my dreams. The fear of coming in contact with a mirror. I shuddered before I could stop myself.

"Not like Eliza." Stephen Williams must have decided to join back in our little interview. He grinned at the wall behind me like the Cheshire cat. "She's my soulmate. I'm sure of it."

"Ok." I breathed out the word. I had to focus on filming the interview, not the sideshow my life had become. "Tell us about her, Stephen. When did you meet Eliza?"

"Right away." He nodded. "She's beautiful. Tall. Dark. Her eyes shine like crystals. No, diamonds!"

Our client giggled and I moved further back in my chair to put some more distance between us. Don't get me wrong. I'd been exposed to some real weirdos since we had started *Grave Messages*. But this man?

He creeped me out.

"Did you meet her here? In this house?" I ran my thumb over the corners of the notepad in my lap. "Surely you can't believe that you are in love with a ghost."

"She's not a ghost." Our client slammed his palm down on the arm of the couch. "Eliza is real, dammit."

"Then how did you meet her?" I was proud of myself. I kept my voice level despite his outburst. "Coffee shop? School? What?"

"In heaven." He whispered. The slick smile was back on his face. "My Eliza came to me in a dream. She told me this was her land. Her home. I knew at once she was talking about me."

"I don't get it." I frowned. "How was she talking about you?"

"I'm her home."

"Mr. Williams, have you had sex with Eliza?"

I whipped my head around to stare at Elliot. Surely he was joking. Maybe this was a sick jest to play for ratings. But Elliot's face was stoic. His tone serious.

"Oh, my god, Elliot." I hissed. "You can't ask him that!"

"Why not?" Elliot narrowed his blue eyes at me. "It's a valid question."

"No." Stephen glanced over to his wife. "Not yet. But I will once I join her in heaven."

"Stephen!"

Nancy Williams jumped up from the couch then began to wring her hands in front of her. I felt something brush against my shoulder. I glanced up to see Cyrus pressing a handkerchief in my palm. He nodded towards the woman who was becoming more and more distraught.

Understandably so. But it wasn't until I really looked at her that I saw what my keeper had noticed.

Nancy was crying. Tears were streaming down her cheeks along with the mascara our make-up crew had applied.

"Here." I stood up to take her arm. "Have a seat and take a breath, ok? We'll straighten this out."

"No." She fell in the chair I had vacated. "You don't understand. This was a mistake."

"Calling us?" I glared at Elliot before I turned my attention back to our client. "Or moving to Mississippi?"

"Everything. All of it." She wiped at her face before she started to cry harder. When she could finally speak, Nancy held her chin up as she faced her husband. "I want a divorce."

"Ok. Look," I held up my hands. "Ms. Williams, why don't you take a few minutes to calm down? This has to be very difficult for you to hear."

"No." The woman threw Cyrus' handkerchief in the chair when she stood. "I'm done. Good luck with your show. As for me? I'm going to pack."

I dropped my hands when she stormed out of the room. I watched her go before I looked at the men who surrounded me. Joey, who was determined to capture every second of this drama on film. Elliot was staring at his notebook as if it were the most interesting thing in the world. Even Stephen seemed unaffected by his wife's announcement. Only Cyrus reacted. He reached over the chair, snagged my wrist, and gave me a look that told me we needed a break.

I couldn't agree more.

"Mr. Williams, can we have a few moments, please?" I gave him a thin smile. "Perhaps you should go check on Nancy."

"She'll be fine." He waved his hand behind him. "Better this way."

"Then I'm leaving for a few minutes. I'll be outside if you need me."

I headed out the door to my left. The house was a trailer without a front porch, so I headed towards the car. I sat on the hood of the rented sedan then folded my arms over my chest as I breathed in the muggy November air.

"Are you alright, Little One?" Cyrus appeared in front of me. He stuffed his hands into his pockets as he studied me. "You didn't seem like yourself back there."

"I can't do this, Cyrus." I doubled over to study the gravel beneath my feet. "I can't stand the sadness. The drama. The sheer amount of insanity. I just...can't."

Cyrus was silent for a moment. When he responded, it wasn't with words. My keeper shifted so that he was leaning against the car next to me. He reached out to wrap his arm around my shoulders to pull me towards him.

I stiffened at first, but when he squeezed my arm, I began to relax. It wasn't until I rested my head against him that he began to speak.

"Eva, remember when I told you there was a lot to learn about your new position?" Cyrus sighed. "Consider this a lesson. You were blessed with a great power, but with that power, the Sibyl is burdened with the tragedies of others. Yet, never forget. I am here with you. You will never carry those burdens alone."

"Yes, but those burdens are supposed to come from the dead. People who are nothing more than memories. Stories..."

"Not always." His voice was soft. Soothing. "You will encounter family members who have lost those dear to them. Just as that woman has lost her husband. But it is your job to separate yourself from their emotions. Do your duty and move on."

"Spoken like a true soldier." I dropped my arms. "How? How on earth am I supposed to go back in there to face a man who doesn't give a damn about the woman desperate enough to call *us* to save him?"

"With strength." Cyrus released me. He reached out to tap his knuckle against my chin. "With knowledge. You must find the spirit called Eliza and find out what sort of hold she has on Stephen Williams."

"Nice. But what you're really telling me is to not give up." I frowned at my keeper. "And what happens if there is no Eliza? What if he's just cracked?"

Cyrus glanced past me towards the trailer. I saw his eyes narrow so I whirled around to see what he was glaring at. Elliot was standing on the porch with Joey's camera pointed at us.

"What in the hell are you doing?" I called out to him. "Elliot, put that down! I'm on a break!"

"And let our viewers miss such a heartwarming moment?"

Even across the yard, I could see the sneer on Elliot's face. He lowered the camera to wave me back inside.

"Come on, Sibyl. It's getting dark and they are about to leave."

I felt Cyrus grab my arm to hold me back. I turned towards him to see him studying me.

"Remember what I said, Little One. There may be burdens, but you do not carry them alone."

"Welcome to another episode of *Grave Messages*." I intertwined my fingers in my lap as I sat on the steps of the trailer. "Tonight, we come to you from Biloxi, Mississippi. A state more famous for its terrible statistics than the rich history of these lands."

I approached Joey who gave me a small smile. We were filming the introduction of the episode. Under normal circumstances, I would have my monologue memorized. I would know more about the history of the house or the area. But not here.

Not tonight.

I decided there was something much more important to focus on.

"Now if you're a fan of *Grave*, you know that now is the time you learn about the gory details. The history we hope to validate or dispel with my abilities as the Sibyl. But not tonight. Instead, I am going to share with you the story of our clients, Nancy and Stephen Williams."

I kicked at the gravel as I swallowed down the knot in my throat. I don't know why their separation was affecting me. Not that it mattered. Cyrus was right. I had a job to do. My duty to Apollo. Film the show. Move on to the next episode. Bring more followers to my patron god.

I could do that. I could focus on that. Not the drama that had happened this afternoon.

"Nancy and Stephen met in Charlotte, North Carolina. According to Nancy, it was love at first sight. The two of them were married six months later. They finished college, held great banking jobs, and had a good life. But Stephen wanted more."

I gave a grim smile at the camera. "Don't they always? When Stephen was accepted into the University of Southern Mississippi, they moved to Biloxi to begin their new life together. But the paranormal got in the way."

I tucked my hands into my back jean pockets. "Which is exactly why we are here. Stephen Williams began to withdraw from his wife. He began to ignore his studies. Instead, he began to stay around the house all day. Talking to himself and a spirit he calls Eliza."

Joey held up three fingers. When the last one fell, Elliot moved into the shot behind me. He was so close to me; I could feel the heat coming off him.

"Stephen claims to be in love with a spirit he met through a dream. His obsession with Eliza has taken a deadly turn. According to his wife, he stopped eating three weeks ago. Mr. Williams refuses to leave the house or do anything to take care of himself. He has told Nancy repeatedly that he wishes to die. Why? To join Eliza."

I focused on the tiny red light blinking by Joey's thumb instead of the dread filling my stomach.

"Tonight, we are going to try to contact Eliza." I shifted forward so that Elliot wasn't so close to me. "And while we like to play with modern technology during our investigations, I think we will focus on the one true method we have to contact the spirits."

I brushed against Elliot's arm when I climbed up the stairs. When I had my hand on the door, I gave Joey's camera a little smile.

"Let's begin, shall we?"

I pushed open the door to see the lights had been turned off. Nancy had left not long after my little pep talk from Cyrus. And Stephen had even agreed to spend the night at a local hotel. I was so focused on getting to our equipment cases, I forgot to look where I was going. So when my knee slammed against the sharp edge of a table, I hissed.

"Eva?"

"I'm fine." I muttered. "Hit an end table."

"Do you want to go through the house first?" Elliot again. He must have gotten the hint that I was still pissed at him for his little stunt earlier because he stayed away from me. "Or go straight for the gold?"

"The gold." I waited until my eyes adjusted to the darkness. "No offense, but I want to get out of Mississippi as soon as possible."

I didn't wait for him to respond. Instead, I made my way over to the trunk that Apollo's golden mirror traveled in. I knelt, unlatched the lid, and began to pull it up when the sweet sound of a piano broke the silence.

"What the hell..."

I raised my hand up and Joey's words died in his throat. I lifted myself up slowly and managed to keep my eyes on the end of the hallway.

"We're alone, right?" I turned towards Elliot. "You saw Nancy and Stephen leave?"

"Yes." Elliot nodded. He pulled a small tape recorder out of his pocket. "Is anyone here?"

"Elliot, be serious. EVPs are nothing compared to music being played in an empty house." I rolled my eyes at him. "Come on. Let's go find out where that is coming from."

I checked each room off the hallway. As expected, there was nothing inside. Only darkness and furniture that had seen its better days. I stopped at the last door seconds before Cyrus appeared beside me.

"Here goes nothing."

I took a breath before I pushed open the door. The room was like the others. It was the master bedroom. Large enough to hold a queen-sized bed and a dresser. But where the other rooms were practically bare, this one had a small black piano in the far corner.

A piano that was being played by none other than Stephen Williams.

I watched him for a moment before my temper got the best of me. I stormed across the room to confront the man who had broken his promise to stay away for the night.

"You aren't supposed to be here." I snapped. "Mr. Williams, you are jeopardizing my episode."

Our client didn't respond. He continued to play the slow tune until I reached down to grab his shoulder. The second I made contact with him, he started giggling.

"Eliza called out to me. She wanted to hear her lullaby."

"She's here?" I dropped my hand as I stared at him. "Now?"

"Yes." The man began to bob his head up and down. "My beauty. My heart. She is here."

"Eliza!" I called out to the room that held just myself and my client. The others were standing by the door. Waiting in case I needed them. "Come out, come out wherever you are!"

"Don't tease her." Stephen whispered. "She is too precious to be mocked. A goddess. My goddess."

"Oh, really?" I widened my eyes in fake surprise. "Which one?"

"Stop being so dramatic, Stephen."

I whipped around to see a woman step out of the shadows. She was small. Dark. Her eyes were the clearest shade of blue I'd ever seen. When Eliza saw me, she bowed her head in my direction.

"Eva McRayne. The darling daughter of Apollo. I hadn't hoped to garner your attentions."

"My attentions?" I shook my head. "I had no idea I was so popular amongst the spirits."

"Ah," The woman giggled. "But the human is correct. I am not a spirit."

"A nymph." Cyrus broke in. He had joined me next to Mr. Williams. "What is your business here, Nereides?"

"Near-what?" I tilted my head at my keeper. "What did you call her?"

"A nymph of the sea." Cyrus explained, but he kept his eyes on Eliza. "As a Keeper in Apollo's service, I demand your answer."

"Fine." The woman rolled her eyes before she crossed the room. She sat on the edge of the piano bench next to Stephen. I didn't miss how she ran her fingers through his hair as she spoke. "This man has encroached upon my lands. I tried to warn him. I told him to leave. But the damned fool wouldn't listen."

"So you enchanted him to love you?" Elliot called out from his spot by the door. "Is that how it works?"

"Don't be stupid, human." Eliza smirked. "My beauty alone was enough for his heart."

She paused for a moment. Her smirk shifted into a frown. "I do not want his heart. He began to call out to me during the day. The human would not leave my space. He pined for me. It was a mistake to contact him in the first place."

"So why did you contact him?" I tilted my head. "And what in the hell is wrong with him now?"

"Because this is *my* land." The nymph snapped. She stared at me with those strange eyes until I felt a shiver run down my spine. "He has no right to be here."

"You didn't try to contact his wife."

Elliot again. I took a step back when Eliza rose and I understood at once why she had chosen Stephen.

"Of course, you didn't. Nancy wouldn't have listened to you." I answered for her. "Men are much more susceptible. Pliable. You can control them."

Eliza grinned. "A power you understand all too well, little Sibyl."

"We are not talking about me." I glared at her. "Now tell us what you've done to Mr. Williams and how we can help him."

"Help him?" The nymph giggled. "Sibyl, are you dense? The spell of a goddess – no matter how minor - cannot be undone."

She patted his head when she stood. "You see, the human's attentions were great at first. Really played into my ego. But he became annoying. His affections became as unnecessary as they were unwanted. So I decided to put him out of his misery."

"Out of his misery?" I stared at her in shock. "Surely you don't mean to kill him."

"How else do you get rid of pests?" Eliza shrugged. "At any rate, the fool wasn't afraid. He believed he was sacrificing himself for love."

"Ok. If I can be the voice of reason here," Joey shifted his camera to join our discussion. "You haven't killed him. Stephen Williams is very much alive."

"Ah, but that is the magick. The poison, if you will." Eliza blew a kiss in Joey's direction. "He is wasting away. Sick and tainted by unrequited love. The human's body is still here, but his mind is too far gone. He is already dead."

"How can you…"

I started to question the nymph, really, I did. I wanted to know how she could be so cruel. I wanted to know how to help our client.

I never got the chance. Stephen Williams began to cough. Even in the darkness, I could see the dark fluid that flowed out of his mouth.

Blood.

"Joey, hit the lights!" I shoved my way past Cyrus to grab his shoulders. "Elliot, call 911!"

"What the hell, Eva?" Elliot snatched his cellphone when he saw that our client was in trouble. "On it."

Cyrus grabbed the man and lifted him to the floor. "Roll him on his side."

Stephen stayed still for only a moment before he began to go into convulsions. I grabbed onto his shirt and stared at Cyrus in horror.

"Cyrus, what do we do?"

"There is nothing you can do." Eliza smiled sweetly at me from over my keeper's head. "His heart has failed him."

"You," I snapped. "Make this stop! You're killing him!"

I let the words hang between us when Stephen stopped shaking beneath my hands. I leaned over him to see his eyes had rolled back into his head. I didn't realize I was shaking until I felt for his wrist. My fingers slipped twice against the man's chilled skin before I hit the spot where his pulse was supposed to be.

There was none.

I dropped his wrist and started to scream. I couldn't stop myself as I shoved myself back.

"Eva!" Elliot reached for me. "Is he gone?"

"Little One," Cyrus caught me. "Come on. We'll wait for help outside."

"There is no help for him, Cyrus." I sobbed. "There never was."

I clung to my keeper until he sat me down in the grass away from the house. He knelt in front of me. Cleaned the blood off my hands. The tears that refused to stop for a man I didn't know. For the love that he had believed in and lost.

I wept for him. For Nancy. But most of all?

I wept for myself and the horrors I had been forced to face thanks to a selfish god with an enchanted golden mirror.

"Evie, you ready to head out?"

I looked up to see Elliot leaning against the door of my hotel room. He was watching me with a concern I found completely unwarranted, so I slammed the lid of my suitcase down with a huff.

"I'm fine, Elliot. Stop staring at me."

"You're not fine." He crossed the room to grab my arms. "You haven't had a chance to process what happened at the trailer."

"First off, stop touching me." I jerked myself out of his grasp. "In case you've forgotten, our friendship is done. And second? There's nothing to process. The man is dead. It's over."

Elliot didn't respond, but he glared at me. After a few moments, he stormed out of the room. I dropped down on the bed next to my suitcase to bury my head in my hands.

"You're afraid."

Cyrus stepped out of the shadows, but he didn't approach me. He stayed in the corner of the room to watch me.

"Yes, I'm afraid." I snapped. "Wouldn't you be if you had someone die in your arms?"

"It is a feeling one never gets used to." Cyrus took two steps forward and stopped. "Yet, it is a feeling one will do anything to avoid."

"You mean, like fighting?" I dropped my hands. "Cyrus, I don't know if I can do that."

"You can and you will." My keeper finally crossed the room to place his hand on my head. "There is a great deal of strength in you, Little One. What occurred was unfortunate, but it cannot be undone."

I shuddered from the memories I wanted to forget. The sound of the piano. The sight of the blood on the keys. The feel of Stephen's clammy skin beneath my hands.

"Yet, you can learn how to fight. You can learn how to save those consumed by the magick of our world." Cyrus shifted his hand down until he lifted my chin up. "Become a hero, Little One. Save those who cannot save themselves. That is the true power of your position."

I closed my eyes at his touch. His words. Cyrus was right. He always was. I had to accept that death was a part of my existence. And I could learn to help those who didn't have the power to help themselves.

But I'd be damned if I let this one go.

"What happened to Eliza?" I caught his hand beneath my chin and pulled it away. "How can I meet up with her again?"

"She took advantage of the distraction caused by the human's death." Cyrus sighed. "The nymph is gone."

"But this is her home. Her land. Surely I can find her."

"Do not." Cyrus raised his eyebrows as he looked down at me. "Eva, not every villain is a villain. And not every fight is worth the effort. Take this tragic story as a lesson. Remember the pain you felt. The fear. Use it in the future."

My keeper lifted me to my feet and took my suitcase from the bed. He led me to the door then held it open so that I could cross the threshold. Yet, I stopped when he spoke once one.

"Separate yourself, dear Little One, from the pain and heartache you feel. For it is the only way you will survive in this life."

SEVENTEEN

SEASON 1, EPISODE 6: OGUNQUIT, MAINE

"THE GOVERNMENT IS GOING to shut me down if the suicides don't stop."

I snapped my head up to see Melannie Sawyer tapping her fingers against the chair she sat in. Even I had to admit, this latest location for *Grave Messages* was strange. Not the building itself, mind you. The Red Rose Bed and Breakfast was gorgeous.

Meticulously restored to its 1920's splendor. But its past was dark. Filled to the brink with death.

The best locations always are. Right?

I frowned. "Ms. Sawyer, tell us about why you called *Grave Messages* here. Do you believe your inn is haunted?"

"No." She whispered so low, I hoped her mic had picked up her answer. "Not the whole inn. Room 23B. That's where they all die."

"When you say 'they'," Elliot Lancaster leaned forward in his chair. "you mean the people who stay in that room, right?"

The woman nodded. Her dark hair bounced around her face with each movement before she studied her hands. I could tell she was nervous. But what I couldn't tell was if it was because she was on camera, or if she was shaken by the story she was telling us.

Hell, it was probably both.

"Ok." I glanced up to Joey before I tossed my notebook of questions onto a neighboring Queen Anne table. I focused on the woman. "Start from the beginning. Before the suicides started."

The woman must have heard the edge in my voice because her head jerked up. She was pale. Her eyes were large. But she started talking.

"I bought this place in 1992. It was a steal back then because it had been left abandoned since the 1950s." She swallowed. "I wanted to start a new life. Away from my corporate job in New York. Maine and The Red Rose gave me the escape I had been looking for."

"What attracted you to this place?" My co-host turned to look out the massive bay window. "The location?"

"Yes." She nodded. "We're right on the cliff's edge. I thought it would be a peaceful getaway for those who wanted to leave their crazy lives behind like I did."

"Leave their crazy lives behind?" I raised an eyebrow at her. "That's a strange choice of words considering you've had twenty-five suicides in the last two years. How many deaths have you had here since you opened the Red Rose in 2001?"

"Two hundred."

The woman choked back her tears and my mouth dropped open. Surely, she wasn't serious. Two hundred suicides in fourteen years?

Maybe I misheard her. Maybe she was playing it up for the camera. I cut my eyes over to Elliot to see that he was jotting this little bombshell down on his notepad. When he met my gaze, I knew he was thinking the same thing I was.

We'd have to research those numbers.

"And they all happened in 23B?" I cleared my throat when my question came out as a squeak. "If so, why haven't you closed that room off?"

"I didn't want to believe it." Our client shuddered. "And once the news got out about the suicides, my customer base exploded. Most wanted to stay the night in 23B. They wanted to try to figure out what was causing the suicides. So, I tripled the price of that room. I had them sign waivers that cleared the Red Rose of any liability if anything happened to them. I made my clients turn over letters from their doctors that declared them of sound mind and body."

"And still, the suicides continued." I narrowed my eyes at her. "When you were researching this place, did you see anything about deaths here before it was shut down the first time?"

"Of course. I found a box full of old newspaper articles in the basement." Melannie nodded. "But it's a hotel, Miss McRayne. Every hotel has suicides."

"Not to this extreme they don't." I saw Elliot pull out his phone. "What on earth are you doing?"

"Texting the boys at Research." He responded, obviously oblivious to the fact that Joey was still filming. "I want them to verify the suicides here. Both past and current ones."

I saw Joey lower his camera and I wiped my hands against my jeans when I stood. "Ms. Sawyer, do you still have that box?"

Our client nodded as she joined me. "Yes. I put them in my office. I can get them for you if you'd like."

"Yeah." I stretched before I gestured so that she would lead the way. "The boys in California aren't the only ones who can dig through the dirt. Let's go."

"This place is morbid, Little One."

I tore my eyes away from the newspaper article I was reading to smile up at Cyrus. My Keeper was ancient. He was annoyingly persistent on keeping me safe. But he was much more than a simple guard to me.

Cyrus had become a friend. One of the few I knew I could count on to be there when I needed him.

"I think 'morbid' is an understatement." I handed him the clipping I had been reading when he appeared beside me. "Two hundred suicides since 2001. At least seventy-five reported prior to this place shutting down in 1952. It's like a horror story come to life."

"Two hundred?" Cyrus whistled as he skimmed the article. He handed it back to me with a shake of his head. "And I suppose you are going to stay in the room where these suicides occurred? Because you're hardheaded?"

"No." I scrunched up my nose at him. "Because I want to find out the truth. Because I have to try to make contact with any spirit who is actually here. Because..."

"Because you're stubborn. And intrigued. And you won't take 'no' for an answer." Cyrus tapped his finger against the tip of my nose. "Will Elliot or Joey be with you?"

"I don't see why not." I shrugged. "There aren't any banshees here to keep them occupied."

Cyrus chuckled at my little joke before he fell into the chair next to me. He reached over the careful piles I had made to pull one towards him.

"1939." I answered before he could ask. "I separated them all by year."

"Ok. When did the suicides start?"

"1925. Two years after the hotel opened." I scribbled down the name and vital information of victim number one on my notepad. "Margaret Gillotson. Flapper. Good time gal. Slit her wrists in the bathtub at the age of 21."

"Sounds charming." Cyrus snagged my notepad from me to rip out a sheet of paper. "And I suppose you hope to contact the spirit of Miss Gillotson."

"Not necessarily." I took my notepad back and passed him a pen. "Cyrus, could there be one of your monsters behind this? A demon? Or is it all just one big coincidence?"

"First off, I don't believe in coincidences." He tilted his head towards me. "Secondly, anything is possible. Perhaps Miss Gillotson was dabbling in powers far beyond her control."

"And it scared her enough to commit suicide?" I snorted. "No offense, Cyrus, but nothing paranormal could ever be that scary."

"Nothing paranormal?"

I didn't respond as I went back to my task. I wasn't going to get into my own demons with Cyrus. Not here. Not now.

"We will see." He turned his focus onto the paper in front of him and began to write. "But why are you in here alone? Where are the others?"

"Setting up cameras." I shrugged. "Elliot jumped on his phone before the interview was even over. By the time he got done, I was in here. Joey hung out for a minute before he decided to get busy with setting up. So here I am. Doing the dirty work."

"That you are." Cyrus held up his fingers to show me the ink that had come off on his hands. "That you are."

"Eva, I want you to stay in 23B alone."

I was in the process of returning the newspaper clippings back into the box when Elliot burst into the office to make his grand announcement. If he was expecting me to pitch a fit, or demand that he and Joey stay with me, he was sorely disappointed. I shrugged then dropped back down in my chair.

"Ok. But what are you and Joey going to be doing?"

"Monitoring you from the kitchen." Elliot rifled through the articles I'd so carefully catalogued. "The audience is enamored with the great Sibyl. I want to see what you pick up without us getting in your way."

Getting in the way? Right.

I leaned back as I narrowed my eyes at him. *Grave Messages* was his idea. It was produced by his dad's company. But Elliot had been finding ways to skip out of being involved in the actual investigations we filmed. Part of me wanted to chastise him for being lazy. But a part of me wondered if he was doing this as some sort of punishment.

"Fine." I stood up then pushed past him. "You know, if you don't want to film *Grave Messages* with me, Elliot, all you have to do is say so. It's not like I need you or anything."

"Excuse me?" His face darkened as he turned to look at me. "What are you saying, Eva?"

"Nothing." I gave him the sweetest smile possible as I opened the door. "Not a damned thing you don't already know, Elliot. Not a damned thing."

I stepped out and ran nose-first into Joey's chest. He caught me by the shoulders with a whistle.

"If you wanna snuggle, Evie, all you gotta do is say so." He grinned down at me until he saw how angry I was. "So...I take it Elliot just told you the news."

"Yeah." I grabbed Joey's arm to pull him away from the office. "Joey, I think Elliot is trying to set me up."

"Set you up?" My cameraman frowned. "Why on earth would you say that?"

"Two hundred suicides?" I stopped to face him after we'd turned the nearest corner. "All in the same room? That he wants me to be alone in? Given my history, that doesn't seem like the best idea."

"Ok. So that's weird," Joey ran his hand through his hair. "But from the entertainment perspective, it makes perfect sense. You may not realize it, Evie, but you have become the face of this show. A face that the audience loves. Elliot could run around naked and they wouldn't give a damn unless you were running along with him."

"I don't run." I punched him lightly on the arm. "And certainly not naked."

"Maybe you should give it a try one day." Joey wiggled his eyebrows at me until I punched him again. "Ok. Ok. Kidding. But in all seriousness? You got this, Evie. We'll go in. Film you being fabulous and have a massive lobster dinner to celebrate for breakfast."

I crossed my arms with a sigh. "And you have the entire room decked out with cameras?"

"Yeah. Even the bathroom." He pointed his finger at me. "So don't do anything you wouldn't want the world to see."

"Oh, you mean like...use the bathroom?" I rolled my eyes. "Ok. Great. Thanks for that."

"Anything for you, Sunshine." Joey tapped me on the chin with his knuckle. "It's almost dark. Let's grab Mr. Brooding Co-Host and get started, shall we?"

"Yeah. Sure." I huffed. "You go get him. I'm going to go find Cyrus."

"He was up in the room last time I saw him." Joey pulled out an earpiece and handed it to me. "Scared me to death when he appeared out of nowhere."

"Yeah. Cyrus told me he wanted to check the room out before I got up there. Said he had a feeling that Elliot would try to throw me to the wolves."

I gave Joey one last squeeze on the arm before I went around him. By the time I reached the lobby, I had worked the earpiece in. I was so focused on getting the stupid volume adjusted that when Melannie cleared her throat, I jumped.

"Jesus." I muttered as I recovered. I shook my head at her. "Sorry, Ms. Sawyer. I guess I'm more nervous than usual."

"I overheard your friends talking." She wrung her hands in front of her. "The tall dark one said you were going to stay in 23B alone?"

"Yeah." I nodded. "But it's just for the night. We won't be longer than that."

"Miss McRayne, I know I signed a contract with Theia Productions for you to film here. But would you mind signing mine?" Melannie crossed over to the counter. When she came back, she handed me a single sheet of paper. "It's the Waiver of Liability form. I need to make sure you won't sue me if something happens to you."

Was she serious? I managed not to throw it back at her as I looked over the contract. As the Sibyl, my main gift from Apollo was the ability to speak with spirits through mirrors. But along with that particular talent came immortality. There was no way I could commit suicide without first passing on the mirror that had granted me my abilities in the first place. Since Cyrus had the relic in his possession, there was no way that was going to happen.

At least I had that going for me.

"Yeah, ok." I pulled out my pen from my back pocket and signed the waiver. "I get it. You've put your entire life into this place. I'm not looking to take that away from you."

"Thank you." Melannie released a sigh of relief. She took the paper back then clutched it to her chest. "You understand, then. You understand why I can't let the government take the Red Rose away from me. It's all I have."

"Yeah. But if the suicides don't stop, there is nothing we can do to stop them from shutting you down." I pointed at her. "This place could be condemned as a health risk. Your best course of action? Close off that room, Ms. Sawyer."

"Let's see what you find first." She went back over to the counter. "Maybe you can figure out a way to stop all this nonsense once and for all."

"Maybe." I tucked my hands into my pockets. "But can you tell me how to find 23B? I'm sure the guys are already set up in the kitchen. They are waiting on me to get started."

"I'll take you there."

Our client led me through a series of carpeted halls until we were standing in front of a wooden door labeled 23B. I ran my fingers over the small bronze plaque that hung just below the numbers.

Stay in this room at your own risk!

"Cute." I turned back to see the woman was gone. "And not creepy. Not in the least."

I pressed the button in my right ear to turn the microphone on. "You guys there?"

"Yeah." Elliot's voice filtered through. "Hurry up, McRayne. It's already dark."

"Sorry. Paperwork."

I muttered as I opened the door. I don't know what I was expecting, but I was pleasantly surprised at the room that greeted me. Single queen size bed. Cute quilt. A small desk by the window overlooking the cliffs outside. It was the standard affair you would find in any bed and breakfast across the U.S.

Except this room had seen more dead bodies than the town morgue. I was sure of that after reading through the clippings Melannie had provided.

"Cyrus?" I shut the door behind me to step further into the room. "You still here?"

"Yes." My keeper stuck his head out of the bathroom with a wave. "So far, I have encountered nothing, Little One."

"So you're not ready to kill over yet?" I teased when I joined him. "What are you doing in here?"

"Covering the mirror," He gave me a dark look. "I'm sure your Elliot simply forgot to cover it before he left earlier."

"Forgot." I shook my head. "Right. I told Joey I thought he was setting me up."

"It would be ironic if nothing happened in here tonight." Cyrus placed his hand on my lower back to lead me out of the bathroom. "But since the cameras are rolling, what would you like to do first? Examine each nook and cranny?"

"That's a start." I chuckled. "But no. Let's just hang out. Pretend like we're normal guests. See what happens."

"Hang. Out." Cyrus raised a single, dark eyebrow at me. "Here? I thought you'd be focused on working."

"I am working." I snagged his hand and pulled him down on the bed beside me. "But we're friends, right? Since I'm waiting on the boogieman to tell me to come off myself, I might as well enjoy your company."

Cyrus chuckled, but before he could respond, we heard a knock on the wall.

No, scratch that. We heard three knocks. I grinned at my friend as I jumped off the bed.

"It's show time, folks." I picked up the handheld camera Joey had left for me on the nightstand. "And I've only been in here for five minutes. The Red Rose isn't particularly known for its haunting, but with so many suicides, how can it not be?"

I moved over to the wall when the knocking resumed. I swept the camera around to make sure each angle around me was covered.

"As you can see, it's just me and Cyrus in the room."

"Tell Cyrus to leave."

I jumped at Elliot's voice in my ear. But I'd like to think I recovered nicely. I started laughing so hard at myself, it took a minute for me to stop.

"If you're wondering where my fellow ghost hunters are, well,

Elliot thought it would be best to send me up to room 23B alone. Why is that so scary? Two hundred suicides. All between 2001 and 2014. If that's not frightening, I don't know what is."

I heard another series of knocks. As I panned down the wall, I noticed something I had missed before. An antique air vent cover.

"For the sake of being thorough…" I knelt to train the camera on the stupid vent. "But Elliot, I'm warning you. I see a rat? I'm screaming in your ear as loud as I can."

I turned the camera towards me so that my co-host could see my face.

"And Cyrus stays."

I could practically see Elliot rolling his eyes at my little gesture. But I couldn't give less of a damn if I tried. I turned my camera back onto the wall and bent down to look inside the vent.

"Hey, Cyrus." I hit the 'zoom' button on the camera. "Can you come here a second?"

"Of course." He knelt beside me. "Did you find something?"

"I think so." I muttered as I tried to make out just what I was seeing. The small camera screen was dark, except it wasn't the right kind of dark. Instead of the pitch black I was expecting, it appeared to be brown. "I think there is something behind this wall."

I flipped on the small light and focused towards the edges of the vent. The ornate piece of metal was fastened on by clips.

"I maintain. I see a rat, I'm screaming. I touch one, and you'll be toast, Mr. Lancaster."

I heard Elliot snort into my ear when I pushed the clips aside. Well, I started to. Cyrus batted at my hand then gave me a dark look before he took over. He freed the vent cover and set it aside. I laid out on the hardwood floor to shine the light inside.

I was right. There *was* something hidden within the wall. I winced as my hand went through a mass of cobwebs.

"Hazard pay. Right there." I pressed against a flat piece of wood. It took some doing, but I managed to get the damn thing free. I glanced over to Cyrus as I worked it out of the wall. "I'm really hoping that isn't a support beam or something."

My keeper didn't say a word as I handed him the board. Cyrus whistled between his teeth as he flipped it over.

"What is it?" I rose up to my knees to focus the camera on it. "By god, don't tell me it really was part of a support beam. The whole place could come crashing down…"

"Ouija." Cyrus tilted the board away from me to blow away the dust. What he couldn't blow off, he swept away with his hand. "See?"

"A Ouija board?" I leaned in closer. "Ok. Even I know that's not a good sign."

"No, dear girl, it is not."

Cyrus gestured for me to bring the light closer and as he examined it, so did I. The drawings seemed to be burned into the wood surface. So too did the letters and numbers. I couldn't explain my next action, but I did it nonetheless. I reached out then traced the letters of my name.

"Eva, what are you doing?"

I heard Elliot, but I didn't respond. I went over to the table by the television to grab a small glass off the tray Melannie had left behind. I dropped down to my knees by the board before I turned the camera towards it. Cyrus stayed silent until I put the glass down in the center. My keeper grabbed my wrist to stop me before I could place my fingers on it.

"Eva, stop." Cyrus frowned at me. "You cannot use the Ouija board. It is much more dangerous than a mirror."

"How?" I matched his frown. "It's just a stupid piece of wood, Cyrus."

"That you found in the wall of a room known for its suicides." My keeper shook his head. "Think, Eva. Think before you act."

When he released my hand, I dropped it down by my side. But I was still drawn to the Ouija board. I wanted to touch it. I wanted to talk to it. I wanted to play with it to see what secrets it held.

Secrets that I could find out through any mirror.

I stood up, grabbed the camera, and turned it on me. I took a shaky breath before I began to speak.

"Ok. In the spirit of documenting everything, you just saw that we found an old Ouija board in the wall. I think that whoever is in here wanted us to find it. But now that I've touched it, I'm drawn to it. I can't explain the desire to use the relic now. It's like a strong need; more than anything I've ever experienced before. That includes my physical addiction for coffee. And wine."

I knew my joke fell flat, but I didn't care. I turned the camera back onto Cyrus and the board. "Cyrus, can you do the vanishing thing you do and get that thing out of here?"

My keeper gave me a nod before he picked up the board. He stepped into the shadows and disappeared.

The second Cyrus vanished, all hell broke loose in the room. The television began to flicker on and off. So too did the lights. I moved back until I was up against the wall. I kept my camera trained on the madness that was going on around me.

I was so focused on what I was filming, I forgot about the massive hole that remained uncovered in the wall behind me. I gasped when I felt a hand wrap around my ankle to jerk me down to the floor. I landed with a thud as my camera clattered across the floor.

"Where is it?"

I blinked back the stars in my eyes as I looked up to see a woman standing over me. She was translucent, but as she reached down for me, I could see the jagged wounds over her arms.

"Where is it?" She shrieked. "The board. I need the board!"

"Margaret." I was surprised when I was able to knock her arms away. I had expected my hands to go right through her. "You're the one responsible for the suicides."

"I was the first. The first to sacrifice. The first to die." She leaned down and I scrambled to get away from her. "But you…you will join the others."

I couldn't move fast enough. The spirit grabbed each side of my head. I whimpered as a wicked sense of cold washed over me. But that was, by far, the best part of the whole experience. I felt something like ice encase my mind. I was hit with the strongest sense of depression I'd ever experienced.

I would never be good enough. I wasn't good enough for Elliot. I had failed with him. Failed my mother time and time again. Failed myself when I gave myself over to my life as the Sibyl. I was nothing more than a monster.

A monster who would have blood on her hands. Strange flashes blinded me as I saw funeral after funeral. I saw people weeping in the streets over something I had done. I saw a charred body and knew it was someone I had loved.

People would be killed because of me. Families would be torn apart. The very thought ripped my heart to shreds.

"You can stop this future." The hateful woman whispered. "Go. Grab the blade. Stop yourself before you destroy everything."

"Everything." I repeated after her. I barely heard the pounding on the door. Or the male voices shouting as I stood up. I knew I was crying, but I didn't bother to wipe my tears away when I walked into the bathroom. "I'm a monster. An abomination."

I felt her come up beside me when I locked the bathroom door. I opened the medicine cabinet door and saw exactly what I was looking for.

A single razor blade. Resting on the metal shelf. Waiting for me.

I didn't even have to free the metal like I had before. It would be so easy. So quick.

I snagged the sharp piece of metal and ignored the pain in my fingers when I touched the blade. I dropped down on the side of the tub and raised the razor up until it was pressed against my skin.

I felt as if I were in a dream. A horrible dream where I couldn't control my actions. I switched my grip on the blade and did as I had been instructed.

The pain was instantaneous. I whimpered as the blade slipped from my fingers and landed on the floor. I heard the spirit scream so I glanced up to see Cyrus standing behind her. His sword?

It was through her. She was gone within moments.

"Eva, dammit!"

Cyrus grabbed a towel off the wall to wrap it around my wound. I was still crying. My heart was still heavy as he leaned his head against mine and whispered.

"It's alright, Little One. You'll be fine."

"Cyrus, I'm horrible. I'm a monster. You don't..."

I started to sob when he wrapped his arm around my neck to pull me into him. Cyrus held me against him as he whispered against the side of my head.

"You're beautiful. You're strong. You're a hero, Little One. You don't have to do this."

"Eva!"

Elliot and Joey burst into the bathroom to see me sobbing against Cyrus. I ignored them while the terrible sadness that had filled me began to fade away.

"Let go of her." Elliot snapped. He dropped down next to Cyrus to reach for me but pulled back when his knee landed in a pool of my blood. "Oh, god."

"She'll be fine." Cyrus didn't let me go, but I didn't miss the steel in his words. "Despite your antics, Lancaster, Eva's healing abilities have kicked in. You got your damn episode. Now leave Eva alone."

Elliot must have listened to Cyrus because he stood. I forced myself to pull away from Cyrus long enough to watch Elliot storm out of the room. Joey was pale. He was visibly shaking, but he dropped down to where Elliot had been before.

"Evie," Joey put his hand on my knee. "Baby girl, it'll be alright. I've called EMS. They will be here within a few minutes."

"Joey." I whispered. "I...I don't know what happened. I..."

"Save your strength, Little One." Cyrus released his grip on me as several men in white appeared in my line of vision. "We'll discuss this later."

I nodded when my keeper stood. He spoke to the EMS workers, who went to work on my arm. When they insisted I needed to go to the hospital, I tried to protest.

My protests were duly noted but ignored. I found myself being taken downstairs. Past a visibly upset Melannie Sawyer. Through the large front door.

I couldn't shake the feeling that the spirit had been right. I was a monster. An abomination because of what I was.

And I was shaken to the very core by the revelation of it.

"If I wasn't the Sibyl, I would have died on Monday night."

I was sitting on the porch steps of The Red Rose as Joey filmed me. Both he and Elliot had promised the footage they captured would be scrapped. That we didn't have to air what had happened to me.

But I refused. I'd be damned if I didn't show the world just how evil the dead could be.

"We join you from Ogunquit, Maine. Home of some of the most beautiful scenery I have ever seen. Behind me is The Red Rose Bed and Breakfast." I gestured behind me as Joey panned out to get a shot of the building. "Built in the mid-1910s, The Red Rose operated from 1923 to 1952. It shut down after the inn received a well-deserved bad reputation as the Suicide Sanctuary."

I stood up, dusted off the back of my jeans, and ignored the bright white bandage over my right arm.

"I'm not making that nickname up, folks. That's actually the nickname this place earned after seventy-five people took their lives here. But there is more. So much more."

I started to walk forward. Joey moved back as I kept talking.

"Melannie Sawyer bought the Red Rose in the early nineties in the hopes of restoring it to its former glory. And believe me when I say the Red Rose is stunning. She spent eight years to ensure that every detail was perfect before she opened the doors to the public in 2001. Yes, she knew its history. But the need to start her life over was far greater than any morbid story."

I glanced up at the sky before I turned my attention back to Joey.

"In truth, it wasn't the inn itself that was haunted. Just a single room. 23B has hosted some two hundred suicides since 2001. Different methods, but each violent. Each with the same result. Death. It has gotten so bad that Maine's Department of Health has threatened to shut the Red Rose down for good."

I studied the gravel beneath my feet for a moment. I considered my next words. I knew my parents would be watching. I knew they would threaten to have me thrown into the next mental ward if it meant I stayed safe. But it didn't matter. I wanted to tell my audience the truth.

No matter how much it hurt.

"I met the spirit who was behind the suicides. You will, too, throughout the episode. Margaret Gillotson was obsessed with the occult. She didn't worship God. Or spiritualism. She worshiped her Ouija board. Seriously. She took advice from it. She ended her life in room 23B on its suggestion. How do I know this?"

I pulled out a newspaper clipping from my back pocket.

"Let's just say the newspapers back in the day were better than TMZ today. They could find out anything about you. And when you kill yourself in a ritzy getaway for the rich? All your secrets are exposed. In black and white."

I could see Joey giving me the signal to cut it short so I held up my bandaged arm. "I'm not depressed. I'm not suicidal. But I tried to harm myself thanks to Gillotson's control over my emotions. So let this episode be a warning. A lesson to any of you who wish to delve into the world of the paranormal."

I dropped my arm. I took another look at the inn I was more than happy to get away from. I turned back to Joey with tears in my eyes.

"The past doesn't rest. Whether its actual ghosts or your own memories, the past will tear you down. Destroy your sanity. Your sense of self. But only if you let it. I know this from personal experience, after all. I don't care who you are or what you do. Believe in yourself enough to know that you will survive the heartaches in life. If you are considering suicide, reach out to someone. Get help. But whatever you do?"

I wiped away the tears that were falling down my face; smearing my makeup all to hell in the process.

"Don't give up on yourself. Ever. That's the worst thing you could possibly do."

Joey waited a good five seconds for dramatic effect before he began his silent countdown. When he lowered the camera, I moved over to him.

"Personal, touching, informative," He nodded. "That was good."

"Yeah, well, maybe it'll reach somebody who needs it."' I started to move around him as I unsnapped my microphone, but Joey caught my arm. "What, Joey?"

"Look, I know about what happened in Georgia. And we all saw you in Kansas. Suicide seems like an easy choice for you and that shouldn't be the case."

"What are you getting at? Because we have to be at the airport-"

"All I'm saying is that if you ever need to talk, I'll listen. I don't give the best advice sometimes, but I'll try to make you laugh."

I studied Joey for a second before I pulled him into a hug. Despite my friendship with Elliot, he'd never actually offered to listen to me. I was touched by Joey's words. I really was.

"Ok?"

"Ok," I released him with a small smile. "I'll take you up on it."

Joey grinned as we fell in step with each other. Elliot was still inside with Melannie, so we had a few minutes by ourselves at the car.

"So do you think Elliot's gonna ease up on you now?" Joey asked as he popped the trunk. "I mean, he did freak out when he saw you."

"Elliot was the one who found me in Georgia." I leaned against the bumper and crossed my arms over my chest. "Plus, the incident at Black Hollow. So no, I don't."

"Where are we going next?" Joey looked up at me as he rearranged the equipment bags. "Because if we can gang up on him, maybe he'll back down."

"Elliot said something about New York." I shrugged. "I have no idea. I guess we'll find out on the plane. Seems to be how he likes to do things."

"True," Joey sighed as he closed the trunk lid. It made a loud thud before he continued. "Hey, we've survived so far. We can last a little longer."

"I hope so," I returned his fist bump. "I hope so."

EIGHTEEN

SEASON 1, EPISODE 7: LAKE NESSIE, NEW JERSEY

"THERE IS NOT enough coffee in the world to be on television at six a.m."

I grumbled while I stood between Elliot and Joey, waiting in the darkened wings of the studio where they filmed *Rise and Shine*. Unfortunately for me, Connor had called Elliot before we left Maine to detour us for an appearance on a popular morning show.

Hence, Elliot's mention of New York. It didn't have anything to do with filming an episode and everything to do with promoting the show.

At six a.m. Which meant a two a.m. wake up call so that we were at the studio by four to be primped and prodded to perfection.

"Jesus, Eva." Elliot hissed in my ear as the crowd erupted in applause. "Can you not complain about everything I ask you to do? This is for *Grave Messages*."

"No." I twisted my head just enough to glare at him. "This is for you. Seems to me, you like playing the big shot. You like to play it up for the cameras because you think it makes you look good instead of actually working on the show."

Before our argument could escalate, a man with an earpiece and clear clipboard approached us. He jabbed a single finger in our direction before motioning for us to follow him.

"We'll finish this later, Eva." Elliot threw me a scathing look. "For now, just behave."

He stormed towards the stage and I tried to resist the temptation to flip him off. It was a temptation I gave in to. I heard Joey snicker when he threw his arm around my neck seconds before our names were called out by the host Amy Morrison.

"It's showtime, Evie." Joey grinned as we walked out onto the set. "Time to shine, baby girl."

I plastered the biggest smile on my face and waved to the audience. Don't get me wrong. I'd been trained on how to conduct myself on television by the best Theia Productions had to offer. I knew what to do when the spotlight hit. So when Amy released Elliot, I clasped her hand into mine and conducted the customary air kisses on each of her cheeks.

"Amy! How wonderful to see you!"

I folded myself up in the seat closest to her. I knew Elliot was glaring at me when he took the seat next to me. After all, I had just stolen the best chair on the stage. I knew I was going to pay for that little move later, but right now?

I was thrilled. Let Elliot stew in his anger. If he wanted to pick a fight with me this early in the morning, I'd be damned if I backed down from it.

"Eva, Elliot, Joey." The woman flipped her perfect brown ponytail over her shoulder. "Welcome to *Rise and Shine*. We're all thrilled to have you here."

Yeah, yeah. I resisted the urge to roll my eyes when she began to ask Joey how he felt going to locations known for their ghosts. I bit my tongue when she spoke with Elliot about how he felt filming for the first few shows had gone. My co-host was halfway through his answer when she turned to me.

"Eva, you claim to have been gifted by Apollo. Tell us. Is that true? Do you really see spirits?"

I blinked back the flashes of memories which played behind my eyes. Blood. Angry women. Fearsome spirits. I swallowed back the fear that plagued me since we'd left Maine the day before. I'd tried to slit my own wrists thanks to the influence of the hateful spirit that resided at the Red Rose Inn. In fact, I still had to cover the fading wound with a bandage.

"I do." I spoke slowly. Careful. "Amy, I have to warn your viewers that not all spirits are grandmothers wanting to talk to their beloved families. The ghosts I have encountered have been...twisted."

"Like in a horror movie?" Her blue eyes widened. "I've been watching *Grave Messages* since it first premiered. Some of the things are a little hard to believe. Are you telling me that you are documenting real occurrences of the paranormal?"

"Of course, we are." Elliot leaned forward to break into our conversation. "When Eva became the Sibyl, she became a lightning rod of sorts. Spirits of all sorts flock to her."

I cut my eyes over to Elliot before I turned my attention back to the host. "Elliot is right. Sort of. The role of the Sibyl is to be a messenger of the dead. *Grave Messages* has allowed me to share their messages with the world."

"Let's show the audience a clip from your latest episode." Amy was practically bouncing in her chair as she turned to the screen behind us. "This is footage sent to us by Joey yesterday. It's an exclusive preview of the episode that will premiere this Thursday."

The audience cheered as the screen shifted into the night vision Joey had used so that we could film in the darkness. I gripped the chair arms as I watched myself swing the small camera around the room as all hell had broken loose around me. Hell that broke loose seconds before my body was jerked to the floor. The perimeter cameras had caught the look of utter fear on my face as a white mist appeared over me.

I didn't remember the mist. I remembered Margaret Gillotson's angry eyes. Her conviction when she claimed to be the first to sacrifice herself to a Ouija board. The jagged wounds that ran up her arms.

I watched in horror as I began to sob on the screen. I saw the white mist shift back when I stood up. I heard Joey and Elliot screaming through the hotel door as I said the same phrase over and over again.

"Monster. I'm a monster."

The clip ended when I went into the bathroom to slam the door behind me. I'd been so caught up in my memories of the horrible place that I'd forgotten where I was. I jumped when *Rise and Shine'* audience erupted into applause and cheers.

"Eva," Amy leaned forward to clasp my arm. "Can you tell us what happened? What was going through your mind at the time?"

"You see a mist. But for me?" I tore my eyes away from the screen. "I saw the apparition of a woman named Margaret Gillotson. She committed suicide in 1925. She was the first of two hundred suicides which took place at the Red Rose."

"Were you frightened?" Her grip tightened. "Were you possessed?"

"No, not frightened." I admitted. "I was too wrapped up in the spell she cast over me. And no. I wasn't possessed. I'm not even sure if that's possible."

"I don't want to be possessed." The woman patted my arm. "So you'll have to let me borrow Cyrus to make sure that doesn't happen."

I blinked. Borrow Cyrus? He was my keeper. My guard. He wasn't a possession to be passed back and forth. And why the hell would she need him in the first place?

Apparently, my question was written all over my face because she giggled.

"Elliot, darling. You haven't told Eva yet, have you?"

"Told me what?" I shifted in my chair to look at my co-host. "I'm all ears, Elliot."

"Amy is going to accompany us to our next location." Elliot threw me a smirk. "I thought it would do us some good to have an extra party member to witness your theatrics, Sibyl."

"Theatrics." I spoke through gritted teeth. "Thanks for that, Elliot. Your support has always been the stuff of legends."

My words were drowned out when Amy started to talk about

how excited she was to join us. She then stood and clapped her hands.

"It is time for *Break Fast with Stephen Masters*. Eva, Elliot, Joey – won't you join our celebrity chef for this segment? It's the least I can do to say thank you."

"Wait." I jerked my arm back when Elliot tried to pull me to my feet. "I don't cook."

"Don't worry, silly. Stephen will take care of you." Amy flashed me a million-watt smile as a tall man dressed in white bounded over to us. "Won't you, Stephen?"

"Absolutely! You can knead the dough. A harmless exercise to be sure." He looped his arm through mine before he addressed the audience. "Don't you think Eva will do a fabulous job?"

The resounding cheers told me these people had paid good money to see us. To see me make a fool of myself. I glanced back to Joey, who was hiding his laughter behind his hand. Elliot took my other arm and leaned in to whisper his warning.

"Behave. The audience is watching you."

I took a deep breath when we approached the cooking station. A large bowl of flour had been set up on the counter. Stephen deposited me in front of it before he turned to the cameras.

"We'll do something simple this morning. Crepes. Who's ready?"

More applause. More cheering. Whistles. How people could be this energetic so early in the morning was beyond me. But as Stephen added the ingredients in the bowl, I got an idea.

"So what do I do again?" I stepped up beside him. "You said something about kneading?"

"Yes." The chef reached under the counter to pull out an identical bowl. Inside was a mass of yellow dough. "How does that look, Eva?"

"Hmm." I reached in and poked at the food with a single finger. "It's weak, Stephen. Reminds me of someone I work with. Never rises to the occasion."

I heard Elliot clear his throat behind me. I knew I hit home. Good. The bastard had gotten away with far too much this morning in my opinion.

I turned to Elliot with my most innocent expression. "Maybe we can make something else that doesn't remind me of you, Elliot."

The audience screamed with laughter. I saw the tips of Elliot's ears turn red when he reached into the bowl to pick up a handful of dough.

"I think it's just fine. Very malleable. You can mold it into anything you want it to be."

"A decent human being? I seriously doubt that."

I picked up a bowl of flour then tossed it into Elliot's face. He ducked but I still managed to cover half of him with the powder.

The rest of it?

Poor Joey was going to have a time washing the flour out of his curls. He gasped before he reached over to grab a bottle of honey. My friend slung it towards us. I burst out laughing when it hit the famous Stephen Masters square in the face. The chef cried out seconds before he joined in our food fight.

As the food went flying, Amy tried to intervene, but we were too far gone. By the time we ran out of ammunition, the entire cooking station was covered in food. We were filthy. And our precious audience? The one that Elliot told me to behave in front of?

They went wild.

"Genius." Amy was sitting in the makeup chair next to me. "The food fight was pure genius, McRayne."

I risked getting poked in the eye by the make-up witches when I glanced over at her. "Thanks. I think."

"You've got a real hold on what makes this business tick." She closed her eyes as the stylist went to work on her hair. "You know the viewers want to be surprised. *Rise and Shine* gets publicity, sure. But your little stunt has been viewed over a million times on YouTube. Not to mention the coverage we gained on other stations who aired footage of your exploits. I'm thrilled with everything that has happened so far."

Uh huh. I bet she was.

I felt Natalie, Theia's head make-up witch, poke me in the temple so I closed my eyes when I responded.

"Why did you want to come with us?"

"Why not?" The woman sighed. "This will be a great opportunity for cross promotion. You will gain my viewers. I could potentially gain yours."

"True." I muttered. "But I have to tell you, Amy. You said during the interview that you were going to have to borrow Cyrus. That's not possible."

"Why not?" She opened an eye to look at me. "He's just a bodyguard."

"No. He's bound to me. I also have more respect for him than to pass him around the room like a shiny new toy."

"You can't be serious." She frowned at me. "Surely you don't buy your own hype. There is no way you really speak with the dead."

"You'll see." I shrugged. "Stay behind Elliot. He will have to take care of you if Cyrus has his hands full with me."

"Fine." She sat up when the stylist moved away from her. "I went over your routine with Joey. Introduction of the place first. Then you go in and try to document the paranormal."

"Yeah. That's pretty much it." I released a breath I didn't know I had been holding. "I'll say something quick to wrap things up at the end, but I'm sure you'll be gone by the time we're done."

I heard banging on the trailer door before Elliot popped his head in. He ignored me when he spoke to Amy.

"We're going to start in about five minutes, Amy. You ready?"

I chuckled while she stood up to follow him outside. Elliot was still upset with me even though my stunt had been a resounding success. He had wanted promotion for *Grave Messages*. I gave it to him. The problem was I had hurt his pride in the process.

"Lancaster will get over his ego, Little One."

I stood up to see Cyrus leaning against the far wall. I grinned up at my Keeper when he shook his head. "Good to see you too. Ready to go play with the ghosts and ghoulies, Cy?"

"More than you could ever know."

Cyrus chuckled. When I started to move past him, he caught my arm then tucked a loose strand of hair behind my right ear before he leaned in.

"Thank you, Sibyl, for standing up for me. I have done nothing to earn your kindness."

"You're my friend, Keeper." I felt my breath catch when I realized how close we were. I cleared my throat before I continued. "I defend my friends. You're not a possession. I don't care what you say about this whole 'slave' business."

Cyrus' expression was soft when he released my arm. He moved behind me as we exited the trailer. I could see dark slashes of metal curving up into the sky. We crossed the parking lot to meet Joey, Elliot, and Amy in front of a broken sign that announced to the world just where we were.

Lake Nessie. An amusement park that had been abandoned in the 1960's after two people died horrible deaths on its grounds.

"You ready, Evie?" Joey slung his camera on his shoulder. "The sun is setting and I need to get you in this light."

I nodded while I joined the other two. Joey raised his hand and dropped his fingers down on the count of three when the light on his camera began to blink.

"Welcome to Lake Nessie, New Jersey!" I gestured to the darkening scene behind us. "We come to you tonight from a broken and abandoned amusement park. I know. I can hear you from here. Come on, Evie. Don't be so clique!"

I smiled at the camera. "Maybe you're right. Maybe this place is clique. But I couldn't ignore the history behind it. You see Lake Nessie was built on a Native American burial ground. Opened in 1926, this was a place for families to come and enjoy themselves. Little did they know their pleasure was taking place on top of a gravesite. Don't believe me? Google it. Archeologists discovered eighteen graves here. That sounds like a recipe for disaster, right?"

"Speaking of recipes," I gestured to Amy from behind my back until she stepped forward. "We have a special guest with us tonight. Amy Morrison from *Rise and Shine* is going to be spending the night investigating with us. Amy, have you ever been ghost hunting before?"

"No." She flashed Joey's camera a smile. "I'm a little nervous to be so close to the Sibyl in action."

"I'm sure." I felt Elliot come up behind me. He grasped my shoulder so tight, I had to bite my lip from wincing. "Elliot, why don't you tell us about the ghosts here?"

"Gladly." He released my shoulder. "There are two documented deaths here at the amusement park. The first died when they were thrown from a roller coaster in 1953. The last was a man who drowned in the lake in the middle of the park. After the gentleman's death, the park was shut down for good in 1966. Yet, their spirits are still here. Trespassers and ghost hunters have reported hearing laughter. Screams. Lights when there hasn't been power at this location for decades. Swings moving without anyone close to the equipment."

"Could be residual energy." I twisted around to look up at him. I raised an eyebrow at his surprised expression. "What? I can do research too, you know."

"That may be," He gave me a tight smile. "As it stands, we hope to document any paranormal occurrences that we come across. And we'll do what we can to keep Eva away from the Funhouse mirrors.

I felt the blood drain out of my face. Elliot's remark was more than a blow. He knew better than most my abilities were triggered by mirrors. I couldn't handle a single reflective surface without Cyrus' help. So to tease me about an entire building full of mirrors?

It was cruel.

"You do that."

I responded before I turned on my heel. I had too. I didn't want Elliot to know he had rattled me. So I pushed the rusted gate open and slipped inside.

Only to stop with a short scream. I stumbled backwards into a chunk of concrete. In the end, I landed on my butt in the middle of overgrown weeds.

Yay. Go me.

A woman was still standing two inches in front of my face. She was pale. Half of her face was darkened by shadow. Her prim blouse was buttoned to the neck, but it was covered in black stains.

"Eva?"

"What's going on?"

Cyrus appeared beside me as the woman disappeared. He took my arm before he looked at me with concern.

"Are you alright, Sibyl?"

"Fine." I pushed myself up. "Just wasn't expecting a damn ghost two inches away from my nose."

"You saw a ghost?" Amy pushed past Elliot. "What did it look like?"

"A woman. Dark hair. Bloody blouse." I frowned. "At least, I think it was blood. The shirt was white with dark stains. She appeared right in front of me."

"Ok." Joey spoke up from behind us. "Let's go in. Maybe we'll come across her again."

I couldn't tell him that running across the spirit was the last thing I wanted to do. I nodded and stepped around a pile of trash that lined the path.

How can I possibly describe what it was like to be in an abandoned amusement park so late at night? Thanks to the full moon overhead, enough light filtered down so that we could see where we were going. Stands that promised prizes and concessions were broken husks covered in peeling paint. Buildings collapsing in on themselves lined the cobblestone path we walked.

I tried to keep my composure, but I had to admit that the spirit had rattled me. I was shaking by the time we stopped in front of a moldy map.

"The swings are to the left." Elliot spoke up behind me. "Let's go there first."

I started to follow him and Amy when a shrill shriek filled the air around us. Our guest screamed before she latched onto Elliot's arm. Even Cyrus whipped around towards the sound. But my reaction was completely different.

I took off towards the scream. Somehow, I managed to dodge the rusted pieces of metal that lined the path when the scream resounded again. This time, I could tell it was coming from a building not far from the entrance. I didn't stop until I was inside. When I slid to a stop, I wished I hadn't.

The room I found myself in was lined with mirrors. Each one broken. Some shattered. I clasped my hands over my ears when the whispers of the dead began to fill my mind. I tried to back out of the room, but each step I took seemed to pull me closer to the mirrors.

"Ok." I took a breath. I kept my eyes shut. "I can do this. It's just a room, Evie. You got this."

My pep talk fell silent when I heard a woman sobbing. I dared to crack open one eye to see the woman I had met at the gate through a distorted mirror. Her horrific face was elongated. Her body twisted by the glass.

"Help me." She whispered. "Lost. I lost so much."

"How?" I dropped my hands as I heard footsteps behind me. "Who are you?"

"Amelia." She buried her face in her hands before she started sobbing. "Amelia Richards. They forgot me. Left me lost."

"What the hell, Eva?"

I heard Elliot when the group joined me. I held up my hand to silence him.

"Amelia. How can we help you?"

"Find me. Please. Let me rest in peace."

"Is she doing her thing?" Amy spoke out loud, but I ignored her. I focused on the woman. "Surely she can't see anything..."

"Where can we find you, Amelia? Can you tell me where?"

"I died. I know I did." She dropped her hands. "I fell so far. So far. Then darkness."

"Ok." I breathed out the word. "Where did you fall?"

"I don't..."

"Show me."

I reached for the glass when I felt Cyrus grab my arm. My keeper pulled me back then wrapped his arm around my neck to whisper in my ear.

"Little One, are you crazy? You cannot take on her memories. Do not allow her to pull you into the glass."

"Cyrus," I relaxed against him. "Let me help her. Please. Just... stay here. Be here just in case."

My keeper tightened his grip around me for a moment before he let me go. Not that he had a choice. Cyrus had learned there was no way to keep me from doing what I wanted once I set my mind to it.

I approached the shattered glass and pressed my palm against it. The spirit didn't move. She stared at me with the same fear I had felt for her.

"Help me find you, Amelia." I whispered. "Don't pull me through but show me what you remember."

The ghost needed no further instruction. She pressed her palm against the glass until her hand slipped through. The second she made contact with my skin, my world shifted. Gone was the twisted metal and piles of trash. Gone were the peeling signs. I found myself at Lake Nessie amusement park in its heyday. People swarmed around me until I lowered myself down into the seat of the roller coaster.

"Joan, this is so silly." I turned to a girl with pointed glasses. "I have class first thing in the morning. What if my students saw me on a roller coaster?"

"Amelia, you are such a stiff." The girl laughed before she pulled the bar across her lap. "Just live a little! It's not like I'm asking you to do drugs or anything. Just sit back. Join the ride. You'll have fun."

The ride jerked forward and we were off. I felt my stomach lurch when the cart clanked its way up the rails. I glanced down from the top to see Lake Nessie beneath us. I felt my body relax when the cart stopped. I tried to enjoy the view of the lake.

The peace I felt lasted for all of two seconds. When the cart began to race downhill, I felt the bar across my lap snap. I went limp. I began to fall. My scream drowned out by the winds before I felt my body slam against the ground below.

"Evie? Evie, honey, you still with us?"

Amy knelt in front of me. I recognized her pretty face the more my vision cleared. At some point, I had ended up on my knees in front of the mirror. I blinked at her twice before I turned to Cyrus.

"Amelia Richards. 25 years old. Not married. She died here in July of 1966. A month before New Jersey shut this place down."

"Ok." Cyrus knelt beside me. "What does she want of you,Eva?"

"To find her." I took the hand he offered me. "This land is littered with bodies. But she is more concerned with her own."

"There is no way we are going to find a body." Amy dusted off her jeans when she stood up. "We didn't see anything. Just shadows shifting."

"Come on, Joey."

I ignored the television host before I walked out of the room. This time, there were no whispers. There was no confusion. It took about five minutes, but I emerged into the moonlight. The more I walked, the more Amelia's memories surfaced. This time, they were memories of sadness. Actions witnessed after her death. So I followed the scenes she showed me. When I stopped, we were standing in the middle of an old souvenir shop.

"She's here."

I moved behind the counter then fell to my knees. "Cyrus, you wouldn't happen to have your sword handy, would you?"

"Eva, you can't just bash your way around here." Elliot spoke for the first time since they'd joined me in the funhouse. "This land is owned by the state. Any damage you do will have to be paid for by Theia..."

"How in the hell are they going to be able to tell?" I snapped. "Seriously, Elliot. If you'd stop being so self-absorbed, you'd see this place has already fallen apart. I don't think one hole in the floor is going to make much of a difference."

Cyrus moved around the counter to stand across from me. I could feel Joey and Amy leaning over my shoulder to get a look when Cyrus slammed the hilt of his golden broadsword against the rotten wood.

It gave away with an audible snap. He hit it twice more before I reached over to pull the wood away. I could see the shadow of something beneath the floor. I knew it was big. I just prayed it wasn't a rat.

"I maintain you are wrong, Eva. Nice trick, though. This makes for one hell of a story..."

Amy's words were cut off by her scream when I pulled the final board free to expose the one thing I had been looking for.

A decomposed corpse rested in the dirt. Her white blouse was stained with mud. Her bony hands were folded over her stomach. I swallowed back my own scream when the sky lit up and music began to blare around us when the park came to life.

"What the..." Joey whirled around with his camera. "Evie..."

"You're welcome, Amelia." I whispered to the corpse before I pulled my cellphone out of my back pocket. "We have to call the police. Amelia saw her burial after her death. She came here with a friend of hers who was paid off by the park officials to keep her death secret. There are others like her. People whose families forgot about them for the money they gained from the park after their deaths."

"What..." Amy was clutching to Elliot as I dialed 9-1-1. "What was her message to you? Did she have one?"

"Yeah." I stared at the body beneath us before I focused my attention onto Elliot. "Don't trust your friends. They will be the first to sell you out."

NINETEEN

SEASON 1, EPISODE 8: MANSVILLE, KENTUCKY

"DAMMIT!"

I turned to see Elliot drop his bag of recording equipment to the floor and grab his arm. My co-host grumbled a curse before he noticed I was watching him.

"What?" He snapped. "It's heavy. If you would help instead of prancing around here like a damned princess, you'd be cussing to."

"Poor baby." I rolled my eyes at him. "Last time I checked, you and Joey wouldn't *let* me carry anything. Something about me being a girl, was it? So, before you start jumping down my throat, you might want to check your own misogynistic tendencies."

I saw Joey step in to drop his own set of black bags next to Elliot. When our cameraman shook out his shoulders, I decided to take pity on them.

"How many bags are left? I'll get them."

"Don't be silly, Evie." Joey narrowed his eyes at Elliot. "There's only one more left. I'll get it since Elliot is obviously out of commission."

I sighed when Joey left us. The tension in the air was so thick, you could have cut it with the proverbial knife. Maybe it was the location. Mansville Sanitarium was known for its ghastly history. Or maybe, it was the resentment that had set in between me and Elliot.

I decided to play nice when Elliot began to wince each time he moved. I crossed the dusty lobby then snagged Elliot's arm before he could protest. I pulled up his sleeve to expose his shoulder.

"What do you think you are doing?" He glared down at me. "I don't need your help, Eva."

"You never do." I pressed my fingers against his skin. "Where does it hurt? Here?"

"Yeah." He grumbled. "It's just sore."

I didn't say another word while I rubbed my hand over his shoulder. It took a minute, but Elliot relaxed beneath my touch with a sigh.

"Better?"

"A little." He tugged his sleeve back down. "Thanks."

Elliot ran his hand through his dark hair when he looked down on me. For a second, I felt pulled to him. It was the same attraction that had kept me by his side for so long. I reached out, caught his hand when it fell, and squeezed it.

"Elliot, listen. I know there's been nothing but tension between us. But we can still be friends if you stop acting like such an ass."

"Can we?" His dark eyes studied me for a moment. "I'm not so sure about that."

"Ok. Look. I get that you're stubborn. And your damn pride gets in the way every single time. But we still have to work together. It'd be better if we tried to get along. Easier."

As I was speaking, I felt the strong sense of security that surrounded me each time Cyrus made his appearance. I saw Elliot's face grow cold when he realized we were no longer alone.

"I'm going to see what's taking Joey so long."

"Elliot!" I watched him leave then stomped my foot in frustration. "Dammit."

"Perhaps it is for the best." Cyrus took his place beside me. "Elliot seems disturbed lately."

"You noticed that too, huh?" I crossed my arms over my chest. "I don't get it, Cyrus. You'd think he'd be happy. *Grave* is at the top of the ratings. We're doing great. Better than great. So why is he so damned determined to act like a two-year-old who hasn't gotten his way?"

"Because he hasn't." Cyrus pulled out his cell phone. When he passed it over to me, he gave me a small smile. " *Grave Messages* was his show, Little One. Yet, there is very little mention of him in the press. I believe that he has become jealous of you."

I took his phone and scrolled through the list of articles he had pulled up. Some were from crappy celebrity sites that thrived on the drama that went on behind the scenes. But there were news articles too. Ones that proclaimed me as 'America's Ghost Girl'. They touted my successes with each location we went to. They took a journalistic approach to what we had filmed so far. I let my thumb hover over one that read *Ghost Girl Finds Human Remains* before I hit the 'close' button.

"That's ridiculous." I passed the phone back to Cyrus. "Elliot has nothing to be jealous of. I'm not trying to steal his show from him. I can't help it if he's decided to stay in the background."

"If you're done talking about me behind my back, we need you outside."

I whirled around to see Elliot was leaning against the front door. He gave me a glare that spoke volumes. I decided to ignore it. After all, I didn't say anything to Cyrus that I wouldn't have said to his face.

"Alright." I squared my shoulders. "Let's do this."

"Mansville Sanitarium." I gestured to the building behind me as Joey took a few steps back. "What can I say about this place that hasn't been covered on the other ghost shows that have filmed here?"

I smiled. "The thing is, I don't know yet. I am going into this place blind, folks. I have no knowledge of the paranormal activity that has occurred here. But I did take the time to learn a little bit about its history."

I started up the steps. Joey began to follow me. I turned towards him to face the camera once more when I had my hand on the door.

"Mansville Sanitarium is the product of a diseased population. You see, Mansville, Kentucky is a great town. But it's built on a marsh. Which means bugs. Which means diseases. Tuberculous ran rampant here in the early 20th century. So much so, the local hospital couldn't handle the influx of patients battering down their door."

I leaned against the door as I continued the monologue I'd prepared the night before.

"Mansville Sanitarium opened its doors in 1923. It was believed to be the most advanced medical facility to treat tuberculous. Not that their fancy equipment mattered. Their patients still suffered horribly before they finally succumbed to the disease. Balloons were inserted into their lungs to help expand them. Ribs were removed in the hopes that the patient would be able to breath better. And let's not talk about the numerous pictures of patients covered in ice while they sat in front of open windows. Why? Because fresh air was believed to be a cure for the white death."

I opened the door to show off the impressive lobby. Or, at least, it had been impressive. The years hadn't been kind to Mansville.

"Thankfully, the outbreak of the disease began to decline as new medicines were discovered. By the 1960's, this place became a home for the elderly. But that little venture only lasted for twenty years. Mansville was left to rot after reports of abuse and neglect shut down the nursing home in 1986."

Joey held up his hand as a signal for me to stop. I moved to sit behind him on one of the equipment cases when Elliot came into view. He leaned against the counter as Joey counted down on his fingers. When our cameraman's hand became a fist, Elliot started talking.

"Eva may be blind to the paranormal activity here, but I'm not stupid. I took the time to look up the entities we might run into tonight. Whether she does her little mirror trick or not." Elliot's tone was nothing but condemnation. "It's true that a large number of paranormal investigation teams have had their fun at Mansville.

Many reported that they heard voices. Caught apparitions in photos and on film. Yet, others claim that there is a shadow person who has taken up residence here. One that has been seen walking on the ceilings. Or climbing the walls. That, my friends, is what I'm after tonight."

"Stupid, am I?" I stood up and walked right into Joey's shot. I heard him hiss for me to get out of the way, but I refused. I jabbed a single finger into Elliot's chest. "Mirror trick? What the hell, Elliot? You know what I can do. You've seen me talk to the dead how many times now?"

"The infamous Eva McRayne, everyone." Elliot's smile was grim, but he didn't face the camera. He kept his eyes trained on me instead. "The ghost girl who has taken *Grave Messages* to a whole new level thanks to her abilities to talk to the dead. And has the most amazing talent of getting herself in danger. Maybe we'll see that again tonight. After all, who knows what will happen?"

"Are you threatening me?" I raised my eyebrow at him. "Because if you are, then I don't want to be anywhere around you tonight."

"Fine." Elliot pulled out a small camera then tossed it over to me. I barely caught it against my chest when he pulled out another one. "You and Joey go one way. I'll go the other. We'll meet back here and see who has the best footage."

I didn't get a chance to respond. My 'co-host' took off to the right. Joey released a deep breath from behind me.

"I've filmed some crazy reality shows before. *Love' em or Leave' em. Give Me Your Money.* But I can honestly say none of them had as much drama in one episode as you and Elliot have in a single minute."

"Ha. Ha." I frowned. "Joey, what has gotten into him? Elliot has always been a pain in the ass. But before, it was manageable. Funny even. Now, he's conniving and just plain..."

"Mean." Joey lowered his camera to the floor then came over to stand beside me. My friend threw his arm around my shoulders and squeezed. "Face it, Evie. Elliot has let his jealousy get the best of him. If he's smart, he'll learn to let it go. If he's not, he'll leave the show."

"Leave the show?" I shook my head. "Never. He'd fire me first."

"Nah. Theia won't let you go now that you've skyrocketed *Grave* ." Joey took the handheld camera from me. He began playing with the buttons on it. "So...what's the deal? We gonna show him up again?"

"Don't we always?" I took the small camera back as Joey picked up his own. "Let's go."

Three hours and two hospital wings later, I was exhausted. So far, neither one of us had heard a single whisper. We hadn't picked up anything on the cameras. And the spirit box Joey had brought along?

Silent.

I circled around the room I had found myself in and grumbled in frustration. Spirits, monsters...whatever you wanted to call them... were usually crawling out of the woodwork to talk to me. I turned one last time to get a final shot of the abandoned hospital room when I bumped right into Cyrus.

I'm not too big to admit that I was startled. I hadn't seen my keeper since the cameras had started rolling, so the last place I expected him was to be right behind me. I let out a gasp of surprise.

"Hush, Little One. It's just me." Cyrus caught me by the shoulders. He gave me a look of concern. "Are you alright?"

"Fine. You just gave me a mild heart attack, but I'm fine." I took a breath to calm my beating heart. "Where have you been? I thought you'd come out to help when you realized that Elliot wanted us to split off into groups."

"I was watching your Elliot." Cyrus' face seemed to darken. "I do not trust him, Eva."

"None of us do at this point." I sighed. "Where is he?"

"No." Cyrus shook his head. "I don't think you understand. I have obtained information that there are forces attempting to contact him. You must be on your guard."

"Forces? Like the paparazzi or something?" I laughed. I couldn't help it. Cyrus sounded like he was talking about a conspiracy show.

Or one of those military documentaries he was so fond of. "Be serious, Cyrus. I'm on Elliot's bad side right now, but he's not my enemy. He's just having a hard time adjusting, that's all."

"Why are you so quick to defend him?" Cyrus crossed his arms over his chest. "Be honest with yourself, dear girl. The man has abandoned you more than once. He has repeatedly put you in situations where you could have been injured."

"It's all part and parcel of the show." I shifted my grip on the camera then patted him on the arm. "Besides, isn't that what I've got you for? To save my neck whenever needed?"

"Yes, but my job would be much easier if you didn't insist on coming to these places." Cyrus relaxed beneath my touch. He caught my hand against his arm. "I do not wish to see you hurt, Little One. By anything or anyone."

Anyone. Right.

I wasn't stupid. I knew he was referring to Elliot. I let him hold my hand as he led me out of the room.

"Joey?" I lifted the camera up to use the night vision screen. Despite the large windows, Mansville was dark. "Joey, where'd you go?"

"Perhaps he went back to the lobby to wait?" Cyrus frowned. "Or perhaps he is in another wing of the building?"

"Maybe." I bit my lip as we walked. "But it's not like Joey to leave me alone. He's almost as bad as you are."

Cyrus chuckled when we came to the end of the hallway. I looked up to see a small figure on the ground below. I released Cyrus' hand then wiped away a layer of grime with my sleeve to get a better view. I could see a fountain. A pond.

And Joey turning in circles with his arms raised.

"Joey?" I glanced over at my keeper before I turned back to the scene in front of me. "What is wrong with him?"

"Go back to the lobby, Eva." Cyrus grabbed my arm to pull me back down the hallway. "I'll go outside and see what is wrong."

"No." I jerked my arm out of his grasp. "Cyrus, Joey is my friend, too. I'm going with you."

"Eva, it could be…"

"Dangerous? Yeah. I figured that part out. Now let's go."

I didn't give Cyrus a chance to respond. I took off down the hallway. It took some time, but I finally reached the door which led out to the gardens. When I opened it, I was hit by a blast of cold air. But when I heard Joey chanting, my heart froze in my chest.

"He is me and I am he." Joey giggled as he turned. "I am free. Free from the solitary confinement within."

"Joey?" I sat the camera down on a bench then took a step towards him. "You alright?"

"Ah." He released a sigh when he turned to face me. "The little Sibyl. We had heard of your intentions. You wished to dispose of us. And yet, you brought us a vessel instead!"

"What intentions?" I held my hands out to show that they were empty. "What vessel? Who are you?"

"The Creeper. The Shadow Man." Joey purred as he approached me. He stopped just short of where I was before he reached out to caress my cheek. "There is such life in you, Sibyl. Such energy! I could feed for centuries..."

"You are not allowed to touch her." Cyrus knocked Joey's hand away from my face. He had his sword held close to his side when he came between us. "Release the boy, Shadow. Then I will truly set you free from this world."

"Keeper." Joey hissed Cyrus' title and bent at the waist. For a second, I was afraid he was going to be sick. "No. No. No."

My friend darted by Cyrus to grab my hand. He jerked me around until I was pressed against him. Joey's arm tightened his arm across my throat.

"No." He hissed again. "I have been captive here for far too long. I was promised a place in heaven. A seat by the throne of God himself. Yet, I remain. I remain."

Cyrus began to circle us. He bounced his weapon in his hand and I knew at once what he was doing. My keeper was looking for an opening. A way to get me out of harm's way before he attacked.

"Cyrus, don't." I whispered. "Don't hurt Joey."

"You heard your mistress, slave." My friend laughed before he pressed his cheek against the side of my head. "Don't harm her friend. Your Apollo has failed greatly in this creature. She is too softhearted. Too weak."

"What in the hell is going on?"

"Elliot!" I widened my eyes. "Get out of here! Something's wrong with…"

Joey screamed behind me. He shuddered, but he didn't release his grip on me when he stumbled backward.

"Bastard!" Elliot tossed his camera aside. I cried out when he tackled Cyrus to the ground. "You just hurt Joey! I knew it! I knew you were against us!"

I couldn't think. I couldn't breathe when Joey began to laugh once more. He pulled me to the side then turned me to face him. For the first time, I got a good look at the man who had become a staple by my side since *Grave Messages* began.

Joey's dark brown eyes had turned black. His expression was one of hate. Madness. His mouth twisted into a grin.

"Sibyl. Immortal. Daughter of Apollo. You…you will do nicely."

"Joey, stop." I reached up to grab each side of his face. "Stop it. You're scaring me. This isn't you."

"The mortal is gone." He hissed. "Gone."

I didn't know what to do, but I knew I had to act. Cyrus and Elliot were struggling on the grass by the pond. There was the threat that my cameraman had become.

I broke free of Joey's grasp then dodged him when he reached for me again. I took off into a run, but I didn't head back inside. I ran towards Cyrus around the edge of the water. I knew if I could get Joey close enough to him, my keeper could free him from the spirit that had taken over my friend.

I didn't make it.

Joey slammed into my back. I twisted, grabbed his arms, and pulled him down into the pond with me.

For a brief, horrible second, there was nothing. I couldn't see. I couldn't breathe. I felt Joey's hands wrap around my throat as we began to sink deeper into the water. Just when my eyes began to adjust to darkness, I watched Joey arch up. He was struggling to breathe just as I was.

I kept my grip on his arms and pulled him down. Further away from the shore. Joey released my throat then began to claw at his own. I widened my eyes when I saw a dark mass shift out of my cameraman's open mouth. For a moment, I wondered if I had imagined it until a flash of gold broke through the darkness.

Cyrus.

I felt my keeper's arm wrap around my waist as he thrust upward with his sword. Another flash and the shadow began to fade. Cyrus kept his hold on me until his weapon disappeared. He caught hold of Joey's wrist to pull us both to the surface.

I gasped for air when my head broke through the water. I let Cyrus help me to the shore before I crawled out on my knees. I began to cough. But it wasn't until my keeper bent down next to me that I realized I had started crying.

My keeper tugged my soaking wet hair away from my cheeks. He whispered the words he knew I needed to hear. Joey was fine. He was unconscious, but unhurt. I twisted in his arms and threw my arms around his neck.

"Cyrus," I sobbed. "How can you be so sure? What if he's…"

"Hush, Little One." My keeper pressed his hand against my back. "Your friend will be fine. The spirit that attached himself to Joey is gone."

I broke away only to see that Cyrus had dropped my cameraman down next to me. I reached out to brush Joey's dark curls away from his face before I realized there was another body not far from where we were laying.

Elliot was knocked out cold against the ground. Even in the darkness, I could see the wicked bruise on his cheek. I whipped my head around to stare at my keeper.

"What?" Cyrus raised his eyebrows. "I told you before, Eva. You are my responsibility. Not Elliot. He attempted to keep me from my duties."

I took a shaky breath before I snagged his hand. I held on tight while I whispered my next words.

"Cyrus, what was that thing?"

"A shadow, dear girl. A horrible, horrible shadow."

"We will never know if the spirit we encountered tonight was a patient at Mansville Sanitarium. We learned nothing about its history. But we do know that it was evil. And that it wanted to be free from this place."

I was sitting on a bench that lined the pond. Joey and Elliot had regained consciousness a few hours earlier. They tried to insist that we leave Kentucky immediately, but we weren't done yet. I wanted to talk about what happened. I wanted to explain to our viewers what they had seen.

I wanted to record the answers for myself.

"Shadow people aren't new to the paranormal world." I leaned forward to rest my elbows on my knees. "Many who experience them are terrified by their presence. It's a feeling they give off. One of hopelessness and despair. But for other, more stubborn cameramen, they don't run. They keep filming."

I cut my eyes up to Joey. My friend had apologized numerous times to me about what happened. He couldn't stand the thought that he had hurt me. It was sweet. Enduring even.

"As you can see throughout our footage, the three of us were separated at this location. Joey heard a knocking noise in the hallway and when he followed it? He caught the shadow of a human on film. I'll let him tell you his story. Reports claim these spirits are demons. Or twisted ghosts of humans who have endured great suffering. But according to Cyrus, they are far more sinister. Shadow people thrive on the energies of souls. The true vampires of the spirit world. The one we encountered here?"

I stood up then tucked my hands in my jacket pockets. "It was weak. Thank god for that. We could have lost Joey to possession. Or worse."

Joey held up his hand and I went silent. After a few moments, my cameraman dropped his camera down on the bench next to me. He wrapped me up in a hug and I could tell he was shaking.

"Evie, I am so, so sorry. I swear, I never thought," He swallowed.

"I would never hurt you. You know that. I don't know how or what..."

"Hey," I returned his hug. "It's ok, Joey. I get it. Just...don't run off alone again. I don't know what I would do if something bad happened."

He pulled back and winced. I knew he was checking out the bruises he had left behind on my throat. I shook my head.

"Elliot has to be done packing up the rest of the equipment by now." I squeezed Joey's arm. "Let it go, darlin'. I already have."

"Yeah." Joey glanced down at the camera. "I'll try, Evie. I'll try."

TWENTY

SEASON 1, EPISODE 9: FAYETTEVILLE, ARKANSAS

I HADN'T SEEN Hollie Stephens in five years. From what I could remember and what Facebook had to offer, she was taller than me. Thin. We had been acquaintances once, but when she moved to Arkansas and I moved to Georgia, we lost touch.

Until yesterday. I pulled up the message Hollie had sent to me through the *Grave Messages* website and bit the top of my thumb as I re-read her words.

Evie –

It's Hollie. I know it's been awhile. And god knows, I never thought I would need you like this. But I've seen your show and you are the only one who can help me. I'm convinced my little girl, Brandy, is being haunted by something we are both familiar with.

I tried to get your phone number from your mom, but she wasn't sure if she should give it out. Or maybe, she didn't think I was who I said I was. So I thought I'd try this way.

I'm still in Fayetteville. Call me at 479-482-3547 if you can. And congrats on the show. It's really great.

Hollie

I typed in her number twice before I heard a knock on my room door. I knew it was Elliot. He'd been harping on me to get ready to go to the airport for over an hour now. But I couldn't shake the feeling that we didn't need to go to Ohio. We needed to go to Fayetteville.

I jumped to my feet, stormed over to the door, and jerked it open before Elliot could bang on it a fifth time. I glared at my co-host for a minute before I returned to my spot on the bed. I plopped down on the pile of clothes I'd been packing and picked up my phone.

"I'm not going to Ohio."

"Excuse me?" Elliot crossed the room in no less than four strides. He planted himself right in front of me with his hands on his hips. "Eva, you can't say 'no'. You are contracted to do *Grave Messages*."

"I've got something more important to take care of than an old asylum." I pulled up Hollie's message and handed him the phone. "Hollie was a...friend...in high school, Elliot. I have got to help her."

"Yeah? I didn't think you had any friends back then." His voice faltered over the last words as a heavy silence fell between us. When I didn't respond, Elliot sighed and ran his hand over his hair. "Ok, even I'll admit that was low. But Eva, you can't run after everyone who begs you for help."

"Hollie isn't *everyone*." I snatched my phone back from him. "And I'm going to Fayetteville. If you want to film the show, then come with me. Otherwise, I'm taking an emergency side trip. I'll just meet you in Ohio when I'm done."

"What does she mean her daughter's haunted?" Elliot collapsed on the bed next to me. "Does she have an imaginary friend? Or is this a possession?"

I winced at the term 'possession'. It hadn't been forty-eight hours since Joey had been possessed by a shadow person. I rubbed my palm against my throat as I remembered how his sweet personality had turned dark. How his face had twisted into someone unrecognizable. Not to mention how he had tried to strangle me in the process.

"I don't know. I was just about to call her for the details before you came barging in here."

"I didn't barge in. You opened the door." Elliot narrowed his eyes as he took in the mess we were lounging on. "I was hoping you were ready. Our flight leaves in less than an hour."

"No, your flight may leave in less than an hour," I pointed at him. "But I'm not going to be on it. I'll book my own flight to Arkansas."

Elliot was silent for only a moment. His mouth formed a hard line across his face as he studied me. Finally, he responded.

"This girl is really important to you, isn't she?"

"Yes." I flipped over onto my back as I dialed her number. "And my advice to you would be to come with me. Otherwise, you never know what you might miss out on."

I waited through three sharp rings before I heard Hollie pick up. She sounded out of breath when she answered.

"Hello?"

"Hollie?" I held up my hand to study my fingernails. "Hey. It's Eva."

"Eva?" Hollie got so quiet, I thought she had hung up on me. Instead, she squealed. "Oh my god! Girl, it has been forever! How did you end up on TV? What on earth is all this Sibyl business about? Did you get my message?"

"We can catch up when I get there," I sat up. "I did get your message though. What's going on? Are you alright?"

"I don't know how else to explain it." Hollie sounded tired. Her words came out slow. Careful. "Brandy's been playing by herself a lot here lately. But she talks to Ophelia."

I felt my heart stop beating in my chest. I closed my eyes and took a deep breath to keep from shaking.

"Ok." I glanced over to Elliot, who had taken out his own phone.

He was tapping his thumb against the screen. "Imaginary friend? She just turned three, right?"

"Yeah. But Eva, you know Ophelia isn't imaginary." Hollie hissed. "You have to remember…"

"I do." I cut her off when I stood up. I cradled my phone against my cheek, and began to fold a pair of jeans. "But how do you know for sure it's her? I mean, yeah. Ophelia's a weird name, but…"

"Eva, stop. You know what happened. She's here. And she's done something horrible."

I could hear my friend shuffling something around in the background before she came back on the line. I stayed quiet. I waited. Finally, Hollie spoke up once more.

"Brandy's teacher disappeared not long after Ophelia showed up. Brandy told me it was because her teacher laughed at her new 'friend'."

I almost dropped the phone. I dropped my jeans into my luggage instead to catch it against my ear.

"Her teacher disappeared," I swallowed. "And you think Ophelia had something to do with it?"

"Yes." Hollie whispered. "And I might be next. Please, Evie. Hurry. For my sake, and for Brandy's."

Fayetteville, Arkansas was the classic college town. The main street that led to the campus was lined with bars. Restaurants. A used bookstore. I pressed my cheek against the passenger window as I watched it all go by. The town reminded me of Athens. Back when Elliot and I were friends and strange Greek myths come to life had never crossed my mind.

"Penny for your thoughts?"

I glanced away from the scenery to smile at Cyrus as he maneuvered our rental car through downtown. My keeper was proof that the Greek myths I had refused to believe were very, very real. He grabbed my hand to squeeze it when we came to a stop at a red light.

"No deal. I'm a celebrity, Cyrus." I glanced down at the phone in my lap. "My thoughts are worth a buck a piece."

"How much are directions going to cost me?" He returned my smile. "Left or right here?"

"Left. She lives on the outskirts of town." I glanced through the rearview mirror to make sure Joey and Elliot were following behind us. They were driving the SUV that was loaded down with our cameras. I sighed then fell back against the seat. "Cyrus, I've got to tell you something. It's going to sound crazy, so you can't laugh at me."

"Dear girl, I highly doubt that there is anything I would consider 'crazy'." He hit the turn signal and switched lanes. "I am assuming this has something to do with why you've been so anxious today. Don't deny it. I haven't missed how pale you are."

I ignored his comment about my anxiety. After all, what was the point of denying the fact that I was scared out of my mind?

"Back when we were in high school, Hollie was drawn to the occult." I stared at the road ahead of us. "She adored coming over to my house because she wanted to figure out if the rumors about Janet's witchcraft were true."

Cyrus remained silent, so I continued.

"Anyway, when I was fifteen, Hollie and I found a book in the attic. Something about spirit guides. She sat right there in the floor and didn't move until she had read the whole damn thing. When she finally realized I had left her alone, Hollie came looking for me. She wanted to borrow the book."

I glanced down at my phone when it chirped. "Take a right at the next light. Her townhouse is on this street. Number 1435."

"Eva, what happened to your friend?" Cyrus followed my directions, but I noticed his hands were gripping the steering wheel so tightly, his knuckles were white. "What do you know about why she called you?"

I didn't get a chance to respond before he pulled up in the drive. Hollie must have been waiting for us because she bounded out the front door. Seconds later, I was wrapped up in a tight hug as she squealed over me.

"Evie! Look at you! You're gorgeous!" She stepped back to hold me at arms' length. "Course, I know it's not all Hollywood. You were always the golden girl in school. Little Miss Prissy Perfect."

"You haven't changed a bit either, Hollie." I gave her a small smile to hide my grimace at the taunting nickname I still hated. "You're still too damn tall. And when was the last time you got a haircut? I swear, it has to be down to your butt by now."

"Pretty close." She laughed before she stuck her hand out to Cyrus. "And you must be Cyrus from the show. Nice to meet you."

"Pleasure." Cyrus shook her hand as Elliot pulled up behind us. "Ms. Stephens, Eva has told me very little about what plagues your daughter. Perhaps we should go inside."

"Evie!" Joey bounded up to us and threw his arm around my shoulder. "Is this your friend?"

"Hollie, meet Joey." I rolled my eyes. "And Elliot. Guys, this is Hollie."

"Hey." Elliot stuffed his hands in his pockets. "Eva told us a little bit about your haunting, but we need to get set up. Do you mind if we go inside?"

"Sure." Hollie linked her arm with mine. "Go on. Get settled. I figured ya'll would be here for a few days. Evie, you can share my room with me if your crew doesn't mind sleeping in the living room."

"Is Brandy inside? I'd like to meet her." I tilted my head towards my friend. Despite her happy-go-lucky welcome, I could see the lines around her dark green eyes. Her arm was tense. I leaned in with a whisper. "Don't be nervous. You'll be fine."

"I'm not nervous." She whispered back. "Can I talk to you alone? I don't trust your posse."

"My posse?" I raised an eyebrow. "Hollie, the guys are fine. And they need to know what we're dealing with here."

"You know." She stopped to open the door. "You were there, Eva. You know what happened last time. If she's after Brandy..."

"We'll take care of you." I caught sight of Cyrus as he came up behind me. "I promise."

"Brandy!" Hollie opened the front door then gestured for us to follow her. "Come here, honey. There's some people I want you to meet."

I sat my messenger bag on the hall table when I caught sight of a little girl peeking out from around a door frame. Her big brown eyes were wide as she took us in. Hollie must have noticed because she reached out her hand towards the child. "It's alright, baby. Eva and her friends are nice people."

Brandy ignored her mother when she joined us in the hallway. She bypassed us completely to stop in front of Cyrus. I had to swallow back my laughter when the little girl grabbed his hand. She tugged on it until he was forced to kneel down in front of her.

"I'm Brandy." She pointed to herself. "Who are you?"

"Cyrus." My keeper glanced up at me before he returned his focus to the child. "It is nice to meet you, Brandy."

The girl giggled before she ran out of the room. Or at least, she tried to. Hollie snagged her by the shoulders and turned her back to me.

"Brandy, say hello to Eva. We went to school together."

The little girl tilted her head to the side before she narrowed her eyes at me. "No."

"Ah," I chuckled. "It's alright, Hollie. She may just be shy."

"No." Brandy crossed her arms over her chest. "Ophelia says you're dead. She doesn't like you."

I couldn't stop myself. My mouth dropped open when the child broke free of Hollie's grasp. This time, my friend didn't try to stop her as she left us alone.

"What did she mean by that?" Joey whistled. "Cause that? That was creepy."

"I'll go talk to her." Hollie sighed. "Make yourselves comfortable. I'll be right back."

"You want to tell us what this is all about?" Elliot spoke up. "What do you know about the child, Eva?"

"Nothing, really." I sighed. "I know that Hollie had her our freshmen year of college. I know that Brandy is exceptionally smart for her age. But I haven't really kept in touch with Hollie over the years. Between school and now, the show, I don't talk to anyone."

"What about Ophelia?"

Cyrus this time. I frowned as my keeper rose to his feet. I couldn't shake the feeling that they were trying to gang up on me. So I used the one tactic that always made me feel better. Feel more in control.

I went to work.

"Let's go ahead and set up the perimeter cameras. If ya'll want to get a hotel, you can. I'm going to stay here."

"Evie, we can't leave you." Joey stuffed his hands in his jean pockets. "Didn't you just get on my case about running off on by my lonesome? Well, it's time for you to take your own advice."

"Do you want me to help with the cameras?" I ignored Joey's question. "If not, then I'm going to check on Hollie."

"No, we got it." Elliot reached into his pocket to pull out a recorder. He pressed it in my hand. "But record everything. You're hiding something, Eva. I can see it written all over your face."

"I am not." I snapped. "What could I possibly have to hide?"

"I don't know." Elliot studied me for a moment. "But what I do know? You're a horrible liar, Eva. If there's something we need to know..."

I didn't give him a chance to finish. I threw the recorder back in his direction, turned on my heel, and marched through the house. I was furious at him. Furious at Hollie for digging up the past. But most of all?

I was furious with myself. How could I have been so stupid? How could I have let her talk me into bringing up a past I wanted to forget?

I was almost to the back porch when I felt Cyrus grab my arm. He whirled me around to crush me into his embrace. After a moment, he broke his silence.

"Little One, it's obvious that you don't want to talk about your past. I understand that. But if you want to help your friend and the child, then you are going to have to let us help *you*. I will not let you fight these demons alone."

"There's nothing to fight." I muttered against his chest before I pulled away. I glanced down at the floor with a sigh. "Alright. That's a lie. But Cyrus, I don't know what to do. I don't know how to handle this."

"The first thing we are going to do is regroup." He raised his eyebrows at me as he squeezed my arms. "Let's talk to the child and the mother. Then, you finish telling us about what happened between you and your friend."

"Why did she say I was dead?" I interrupted. "Cyrus, surely that wasn't just to creep me out."

"No." He sighed when he released me. "Eva, you have to understand. Death is nothing but a transition. A shift from one form of existence to another. When you became the Sibyl..."

"I transitioned into something else." I whispered. "Something no longer human."

"Eva..."

"No." I shook my head. "It doesn't matter. Not right now. Let's do what you said. Regroup. Talk to Hollie and Brandy. Watch the girl. Tonight when I've had enough wine to float away, then we can sit down to discuss how Ophelia came into being."

Cyrus placed his hand on my back to lead me outside. It was a comforting feeling to have, knowing that he was by my side. But as we joined Hollie and Brandy on the back patio, the fears I had managed to push aside came back with a vengeance.

I was a monster. I just wasn't sure if it was because I'd become the Sibyl, or because it was my fault that a little girl was being haunted now.

"Look at the baby Evie." Joey teased while he pinched my cheek. "You used to be so cute. What happened?"

I smacked his hand away and grumbled as he continued to flip through the yearbook Hollie had managed to find. My old friend was sitting between my newer ones with a grin of absolute delight on her face. When she started to tell them about our days on the cheerleading squad together, I downed my fourth glass of wine and relived the events of the past few hours.

Brandy had been the perfect preschooler for the rest of the day. She insisted that Cyrus color with her, she ignored me, and managed to convince Joey that playing with Barbie dolls was good for him. She even got Elliot in on the game, but my co-host spent more time trying to ask her questions about Ophelia than playing. The only response the child had said was just as creepy as her 'dead' comment to me.

"Ophelia is here." Brandy had busied herself with putting her doll in its car. "She's watching you."

"Watching us?" Elliot acted surprised. "Does she want to play, too? She can have my doll if she wants it."

"No. She wants you to go away. You're bothering her."

"But are we bothering you?" Joey had pushed back the oversized pink hat he had been conned into wearing. "I thought we were having fun."

Brandy went silent before she shook her head. "I like you. You can stay."

I snapped out of my thoughts when I heard Joey whistle. He grinned at me and held the yearbook up so that I could see the picture of my sixteen-year-old self in my cheerleading uniform. I refilled my wine glass and downed it as I took in the skeletal girl in the photograph. I didn't like to think of my childhood or the lengths my mother went to so that I would be deemed 'perfect'.

"I'm thinking we need to get this picture to wardrobe stat. You wear this on the show, Evie? Our ratings will go through the roof."

I snagged the pillow behind me and tossed it at him. My cameraman laughed when I missed. Hollie gave me a strange look before she gestured at me with her wine glass.

"Aren't you going to take your contacts out, Evie? I mean, get comfortable for god's sake. You can't possibly sleep in those."

I blinked until I realized what she was talking about. The only physical attribute that marked me as Apollo's Sibyl was my eye color. Before I took on the role, my eyes had been green. Now?

They were gold. I started to explain to her that I wasn't wearing contacts when Elliot took the book from Joey and closed it. He cleared his throat then sat it aside.

"Alright, you two. It's time to tell us about Ophelia."

Hollie and I looked at each other. When she nodded, I sighed.

"Fine. Hollie, you want to start?"

"Not really." She shrugged. "I've spent the past eight years trying to forget what happened. But if it'll help Brandy, I don't mind."

My friend took a moment before she spoke again.

"I can't remember a time when I wasn't obsessed with ghosts. I mean, I grew up in Charleston. How could I not be? We weren't told bedtime stories. Our folks drenched us in tales of the dead. Of the past. Everybody I knew had a ghost story. Everybody except Eva. She just ignored the rest of us when we told our stories." She cleared her throat. "The rumor at school was that Evie's moma was a witch. That's the sole reason why I became friends with her our freshman year. I wanted to know more about the girl who had more access to magic than I ever could."

Ok, so, this was new. I raised an eyebrow at her as I stretched my legs out over Cyrus' lap. My keeper placed his hand over my ankle and squeezed to let me know he was there. That he wouldn't judge me. Or Hollie.

No matter what he heard.

"Anyway," Hollie waved her hand in the air. "My fascination with your family shifted into a fascination with you. I couldn't get over how you refused to believe in magic. It amazed me that you were so stubborn. As we grew closer, I knew I could prove to you that the paranormal was real. I knew that if you could just see it yourself, then you would believe like I did."

"That's why you wanted the book." I twirled my glass in my hand. "Ok. Let me take over for a second."

Hollie leaned back and I refilled my drink before I continued.

"Hollie and I met when I was fifteen. That summer, we spent what free time I had at my house. By August, my grandmother was bedridden, so she asked for us to go up to the attic to get her photo albums down. She was adamant that she had them close by before she died. So Hollie and I did what we were told. I found the albums. But Hollie found a bunch of books on the paranormal. Ghosts. She pulled out a book on spirit guides and that was it. I didn't see her for the rest of the day."

"It wasn't a book on spirit guides. I just told Eva that to keep her quiet so I could read." Hollie grimaced. "It was a book on conjuring spirits. When I realized what I had stumbled across, I knew I had to have that book. When Eva told me that she didn't care if I borrowed it or not, I took it home. I became obsessed. I told myself that this was it. This was my way of proving to Eva that what I believed in was real."

"So what happened?" Elliot looked between us. "You cast some sort of spell?"

"A séance." Hollie began to pick at the blanket she had over her lap. "We had a sleepover at my place. Eva, me. A girl I hung out with named Charlotte Edgemon. When I lit the candles and pulled out the book, Eva refused to participate. She said there was no way she was to take part in anything even remotely related to witchcraft."

"And I didn't. Seances don't count." I bit my lip. "Hollie convinced us to hold hands around the candles. She said something I couldn't understand. I don't think she understood it either."

"Yeah. Well." I cleared my throat. "Anyway, nothing happened until we went to sleep. Each one of us woke up at 3 a.m. Each of us screaming because we'd had the same dream."

"Ophelia." Hollie swallowed. "I can still remember that dream. I was in a car driving over the old Charleston bridge. Listening to an audio tape of *Hamlet* of all things. I hear a crash behind me. I lost control of the car and went over the edge."

"Into the ocean." I finished for her. "I couldn't breathe. I couldn't see because of the salt water in my eyes. Every part of my body was burning until the world went dark."

"Ok." Joey drew out the word. "And all three of you had this dream?"

"Yeah." I swallowed. "We stayed up for the rest of the night talking about it. We convinced ourselves that it was nothing. Pure coincidence."

"But it wasn't just the dream." Hollie looked over to Joey. "We all started experiencing things around our houses. A woman's voice.

I would rage for no reason. Evie shut down. She refused to talk about it. And Charlotte? She became depressed. Her parents couldn't get her to leave the house."

"So what happened?"

"Charlotte disappeared." I gulped down the wine I'd forgotten about. "No one could find her. The police marked her down as a runaway, but we knew better. And we were right. Her body was found on Sullivan's Island a week later with the word 'Ophelia' written in the sand."

"That explains where the name came from." Elliot stood up.

"Eva, how could this have never come up before? How many late night discussions have we had about the paranormal?

"I don't like to talk about Charleston." I glared at him. "But now? As the Sibyl? I don't have a choice, Elliot. I can't let an innocent child get hurt."

"The hauntings didn't stop after the girl's death." Cyrus tilted his head as he studied me. "The spirit wanted the two of you to join her."

"Yeah." Hollie nodded. "Ophelia hated Eva the most because she said there was something wrong with her blood."

"Not long before Christmas that year, Grandma stepped in." I closed my eyes as I got to the most painful part of this story. "She had Hollie and I come to her room then flat out asked us what was going on. Hollie broke down. She told Grandma about the séance. The dream. We both told her about Charlotte and how she died. My grandmother was furious. She had been bedridden for months, but after hearing our story, she got up. She walked around the entire house with a bundle of herbs, whispering and chanting for protection. When it was done, she pulled out a box of black candles. She divided them between us and made each of us swear that we would burn one in our windows every day for six months."

I swallowed. "When Hollie left, I helped her back to her bed. I thought she was going to yell at me some more, but instead, she grabbed my hands. She told me to embrace my heritage. Embrace my blood."

Cyrus tightened his grip on my ankles, but he stayed silent. So did the others as I wrapped it up.

"That was the last time I spoke to her. Lillian McRayne died in her sleep that night. It was also the last time we had any interaction with Ophelia. I convinced myself that it was all a bad dream. I was so wrapped up in my grief, that I put the whole horrible experience behind me. I forced it out of my mind until I spoke with Hollie yesterday."

"I never stopped believing." Hollie whispered. "How could I? I'd gotten my wish, after all. But as the years passed, I compartmentalized Ophelia, but the nagging feeling that she had returned began when Brandy started talking to herself. Now, the same activity that I experienced as a teenager has returned."

"Including a mysterious disappearance." Joey pointed out. "Brandy's teacher, right?"

"Yeah." Hollie nodded. "Brandy came home one day crying because Mrs. Carter had told her that Ophelia wasn't real. I tried to console her, but she didn't calm down until the next morning. Brandy was giggling and laughing over her toast. When I commented on how happy she was, my little girl gave me the darkest look. She told me that Mrs. Carter wouldn't be her teacher anymore."

"Do the police have any leads?" I reached for the wine bottle and scoffed when I saw that it was empty. "Or are they saying anything at all?"

"Not really. The news had a story on just yesterday about Brandy's teacher. They think she went hiking alone and got lost. The state police have started searching the trails around here for her body."

I shuddered. I couldn't help it. I returned the empty bottle back to its spot on the coffee table.

"So let's draw out this Ophelia." Elliot stopped pacing long enough to rub his hands together. "She should still be pissed off at Eva, right?"

"Yeah." Hollie nodded. "I would assume so."

"Then that's our show. And this," He gestured around the mess we had made of the living room. "This was our interview."

"Elliot, we weren't filming." I pulled my legs off of Cyrus' lap and swung them over the edge of the couch. "Were we?

"We're always filming." He gestured to the three perimeter cameras he and Joey had set up that afternoon. "It's not my fault if you don't notice."

I bit my lip to keep my sarcastic response from being said out loud. I was a mess. We were all in our pajamas except for Cyrus, who wore a suit no matter what time of the day it was. And Elliot knew that I would be exposing my dark secret that night. Of course he would be filming.

Bastard.

"Tomorrow." I finally broke the heavy silence that had settled around us. "Tomorrow night we can have any dog-and-pony show you want, Elliot. But right now? I'm exhausted. I'm a little drunk. I'm not doing anything other than going to bed."

I didn't give him a chance to argue with me. I linked arms with Hollie and pulled her to her feet.

"You sure you don't mind if I crash on the bed with you? I can make a pallet if you want."

"Don't be silly." Hollie was pale, but she gave me a tight smile. "Come on. We'll go get settled in."

We said our good nights and went to her room. We got ready in silence. Teeth brushed, faces scrubbed. It wasn't until we were laying in her bed that my friend spoke up. Hollie rolled over to her side to face me.

"I'm sorry, Eva." She whispered. "I'm sorry for everything that happened. And I'm sorry for bringing it up now."

"I just," I closed my eyes with a sigh. "I thought what Grandma did put an end to Ophelia. I thought it was over."

"It will be. Now that you've got more knowledge about the spirit world than I could ever hope to have." Hollie leaned up on her elbow. "Not to mention Cyrus. I told you I watched the show. I know he'll straighten Ophelia out."

She went silent but didn't move to lay back down. So I cracked open one eye to look at her.

"What?"

"What's up between you and Cyrus?" Hollie smirked. "Don't lie to me, Evie. I can see how he looks at you."

"Nothing. Not a damn thing." I closed my eye again. "Cyrus is a friend. A protector. That's all."

"Right." Hollie's disbelief was evident as she finally laid down. "You know I don't believe that for a second, right?"

"Yeah? Well, it is what it is." I flipped over and adjusted my pillow. "Good night, Hollie."

She didn't respond so I relaxed. I wasn't kidding when I said I was exhausted between the flight from Kentucky to the horrible trip down memory lane. Just as I was about to doze off, I felt the sweet security that surrounded me whenever Cyrus was close by. My keeper brushed his hand over my hair and leaned in to touch his forehead against the top of my head.

"Have no worries, Daughter of Apollo." He whispered. "This new threat will be vanquished. Just like the last."

"Brandy, stop badgering Cyrus."

Hollie was in the middle of making lunch when I finally came downstairs. I wasn't used to getting out of bed before nine, but I was surprised to wake up to see it was after 1 p.m. I made my way to the kitchen to see Brandy hand Cyrus a black crayon.

"You're doing her eyes wrong." The little girl frowned at my keeper. "Use this one."

I leaned against the door frame to watch my keeper take the crayon from the child and press it against the paper. I had to admit, I was seeing him in a whole new light. The Cyrus I was used to seeing was a force to be reckoned with. But here? With Brandy?

He was patient. Gentle. It was endearing and sweet.

"Can I see what you are working on?" I moved over to the table to shake the sudden warmth in my chest. "It looks like you're giving Cyrus art lessons."

Brandy scowled at me before she returned to her paper. Three stick figures were drawn on the page. A small girl with brown hair, a tall male figure with the outlines of a tie around his neck, and a woman standing behind her. The woman's hair hung around her shoulders. Her mouth was a slash of red. Her eyes? Blacked out in a single thick line.

"Can Ophelia see?" I tilted my head at the disturbing image. "Does she know that you and Cyrus are playing?"

"I am not supposed to talk to you." Brandy glared at me. "You talk to funny pictures in the mirror. You're mean to Ophelia."

"Have I met Ophelia before, Brandy?" I kneeled beside her chair and knew that my keeper was watching us. "Did she come to me in a dream once?"

The child resumed her silent treatment so I sighed and stood. Cyrus gestured towards her with his head before he cut his eyes over to Hollie. I knew at once what he was trying to say. Talk to Hollie. Get the girl squared away before we tangled with our tormentor tonight.

"Hollie, where's Elliot and Joey?" I grabbed a handful of strawberries from the bowl beside her. "Surely to God they aren't still crashing on your floor."

"No." She chuckled. "They took a few cameras and decided to get some shots downtown. Joey said you wouldn't be awake for a while though. Something about needing all the beauty sleep you could get."

"Uh huh." I rolled my eyes. "Listen, if we are going to do the investigation tonight, I don't think it's a good idea if Brandy is here."

"I couldn't agree more." Hollie went back to slicing up the fruit. "I'll call my mom. She can stay with her until all this is settled. But between now and then? Let's have some fun. You promised to catch me up on everything once you got here, and we've done nothing but talk about our ghost."

"What kind of fun?" I popped a strawberry in my mouth. I tapped my fingers against my chin while I swallowed. "I tell you what. Let's go downtown, too. Maybe meet up with the guys. I thought I saw a used bookstore I'd love to check out."

"Done." Hollie beamed at me. "Now sit down. Eat something. And we'll get our day started."

By the time night had fallen, I had decided I was in love with Fayetteville. Since the town was nestled in the Ozarks, it had gorgeous scenery. The downtown was just as charming on foot as it had been when we drove through it. But the best part?

I was able to pretend to be normal. Even if it was just for a little while. Hollie and I caught up on each other's lives since our last summer together. We talked about everything from make-up to love lives to career choices. It was nice to have a female perspective on things for once.

The day had gone so well, I couldn't help but be disappointed when we gathered in Hollie's living room to get started on the investigation. Joey, Elliot, and Cyrus had moved the furniture out, which would have given us plenty of room if it weren't for the wires to the cameras Joey had placed everywhere. I had to catch myself more than once to keep from tripping over them as we gathered around a single candle that had been placed in the center of the circle we made. Hollie waited until Elliot nodded to her before she began.

"Ophelia, come to us. Join us in this circle tonight. We wish to speak to you. We wish to rectify all the wrongs done to you so long ago."

The candle flared once before it settled down on the wick. Hollie took a deep breath before she spoke again.

"You wish to haunt me through my daughter. You have harmed two people that we know of. Perhaps more. Come to us. Speak to us tonight. Tell us what we can do to make amends."

I heard a strange rattling behind me. I glanced over my shoulder and ducked seconds before something flew past my head. I whirled around to see Hollie holding her cheek and even in the dim light, I could tell that she was bleeding.

"Oh my god." I broke the circle and knelt down next to her. I heard glass crunch beneath my knee, but I ignored it when I pulled her hand away from her face. "Hollie, you've been cut."

"She's here, Eva." She stared at me with widened eyes. "She's here."

"Like hell she is." I stood up and faced the candle. "Ophelia. What a joke. I don't believe for a second that you are strong enough to harm anyone."

I caught sight of Cyrus' weapon in his hand. I made sure Elliot and Joey were on either side of me in case I was attacked.

"Come out, come out wherever you are!" I turned in a single circle with my arms outstretched. Come pick on someone your own size. Stop messing around with confused teenagers and little kids. Stop being so damned pathetic."

"Eva…hush."

Hollie was as white as a sheet when she stood. But I laughed instead.

"Come on, Hollie. If Ophelia could hurt me, she would have done it by now."

I felt an icy hand brush against the nape of my neck before my head slammed forward into the table the candle was sitting on. Whatever had a hold on me jerked my head back in an attempt to do it again when I heard laughter in my ear.

"You have seen so much, Sibyl, but yet, you know nothing."

I opened my eyes to see Cyrus, Joey, and Elliot circled around me. Cyrus' lips were pressed into a hard line before he reached out to grab my arm. My keeper pulled me against him as the spirit let go of my ponytail.

"You are a clever one, Charlotte." Cyrus kept his arm around my neck as he pointed his sword towards a shadowy figure I could barely make out in the candlelight. I would have stared at him if he wasn't holding me so tightly. "Using the same scare tactics as the wraith that haunted you when you were alive."

Wraith? I clutched Cyrus' arm as my mind began to put the pieces together. But I didn't get a chance to voice them. The spirit laughed as the candlelight dimmed.

"They lived." It hissed. "Lived! Why should they have survived when I suffered so? We called it forth together. We were all haunted. Yet, I was the only one…"

"Who was weak." Cyrus released me long enough to push me behind him. "You were already disturbed, were you not? Your physical mind tainted with madness. It appears that madness remained."

"No! I wasn't...I'm not...I am Ophelia..."

"The wraith called Ophelia was banished to the Underworld by Lillian McRayne."

Cyrus was starting to sound bored as he bounced his sword in his hand. "You witnessed this yourself. You also knew that the spell conducted that night granted protections to your former friends. Which made them untouchable by the likes of you."

"Brandy." Hollie whispered. "That's why she attached herself to Brandy."

"Yes." Cyrus stepped forward. "You will no longer haunt the child, wraith. Your time on the physical plane has ended."

The shadow screamed with frustration before she lunged towards me. But I was too far behind Cyrus for her to get very far. My keeper swung his sword upward and slashed it through the dark figure.

I watched, stunned as the shadow began to shift. I started to step around Cyrus when I realized that a familiar girl was curled at his feet. Charlotte Edgemon appeared as she had the last time I'd seen her. Mousy brown hair in a braid. Jeans. T-shirt. But the image didn't last long. The figure faded just as quickly as it had appeared.

I jerked up when I heard a sob fill the room. Hollie was still on her knees, but this time, she was bent over. I pushed past Cyrus, ignored Joey and Elliot, and wrapped my arms around the girl that had known me first.

"Hush, Hollie. It's over. I swear to all the gods who ever were, it's over."

"Ok. We're ready when you are, Joey."

I tightened my ponytail as I sat down beside Hollie on her couch. This was not my normal position when we were filming. I tended to be outside when we wrapped things up. But it wasn't just my story.

Not this time.

"This location wasn't haunted. But a person instead. Meet an old friend of mine, Hollie Stephens." I leaned forward when I started talking. "Her story isn't all that different from the others floating around the internet. In fact, it's not much different than any classic horror movie. Young girl, obsessed with the paranormal, invites something into her life that she can't control. Now, almost ten years later, the monster that haunted her as a teenager came back. This time, the focus wasn't on Hollie, but on her young daughter."

I took hold of Hollie's hand and squeezed it. "Fear can save you, but it can also destroy you. Charlotte turned out to be proof of that. Her fear of what we had experienced enhanced her depression. She became convinced that her only way out was suicide. But by giving into her fears? Our former friend turned into the very creature that was haunting her. A wraith. A twisted spirit."

Hollie wiped the corner of her eye with a Kleenex as I wrapped it up.

"So the moral of this story? Be curious, but don't be stupid. Don't take part of things you don't understand and by god, don't let your monsters take over. Don't let the fear take over. Because I can guarantee, it won't be pretty."

TWENTY-ONE

SEASON 1, EPISODE 10: AURORA, IOWA

"WAIT." Elliot held up his hand as he swallowed a mouthful of beer. He wiped his mouth against his sleeve before he spoke again. "Are you sick, Eva? Or am I getting drunk?"

"What?" I leaned back against the vinyl booth we had confiscated. "I can't agree with you every once in a while? I think it's a great location."

"I," Elliot took another drink. "I'm just not used to you agreeing with me. I was expecting you to whine more."

"I don't whine." I picked up my pen and threw it at him. "I just disagree with your choices."

"I'm with ol' Eli on this one." Joey Lawson gave me a look of suspicion. "That was way too easy, Evie. Maybe you really are sick."

My friend reached across the booth to put the back of his hand against my forehead. I batted him away with a frown.

"I am not that bad." I grumbled. "And for the record, Sibyls can't get sick. Right, Cyrus?"

"I didn't think so." My keeper smirked at me over his shot glass. "Yet, I am a firm believer in the saying that there is a first time for everything."

"You are all asses." I pointed at Elliot and Joey with my wine glass. "Look, all I'm saying is that a haunted library might be a piece of cake compared to the hells we have faced so far."

Joey winced and I knew why. He still found ways to tell me how sorry he was for attacking me at the Mansville Sanitarium. I grabbed his hand and squeezed it against the table before I continued.

"Think about it. Libraries are for scholars and nerds." I released Joey's hand. "And the story is about an old woman, right? She can't be that mean."

"You've never been around hateful old women, have you?" Elliot joked. "Actually, this one does seem pretty standard. The lady in white, she's called. Believed to be the wife of the founder who built the library in the 1940's. Dr. Rodney Johnston."

"See?" I downed my wine and grabbed the bottle from the middle of the table. "Easy."

We fell into a comfortable silence which was rare these days. Normally, Elliot and I were at each other's throats with poor Joey stuck in the middle. It was nice to call a truce.

Even if it was just for the night.

"Why are apparitions always white?" I wondered aloud as I fingered the picture sitting on top of my folder. It was a still shot from the library's security footage. I welcomed the warm buzz of the alcohol as I nursed my third glass. "I mean, I get why they appear the way they do. Looking like they did in life and all. It's what they knew. But why white?"

"Energy." Cyrus twisted his shot glass between his fingers. "It takes a lot of energy to appear outside of a mirror, Little One. And since white is – technically – the absence of color, it is much easier for a spirit to appear as a white form."

"Or as light." Elliot nodded in agreement. "Parapsychologists believe that spirits pull from the energies of the world around them, right? They exist off of frequencies."

"Ok." I muttered. "I'll just take your word for it."

"Uh huh." Joey grinned. "I think it's time to cut you off, Evie. You're getting all flushed and quiet. The wine must be getting to you."

"Am I?" I shrugged. "Maybe. Or maybe I'm just getting tired. All this running around chasing tragedies can take its toll on a person."

"Two." Elliot finished his beer and pushed the bottle away from him. "You have two more locations, Sibyl. Then you can rest."

I didn't miss the glare my keeper threw at Elliot. Cyrus was staunchly against *Grave Messages*. The fact that Elliot had been trying to work us to death didn't help matters at all.

"Whatever, Elliot." I finished my drink then reached for my purse. "When do we leave for Iowa?"

"Tomorrow morning." Elliot waved away my attempts to leave a tip behind. "Consider this one a business meeting, Evie. Theia can cover it."

"Why?" I narrowed my eyes at him as the world began to get all blurry. I slid out of the booth and he stood with me. "Free drinks just because we talked about work? That doesn't seem right."

"Because, for once, you agreed with me." Elliot gave me a charming smile before he leaned in to whisper in my ear. "Things can go so well for you if you just do as I say, Evie."

"Don't you 'Evie' me."

I studied his face as he pulled back. Elliot winked at me as our waitress approached the booth. I waited until the woman took his credit card and disappeared before I continued.

"I was right." I tugged the strap of my purse up as it slid off my shoulder. "You are an ass."

I turned on my heel as the happy buzz I had was replaced by a dull anger. I wanted to be alone. I wanted to get back to my hotel room and collapse before my anger turned into tears. I didn't want Elliot to see me cry over him.

I'd be damned if he did.

"Eva, wait."

Elliot called after me, but he was too late. I threw a wave to Joey over my shoulder as Cyrus led us out of the bar we'd found close to the hotel. I didn't say a word while we walked back. I tried to let the November night air calm me down. I even held onto Cyrus' arm to keep myself steady. But on the inside?

I was shaking with my anger.

By the time we reached my room, I was livid. I kicked off my flats then threw my purse into the closet.

"Little One..."

"Why?" I whirled around to face Cyrus. "Why does he have to ruin everything? We were having a great night. Even if he insisted on talking about work. So why did he have to pull a damn power play right at the end?"

Cyrus stuffed his hands in his pockets then watched me. I knew he was trying to decide whether to respond or let me finish my rant. In the end, I wiped away the tears burning at the corners of my eyes before they could fall. I dropped back on the bed and stared up to the ceiling.

"Maybe he's right." I whispered. "Maybe my life would be easier if I just did what he said."

"Perhaps." Cyrus lowered himself down until he was stretched out beside me. "Of course, there is a danger in following anyone or anything without question."

"Yeah? Like what?" I turned my head until I was studying my keeper. "You think he will lead me off a cliff or something?"

"Much worse than that." Cyrus propped himself up on an elbow. "You could lose yourself, dear girl."

"I lost myself the moment Kathy Carter gave me that damn mirror." I threw my arm over my eyes. "Otherwise, I'd still be in Georgia."

"And not the Sibyl." Cyrus went quiet, but it wasn't long before he spoke again. "Your fate is your own, Eva. There is no point in regretting the past. You can either embrace it or abandon the choices you have made. Either way, you should be wary of losing yourself in the future. I am afraid that this is exactly what Elliot wishes for you."

"That I lose myself."

"Yes. It will allow him to control you." Cyrus reached over to pull my arm free. "I can only tell you this, Little One. Follow no one but your god. Fulfill the oath you made to Apollo. Everyone else can be damned."

"Not Joey. I like him."

I heard Cyrus chuckle, but I didn't say anything else. Instead, I curled up against his side to consider what my keeper had said. Maybe Joey was right. Maybe I had too much to drink. But I couldn't stop myself as my eyes grew heavy. I snuggled up against Cyrus and breathed in his sweet scent of old liquor.

"You smell good." I muttered. "I like you, too. I think I'm going to keep you."

Cyrus didn't respond as he brushed the hair out of my face with his fingertips. The more he caressed my face, the more exhausted I became. I was dozing off when I heard him break the silence around us.

"Come on. Let's get you ready for bed before you pass out on me."

My keeper was too late. I was asleep within seconds.

"Are you sure this is the right place?"

I pushed my sunglasses to the top of my head and immediately regretted my decision. I jerked them back into place while Joey started laughing.

"Hush." I grumbled. "And this? This doesn't look like the pictures you showed us last night, Elliot."

That much was true. Instead of the two-story building that housed the Johnston Library in Aurora, Iowa, a burned-out brick husk sat in its place. I felt Cyrus come up beside me. My keeper twisted his face as he breathed in the chilly afternoon air.

"The fire was recent." Cyrus glanced down at me. "Within the past week. I can still smell the embers smoldering."

I wrinkled my nose as I realized I could smell it, too. Elliot had been in the process of making a call, but as he dropped his phone back in his pocket, a man popped up from the ruins.

"*Grave Messages*?"

When Elliot nodded, the newcomer jogged over to us. "My name is Sean. Sean Paulson."

"Mr. Paulson." Elliot shook his hand. "It looks as if we are too late to investigate your library."

"Well, it is a tragedy." The man agreed. "But I wouldn't say you are too late. If you can stand the smell, the building is still structurally sound."

"You can't be serious." I crossed my arms over my chest. "This place – or what's left of it – looks like it could fall in at any second. We can't go in there."

"I assure you, it's quite safe." Paulson gave me a sad smile. "Come inside and see for yourself. I think you will find the fire could add to your investigation."

"It would be a creepy background." Joey piped up. "What with the moonlight filtering in through the roof and all."

I turned towards my friend and mouthed my response when Elliot began to follow our client up the sidewalk.

"Not. Helping."

"You're just irritated because you're hungover." Joey teased as he looped his arm through mine. "And off of three glasses of wine? That's just sad, Evie."

"Four." I grumbled. "Four glasses."

"Pitiful." Joey clicked his tongue against the back of his teeth in disapproval. "We gotta work on your tolerance level."

I decided to keep my mouth shut as we ducked under the yellow caution tape across the door. When we walked over the threshold, I could see just how bad the damage was.

The walls were black from burn marks and soot. Waterlogged books covered broken shelves and the floor. I couldn't help but cover my mouth as the smell hit me. It was horrible. The entire place was a mess.

But Sean was right. There didn't seem to be any danger. The walls and ceiling was burnt, but still standing.

"What happened here?" Elliot stopped when we reached the main room. "Accidental fire?"

"The grey lady." Our client answered in a voice that creeped me out. It was too dreamy. Too serene given the environment around us. "The Johnston library has burned down on November 15th every twenty years. We have come to expect it."

"Wait, what?" I dropped Joey's arm and pulled off my

sunglasses. It was darker in here. More tolerable. "Your library catches fire every twenty years?"

"Yes, Miss. McRayne." Paulson turned to me with a smile just as creepy as his voice. "We even budget for it."

"The ghost who haunts your library sets it on fire every twenty years?" I raised an eyebrow. "Seriously?"

"Seriously." He nodded. "I was hoping you could be here to see it burn. But that is for naught. Mr. Lancaster told me you were caught up with your filming schedule."

"Right." I breathed between my teeth. "So much for the gentile old lady ghost you were boasting about, Elliot."

"Oh, Millie won't hurt you." Paulson tilted his head to the side. "She might knock things off the shelves, but aside from the fires, she isn't dangerous."

"So her name is Millie?" I started to drop down in one of the remaining chairs but decided against it. "I'm not sure how much I trust an arsonist, Mr. Paulson."

"Please. Call me Sean."

"Yeah, ok." I shrugged. "Tell us about Millie, Sean."

"Wait." Elliot piped up. "You're here. We're here. Let's go ahead and start filming. The interviews would look great in here."

I closed my eyes and pinched the bridge of my nose between my fingers. I didn't want to admit it, but I really *was* hungover. My head was killing me. My thoughts were all jumbled up. I felt slow. Sluggish. I wasn't ready to do anything other than crawl into the nearest bed to sleep this off.

"Elliot, can't we come back tomorrow?" I dropped my hand. "Really. I don't know if I'm up to playing twenty questions with Sean right now."

"The sooner we get this done, the sooner we can hit our last location before you're off for a month." My co-host turned on his heel to head back outside. "I thought that's what you wanted. To get away from me."

"I never said that!" I snapped. When he kept going, I moved after him. He'd already ducked beneath the caution tape by the time I managed to grab his arm. "Elliot, stop it. You're being ridiculous."

"Am I?" He turned to glower down at me. "Eva, the entire time we've been on the road, you've griped and complained about the choices I've made. You've whined about the locations or tried to do your own thing. Either we are a team or we are not. The sooner you realize that, then maybe we can start having fun doing the show."

"The sooner I start following your orders you mean." I dropped my hand. "Elliot, what happened to you? To us? This time last year, I never would have imagined that we could fight like this."

"Yeah? Well, this time last year, you were still the same girl I fell in love with." He grabbed my arms to stare down at me. "I miss that girl more than anything I've ever known."

"Fell in love-." I stared at him in confusion. "Wait. You were in love with me?"

"I don't know." He released me to head towards the SUV to get our equipment. "I thought I was. But not now. Now, you're just the bitch I have to work with."

I watched him for a few minutes before Cyrus appeared behind me. He clasped his hand on my shoulder to squeeze it. But before he could say anything, I shook him off.

"Let's get back inside. I need to find a set of decent chairs to set up while the guys figure out how we're going to film this thing without power."

I didn't say another word. I didn't know what to say. I didn't know what to think as the dull aching in my heart seemed to sync up with the throbbing in my head. But Elliot was right about one thing. The sooner I got this over with, I would be one step closer to the peace I so desperately needed.

To say that our interview with Sean Paulson was boring would have been a massive understatement. The man's story was so standard, I couldn't help but wonder if he got it out of one of the books at Johnston.

Dr. Rodney and his wife, Millie Johnston built the library after World War II. She worked here every day until her death in 1954. It wasn't long after that the patrons of the library claimed to see her. Books would be moved. Papers would disappear only to reappear in different rooms. The local legend was that she was still here. Still working some fifty-nine years after her death. It wasn't until 1974 that Johnston burned down for the first time. The cause? Bad wiring. It burned for a second time in 1994 and again last week. Both times, the electrical system of the building was to blame.

What I couldn't wrap my mind around was why. If Millie loved the place so much, why would she cause it to burn? And if it was such a staple here in Aurora, why didn't they update the damn electrical system?

These were the questions on my mind as we got started. Elliot had been kind enough to let me sleep the entire afternoon. Now, we were standing in the midst of the main library room. I waited for Joey to give me the signal before I started.

"First off, I want to say do not try this at home, folks." I held my hands out in front of me to emphasize my point. "Trust and do believe, I wouldn't be here if there weren't some pretty heavy guarantees that the Johnston Library was safe after a fire ravaged it on the 15th."

I dropped my hands and glanced around the dark room. Joey had been right. It was the perfect backdrop. The shadows cast around me were pushed back by the moonlight filtering in through the broken windows. The place was a beautiful destruction at its finest.

"Second, I want to say that despite the fire, the ghost believed to haunt the library isn't known for her violence. There was no violent death. No rivalries. No magic. She simply had a love for books that her husband encouraged. That love is believed to be the reason why she continues to stay here. Not at her home. Not close to her family. But with her beloved books."

Elliot stood up from his perch on the table behind me. He didn't look at me as he began to speak.

"The Johnston library has had numerous reports of paranormal activity. Security footage has repeatedly caught Millie on film. It has also caught poltergeist activity. Books are thrown from the tables if left behind. Or from the shelves. There is even a story told around town of a group of school girls playing 'Bloody Mary' in the mirror in the bathroom. No one knows what they saw, but each girl ran out screaming." Elliot gave the camera a cold smile that he turned onto me. "Luckily for us, we have our own Sibyl who is willing to play that game anytime we need her to. We hope to meet Millie tonight."

I returned Elliot's cold smile with the sweetest one I could muster before Joey called out for us to stop. I glanced up to see my cameraman drop his large camera onto the table next to him.

"We'll interject the security footage here. Have Elliot do a voiceover to describe what we are seeing." Joey reached in his pocket to pull out a pack of gum. "So now what?"

"We wait." Elliot shrugged. "I'll try to catch some voices on the recorder, but what I really want is to get her on film."

"You mean, you're not going to throw me in front of a mirror?" I widened my eyes in mock shock. "Elliot, I'm touched."

"Don't push it." He grumbled before he pulled out a recorder from his pocket. My co-host rubbed the front of it before he glanced over to me. "And for the record, I thought you needed a break from the violence. You're in danger too much, Eva. So we'll take it easy tonight."

I blinked back my surprise. This was the first time in months that I'd gotten a glimpse of the Elliot I used to know. I swallowed down the knot in my throat before I squeezed his hand.

"Thanks, Elliot." I tilted my head towards him. "I appreciate it."

He didn't say anything so I sighed and pulled out my own recorder. "I'm heading over to the YA section. Maybe she likes the lighter genres."

"Want me to come with you?" Joey popped his gum. "Or do you want to take a handheld?"

"Handheld." I couldn't explain it, but after Elliot admitted he was concerned about me, I wanted to be alone. I was still rattled by his confession earlier that day where he said he had been in love with me. "You can see me from here, right?"

"Yeah. We can see everything." Elliot gestured over to the corner. "Just don't go too far into the shadows."

"Right."

I pressed the buttons Joey had shown me until the small screen in front of me flipped to night vision. I held the recorder in front of me as I walked through the debris.

"As you can see, this place is a really, really bad mess." I sighed into the microphone. "But the really creepy thing that no one has an explanation for is why it catches fire. What is so important about November 15th ? Not even our client could explain that one."

I could hear Elliot and Joey as they worked from the center of the room, but the further I moved away from them, the more the library seemed to change. The burned walls lightened to a pretty shade of white that gleamed in the moonlight. I could see books lined the shelves around me. I frowned at the screen when I heard someone whisper next to me.

"Watch, Daughter of Apollo."

"What?" I jerked my head up to see that the night had shifted to day. And I wasn't alone. A young man was sitting at a table next to the wall. He ripped off his thick glasses to rub his face in his hands.

"Guys?" I called out. "Cyrus? You might want to get over here."

Nothing. I swallowed as I turned around. The library itself was pure perfection. It reminded me of the one I used to spend hours in at UGA. Yet, the people around me didn't seem to notice me. Nor did they seem to understand that the fashions from 1954 were best left to costume parties.

"Ok." I breathed out. "You want to show me something? Show me."

No voices responded. No strange whispers as the scene played out around me. I felt as if I'd been dropped in the middle of an episode of *I Love Lucy*. Except the world was in color. I switched off the night vision as I kept the camera trained on the table that was in front of me. When the man stood up, I let my mouth drop open.

Sean Paulson was standing in front of me. He loosened the tie around his throat before he turned to pick up the book he had been reading. I watched as he took two steps to his left.

They were the last ones he would take. I screamed as the wall next to him exploded inward. I fell to my knees as the bricks rained down. I ignored the sharp pain that filled my arm as one of them smashed against my elbow. Somehow, I kept the camera steady. I could hear the patrons around me screaming as the smoke began to clear. Then and only then could I see what happened.

A car was sitting where the table had been only seconds before. I forced myself to stand. I forced myself to approach the wreckage just as two men dropped down by the body pinned beneath the undercarriage of the vehicle.

"Oh, my god." I whispered. "How…what?"

"I died."

I whirled around to see our client step up beside me. His hands stuffed into his pockets as he studied the horrors before us. I let my mouth drop open as I stared at him.

"I…" I tried to find my voice, but damn, it was hard. "I don't understand."

"This town adores their Millie." He gritted his teeth. "They remember an old woman when she left Aurora behind for heaven. Yet, I remain. I remain."

I made sure I kept the camera trained on him as he spoke. I tried to keep it steady, but that was harder than finding my voice had been.

"You're the one who sets the fires." I whispered. "You are trying to get people to remember you. Your tragedy."

"I was no one." The spirit glared at me. "I had no standing in this town. No family. I'd come to Aurora for a new start. But it all ended when a damned drunk couldn't find the brakes."

He took another step towards me, so I took a step back. My mind was flying at a million miles an hour as I processed his story. One thing was for certain. I had to find my way out of this. I had to get back to Cyrus. To Elliot and Joey.

"Why?" I glanced up to see him standing directly in front of me. "Why did you bring me here?"

"To show you." He leaned forward to clutch his hands into fists. "You have to understand. You can show the world the truth. There is no Millie. And nothing I have done has convinced these stupid people otherwise."

"What have you done? Aside from set the fires?"

"What have I..." Sean laughed. "The apparition? Me. The poltergeist? Me."

The spirit waved his hand and the row of books next to me flew off the shelves. I cried out as they struck me, but I stayed standing.

"Ok!" I twisted to avoid another barrage of books. "You've made your point!"

"I died! No one remembers. No one wants to remember." He wrapped his arms around his waist and doubled over. "Why? Why was I not remembered? Why was she so damned important?"

I didn't respond with words. Instead, I took his moment of self-pity to dart around him. I took off across the library. Past the people standing around to watch the police as they investigated the accident. I heard Paulson scream seconds before he grabbed me from behind.

"Make them remember." He grabbed my head on either side. "Make them know the truth, Sibyl."

For the second time, I found myself screaming. I swung the camera up in an attempt to get him off of me. I couldn't explain my fear. Maybe it was because I was alone. Maybe it was because this situation was so bizarre. Either way, I struggled against the man determined to hold me down.

"Jesus Christ, Eva. Calm down!"

I blinked to see Elliot had replaced Sean Paulson. The library I had been in was gone, replaced by the mess I'd left behind.

"Elliot? What? Where am I?" I stared at him confused until I realized I was back. I was where I belonged. I sat up to throw my arms around his neck in my relief. "Oh, my god."

"Little One." Cyrus had knelt down beside us. I released Elliot long enough to take in my keeper as he spoke. "Little One, what happened?"

"I don't know."

I pulled away from Elliot to bury my face in my hands. I counted to ten. Then again until my heart stopped pounding. The guys were good to me. They didn't try to say anything. It wasn't until Joey gasped that I realized the camera that Elliot had wrestled out of my hand was no longer on the floor beside me.

"Oh, my god." Joey looked at us with wide eyes. "Elliot, Cyrus. You have got to see this."

Even from my position, I could hear the sounds of the library from its heyday. I could hear the crash as the car slammed into the building. I knew that they were seeing what I had experienced firsthand.

"That's why it burns."

"What did you say, Eva?" Elliot's excitement was so apparent, he seemed to be bouncing on his knees by Joey's side. "How did you get this? How…."

"Make them remember." I dropped my hands to see that Cyrus hadn't joined the others. My keeper was too busy examining my face, his lips pressed together in a harsh line. "He took me back. Back to the day he died."

"He?"

I glanced up at Joey but didn't respond. I could see the shock on his face. Sean Paulson must have come into view.

"Yeah." I swallowed. "That's why this place burns. Sean Paulson died on November 15, 1954. He was jealous that his attempts to be noticed were attributed to the White Lady."

I turned my attention back to Cyrus. "What happened to me? How…"

I let my voice trail off as a glint of light caught my attention just over Cyrus' shoulder. Behind him, hidden by shadow and soot, was a large gilded mirror. Its glass cracked down the center.

"The mirror." I whispered. "He pulled me through."

My keeper didn't say another word. He tugged at my arm until he wrapped his arms around me. I let him hold me as I stared at the broken glass.

I'd been pulled through. I'd been taken back. But the most shocking part wasn't the time travel. It wasn't what I had seen. Or what I now knew to be true.

I had survived. Somehow, without Cyrus or Joey or Elliot.

I'd survived.

TWENTY-TWO

SEASON 1, EPISODE 12: SAN DIEGO, CALIFORNIA

"TELL me again why Elliot wanted to call a meeting so early."

Joey grumbled into his Starbucks cup before he took a gulp out of it. He looked tired. Ragged. And if I was honest, I'd say I was right there with him. Elliot had called each of our rooms the night before and demanded that we meet him in the hotel's coffee shop at six a.m. I shrugged, rubbed my hand over my own heavy eyelids, and took a sip of my latte.

"I have no clue, Joey. Elliot became a mystery to me back in August. There's no telling what he is up to this time."

"Or where he wants us to go." Joey fell back against his chair with a sigh. "Not that I don't love spending time with you, Evie. But I gotta admit. I'm looking forward to our break."

"Me too." I cupped my chin against my hand. The break Joey was talking about was Theia's way of letting us take a rest from filming. From December 1 st to January 5 th , I could do anything I wanted. No planes. No airports. No deranged spirits determined to drive me insane. "What are you going to do? Go see your family for the holidays?"

"Nope." Joey grinned at me. "I'm not doing a damned thing. If I get up from my couch, it'll be a miracle."

"Same." I tapped the side of my cup against Joey's own. "Here's to being slouches for an entire month."

"Speaking of slouches, where is our fearless leader?" Joey peered over me to watch the door. "If he's not here in five minutes, I'm going back to bed."

"Probably gathering up the information he wants to talk to us about." I began to play with my straw. "You know how he is, Joey. Elliot always waits until the very last minute."

We fell into a comfortable silence and I waited for Joey to make good on his word. The truth was, I wouldn't be far behind him. We'd been on the road since August. We'd been filming and making appearances all across the country. Not to mention the emotional toil of being exposed to so many horrible stories.

I was beyond exhausted.

I picked up my cup and started to stand when I heard the door open. I glanced at the clock on the wall then rolled my eyes as Elliot strolled in thirty minutes late. He gestured for me to sit back down before he plopped down beside me.

"Sorry. Connor called. He wanted to know if we planned on taking the break or if we were going to push through the holidays."

"You told him 'yes' to the break, right?" Joey cut his eyes over to Elliot. "Please tell me you said yes."

"I did." Elliot smirked. "But that's not why I wanted to see you two. There's been a change in plans. We aren't going to Denver."

"So where are we going?" I picked up my empty cup and wondered how much caffeine it would take to keep me on my feet. "Back to Los Angeles?"

"Pretty close." Elliot slid two folders in front of us both. "San Diego. The Black Swan Suites."

"Another hotel?" I narrowed my eyes at him. "Elliot, if you don't remember, we already covered a bed and breakfast. If we do another one so soon, we might look desperate."

"Ah, but this one doesn't have a demented spirit attached to it." He grinned at me. "It's haunted by something else altogether."

"Like what?" I waved my hand before I finished my question.

"Wait. Hold that thought. I have a feeling I'm going to need another latte to get through this."

Joey passed me his own cup so I stood up and headed over to counter. Two coffee refills and a bottled water later, I returned to the table. I plopped down in my seat and waited. I didn't have to wait for long. Elliot was practically bouncing in his chair with excitement.

"A nix."

"A what?" I scrunched up my nose. "I don't think I understood you."

"A nix." Elliot tossed a straw wrapper at me. "It's a German water spirit."

"Ok." I breathed out the word. "And what's so special about this spirit?"

"They are shapeshifters born from water." Elliot took a swig of his drink. "Shouldn't Cyrus be here to tell you all this?"

"He had to go to Olympus." I shrugged. "Something about meeting with Apollo and a Council of some sort."

"Whatever." Elliot rolled his eyes. "Anyway, the Black Swan has gotten a bit of a reputation thanks to the nix that frequents it. When I talked to the general manager yesterday, he said that women have started making complaints about a male visitor who seduces them."

"Seduces them?" Now it was Joey's turn to make a face. "I don't get it."

"The nix shifts into someone the victims have a relationship with. Or someone they fantasize about." Elliot leaned forward to gesture with his hands. "He sleeps with them. By the time the women wake up? He's gone."

"I have two questions." I tapped my knuckles against the table to get Elliot's attention. "One, if they think they are sleeping with someone they are familiar with, where does the story of the nix come into play? And two, how do they know it is a nix to begin with? I thought spirits who had sex with humans was called a succubus."

"That's a female." Elliot sat up straight. "And a demon. Nix are harmless for the most part. The legends say they are lonesome. They only want companionship. So they seek out humans to mingle with. As for your second question, there's no telling how many women have interacted with this spirit and never knew it. The ones who figured it out tried to contact their lovers after the fact, only to discover the men were nowhere close to San Diego the night of the encounter."

"And you want to try to catch this thing on film." Joey pushed his empty cup aside. "Elliot, how? If it's a member of the lonely hearts club, I don't think our standard tactics are going to work."

Elliot glanced over at me and I knew at once what he was thinking.

"No." I glared back at him. "You are not going to use me as bait for this thing."

"Just to draw it out." Elliot grinned at me. "You've got nothing to worry about. Me and Joey will be in the next room. You see the nix, you scream. We come to the rescue."

"Rapist." I picked up my cup. "The word you are looking for here is 'rapist'. One that you have no problems putting me in danger of. I'm not doing it."

"I'm with Evie on this." Joey looked between the two of us. "I don't think it's a good idea, Elliot. I'll do it. I'm sure with the make-up department's help, I'd make a great looking woman."

"Eva, nothing is going to happen to you." Elliot ignored Joey as he focused on me. "Seriously, we'll be right there. We'll have the cameras set up to watch your every move. You'll be fine."

"Why?" I snapped at him. "Why can't we just find another location? What is so special about this place?"

Elliot got quiet for a moment. I watched him clench his hands into fists before he placed his hands flat on the table.

"It's different, Evie. We're not just chasing after ghosts anymore." He tilted his head towards me. "We're chasing after legends."

I stared at him in complete silence for a good two minutes before I stood up.

"Fine. But I'm texting Cyrus."

"Didn't realize you needed your guard dog's permission, but ok." Elliot rolled his eyes. "Tell him whatever you want. I don't care. You know as well as I do that this would be a great way to end the first half of the season. People love romance. They eat up anything that is deemed scandalous."

"What does Connor have to say?" Joey pushed his chair back. "Because as much as you like to play the boss man on the field, Elliot, he's the one in charge. I'm sure he'd have a lot to say if you put Eva into this situation."

Elliot turned his head slowly towards our cameraman. "What are you trying to do, Joey? Undercut me? Play the hero? What?"

"No, man." Joey stood with a stretch. "Just doing what I think is right. And sending Eva into that lion's den alone – especially without Cyrus to help her – ain't right."

My friend grabbed my empty cup from in front of me and tossed it in the trash behind him.

"Come on, Evie. Let's get out of here. Before Lord Lancaster comes up with more hellfire to throw you into."

I threw one last glare at Elliot before I moved to follow Joey out of the coffee shop.

We were almost to the door when Elliot called out.

"The plane leaves at eleven. I expect you both to be on it. And you'll do what I tell you or there will be hell to pay."

"What has gotten into him?" Joey was pacing the carpet in front of me. He'd thrown his luggage together in record time then barged into my room to talk about Elliot's plan. "I get that *Grave* is important to him. But if the stories are true…"

"It doesn't matter." I tossed my toiletry bag into my suitcase. "Nothing is going to happen to me."

"Yeah. Cause nothing dangerous has happened to you at all since we started filming." Joey rolled his eyes. "Come on, Evie. Be serious."

I snapped my suitcase closed and dropped down on the bed beside it. I grabbed Joey's arm when he made another pass in front of me to force him to stop.

"Look, I don't like it any more than you do. But I've been thinking."

"About?"

"Elliot's been pissed off at me for months, right? It would be easy to think that he's doing this now as some sort of punishment. But I don't think he is. I think he wants me to prove my loyalty to him. You, too."

"Loyalty?" My friend gave me an incredulous look. "Haven't we proven that time and time again?"

"No. Not really." I released him. "Elliot is convinced that he's losing his show to me. He's convinced himself that Cyrus has taken his place in my life. He feels threatened. Jealous. If I do this – if I put my trust in him – then all will be forgiven."

Joey sat down beside me to rub his hands over his face. Finally, he sighed.

"Is the show really worth it?"

"Yes." I nodded. "To me it is. I love what we do, Joey. I'm not ready to be fired for insubordination yet."

"Do you really think he'd fire you over this?"

"No. But he'd make my life absolute hell if I don't." I interlocked our fingers together and squeezed Joey's hand. "Thank you."

"For what?"

"For being my friend. For sticking up for me back there. You're the best, Joey."

"Yeah? Well, somebody's gotta step in for the big man." He wrapped his arm around my shoulders and pulled me into a hug. "And I know just what he'd say."

"Before or after he smashed Elliot's face in again?"

"After." Joey released me and twisted around until we were practically nose to nose. He hardened his expression then pointed at me. "You don't have to do this, Little One. Just say the word and we'll find a way to get you out of this damned show."

I laughed. I couldn't help it. Joey was no Cyrus, but his impression was pretty damn close. When I composed myself, I grinned.

"That was awesome. Just...please. Don't do that in front of him."

Joey started to respond, but a knock at the door interrupted him. The somber mood that had settled in after Elliot's big announcement returned. I sighed and stood.

"Let's go and get this over with, darlin'. I'm ready to start my vacation."

Suzanna Mathers dabbed her eyes and took a deep breath. She was our fifth interview of the day. One of the countless victims of the nix. If there actually was such a thing.

I tried not to feel sorry for her. She had stayed overnight at the Black Swan during a business trip. The result of that decision?

She was sitting in front of me. Recounting a story that I was having a hard time believing.

"I'm sorry." Suzanna began to play with the tissue in her hands. "I know it sounds crazy."

"It's fine. Take your time." Elliot passed her a tissue box. "We're in no hurry."

"Thank you." She cleared her throat and squared her shoulders. "As I was saying, I came to the Black Swan for a business trip. I live in Phoenix, but my company's headquarters are here. I tried to get out of it. You see, I was going to be here on my wedding anniversary."

"You're married?" I jotted that down on the notepad in my lap. "How long?"

"Four years now. I was here for our second anniversary." She tossed her long dark hair over her shoulder. "That night, I'd been unable to get through to my husband. I tried to call him. I just wanted to speak with him. Then, I received a bottle of wine from room service. I thought it was from Tom, so I drank a toast to him."

"And you were completely alone?" I jotted down another note. "Did you go out on the town at all? Speak with anyone?"

"No." Suzanna whispered. "I arrived here around four that afternoon. I had dinner in the dining hall alone then went to my room to call Tom. It wasn't until I had gone to bed that *it* appeared."

"It." Elliot tapped his pen against his knee. "Can you describe what happened to you?"

"I won't go into details." She shook her head. "It was dark. I felt a man join me in the bed. But even in the dim light, he looked just like my husband. I was groggy, but I was thrilled. I convinced myself that he came to San Diego to surprise me. Especially after I received the wine and I couldn't reach him."

"A logical conclusion." I nodded. "When did you find out that it wasn't your husband that joined you that night?"

"The next morning." Suzanna's face went white. "I woke up alone, but there was sand all over the floor. As if I'd spent the day on the beach and didn't bother to wash my feet when I came back. I picked up my phone in case Tom had left me a message to find out that he had left me a voicemail. From Phoenix. He had worked late and missed my calls. I filed a police report that morning."

Elliot asked her more questions about her experience, but I wasn't listening. I was too busy trying to put the pieces together. After all, we had talked to five women so far. Each one had very similar stories. They were all between the ages of twenty-five and thirty. They had all eaten in the dining room alone the night of their assault. And each of them had received a complimentary bottle of wine from the hotel.

"How do you know it was a nix?" I interrupted Elliot. "Please, don't think I'm questioning your story. I'm not. I'm just curious where you heard about the creature."

"From Mr. Sams." Suzanna's eyes widened. "After I filed my report, I came back to tell the management of the hotel what happened. He pulled me aside and told me I wasn't the first woman to come forward. He explained to me that it was believed the Black Swan was cursed with this horrible being."

"And you believed him?" I pressed my lips together. "Just like that?"

"Eva."

Elliot hissed my name, but I ignored him. I knew I shouldn't have questioned her like that. I wasn't the police. But I wasn't convinced that the rapist at the Black Swan was some lonely water spirit.

"Ms. Mathers, thank you for your time." I tucked my pad under my arm when I stood. She joined me so I shook her hand. "We may contact you in a few weeks to get your reaction of our findings."

"Thank you." She dabbed at her eyes again before she unhooked the microphone Joey had given her. The woman handed it to me then clutched at my fingers. "For not calling me crazy."

I waited until she had left us alone before I turned on my heel to walk out of the conference room the hotel had provided for us to hold the interviews in.

"Eva, where are you going?"

I ignored Elliot when he jogged up to my side. I ignored the fact that Joey was following behind us, still filming. I went up to the front desk to see the man who'd greeted us. The general manager Elliot had made contact with excused himself from the guest he was talking to.

"Mr. Carson Sams?" I tilted my head at him. "I know we discussed the possibility of you taking part in the interviews today. Do you mind if we steal you away for a few minutes? I have a few questions for you."

"Certainly." His teeth gleamed white against his tan when he smiled. "I'll be there in just a moment."

"No. Wc can do it here."

"Ms. McRayne," Sams' smile faltered as he glanced over to the group of tourists checking into his hotel. "Perhaps this would be best done in private."

"Why? The episode is going to air in a few weeks. The truth about the Black Swan will be out. What harm is there in answering a few questions here?"

The man stiffened for a moment before he relaxed. The smile was back less than two seconds later.

"Very well. What can I do for you, Ms. McRayne?"

Shut this place down? Warn every woman who checks into this hotel when she crosses the threshold? Those were my thoughts, but I managed to keep my mouth shut. Instead, I passed him the tiny microphone I'd retrieved from Suzanna. When he clipped it on, I stood off to the side so that Joey could get both of us in his shot.

"Mr. Sams is the general manager here at the Black Swan hotel. Sir, can you tell us when you received the first report of an assault here?"

"Within my first month. September 2010." He glanced over at the camera. "But the legend of the nix has been around since the Black Swan was built."

"Back in 1946, right?"

"Right." The manager's expression was one of concern. "We are quite troubled by these reports. We've called in priests in an attempt to expel the spirit. The Black Swan's reputation has been severely damaged."

"Why haven't you been sued yet?" I gave him my sweetest smile. "I'm just curious. After all, you have no warning signs up. There is nothing on your website. Yet, you continue to allow women to be assaulted."

Sams' froze. His eyes darkened as he glared at me.

"There is a clause in every contract. When you rent a room and you sign on the dotted line, you release the Black Swan of any liability of what happens to you on these grounds."

"Do your clients know this? Like, is it explained to them by your staff? Or is it buried so deep in the legalese the man who wrote that contract would have a hard time finding it?"

"What are you accusing us of, Ms. McRayne?"

"Deception. It seems to me that the Black Swan is just as responsible for these attacks as the nix you speak of."

He started to remove his microphone, but I placed my hand over his before he could.

"Tell us the story of the nix, Mr. Sams. Why is it at the Black Swan?"

"Why should I continue to talk to you?" His dark eyes were still smoldering. "Since you are so insistent that I am lying?"

"I don't think you're lying to us. But I do think you should be more open to the customers who are put in unnecessary danger."

Carson Sams studied me for a moment before he sighed. "Fine. But you must promise to edit out the part about our agreements."

"Yeah, no." I extended my hand to get my microphone back. "If those are your conditions, then I'll just dig through the history of your establishment."

He didn't move. He didn't remove his microphone. In the end, Sams relented. "The Black Swan began as a brothel. The hotel was a front for its high end clients."

I folded my arms over my chest as he began to talk.

"From what I have been told, the girls were expensive, but they weren't treated with the greatest respect. At least three were murdered. Two more committed suicide to escape their professions. They were called 'throwaway wives'. Men would travel to the Black Swan from all over the world to take part in the services offered."

I stayed silent, so he swallowed and continued to talk.

"It is believed that the nix was one of the patrons of the original establishment. It was drawn to the girls. To what they offered. But there was one girl it adored above all the rest."

"How do you know this?" I broke in. "Is this more 'legend' or do you have proof?"

"Proof." Carson Sams tucked his hands into his pants pockets. "The girl left a diary detailing her interactions with a man named John Bruen. She claimed that he confessed his love to her. He would visit her at least twice a week. Each time she refused him."

"Ok. That means nothing. It would hurt business if she fell for a client, right?"

I ignored Elliot's interruption. I didn't have the time or patience for him now that our client had finally started talking.

"Go on."

"On their last night together, John promised the girl that he had powers no ordinary man possessed. He claimed to be a water spirit who had traveled from Germany to the United States. He swore that if she loved him as he loved her, he would be able to transform her into a nymph. He promised her an eternity of happiness. The girl laughed and sent him on his way. We know this," Sams' stressed his last words. "Because she detailed it in her journal."

"Ok. So what happened to her?"

"She was found dead the next morning. Her next client got too carried away. The man was arrested and the police stepped in. They shut the Black Swan down. It took five years for it to be reopened as the hotel you are standing in today."

"And you believe that this John Bruen has continued to return to the Black Swan?" Elliot took out his notepad. "In search of his lost love? Or the companionship she offered?"

"Both?" Sams shrugged. "That's why I called you. I'd seen your show. I knew what your Sibyl could do. I was hoping that perhaps she could talk to him. Convince him that the girl he loved was truly gone and he should go with her."

Well, at least now I knew what was expected of me.

"I'll do what I can." I sighed. "I'll be honest, Mr. Sams, I'm having a hard time with your story in light of what's happened to these women."

"Can we see the diary?" Elliot was still writing, but he stopped as he waited for Sams to answer him. "I would love to have it on film."

"I do not have it on the premises." The manager raised his hands in front of himself in mock surrender. "We donated it to the historical society for preservation. The book is old, Ms. McRayne. I'll provide you with our contact and you can arrange your viewing with them."

I didn't wait around while he and Elliot discussed the details of our viewing of the book. I saw that Joey had turned his camera off. He sat it down on a side table before he beckoned me over.

"Yeah?"

"Have you contacted Cyrus yet?" My friend looked down at me. "Because I'm with you, Eva. I'm not sure if the ghost story is a front for a very real bad guy."

"Spirits are very real, too." I countered. "But no. Not yet. You know how Cyrus operates, Joey. He fades in and out of the shadows. It's not like he's going to have to catch a plane or anything."

"Yeah, but I was hoping he would be able to talk some damn sense into you before you settled in for the night."

"You guys are in the adjoining room, right?" I felt my shoulders relax when he nodded. "And you're all set up?"

"Of course." Joey glanced over my head. "You sure you don't want the cops waiting in the wings with us?"

"No." I chuckled. "I think that's considered entrapment."

"Thanks, sir."

I turned to see Elliot shake Sams' hand. He crossed over to us with a grin.

"A document! A recording of the haunting! Damn, that was a great interview, Evie."

I narrowed my eyes at him but didn't respond. I'd had a really hard time talking to Elliot since we'd boarded the plane for California. So I didn't know what to say now. Not that it mattered. My co-host was so ecstatic, he clapped me on the shoulder.

"Go get ready. Dinner starts in less than an hour. That'll give Joey time to hook you up with the body camera."

"Yeah, because I'm totally going to pass as a regular hotel guest after everyone has seen Joey following me around with the camera." I pulled away from his touch. "And how obvious are you being right now? I'm supposed to be alone."

"Sorry." Elliot rolled his eyes at me. "Anyway, time's a'wastin'."

I stared at him. I waited for him to tell me that I didn't have to do this. That I'd passed his stupid test of loyalty and he'd keep me safe. That we were in this together. I can't say I was surprised when he walked away without a word.

What did surprise me was the tears which burned in the corners of my eyes. I couldn't get over how much Elliot had changed since the premeire. Had it really been a few months ago? It seemed like years.

Joey picked up his camera, threw his arm around my shoulder, and walked me towards my room. It wasn't until we reached my door that he spoke.

"Don't worry, Evie. Even if Elliot's an ass, he still cares about you."

I gave my friend a small smile before I slipped inside. I wanted to believe him. I wanted to think that Elliot had my best interests at heart. Yet, as I pulled out the dress I'd bought for tonight, I knew better.

Elliot had only one goal in mind. Catch the monster on film. Make a damned good episode. No matter who got hurt in the process.

Dinner was horrible.

I'll admit, I picked at the food as I sat at the table alone. I pretended to be engrossed in my phone. I pretended to be preoccupied with my own thoughts. But the truth was much simpler. I was watching the people around me. I didn't know what or who I was looking for. But I couldn't shake the feeling that whatever we were after was already here.

"Ms. McRayne, will you be expecting anyone else tonight?"

I glanced up from my phone to see that the waiter had returned with my wine. He glanced at the empty chairs around me before I understood. The poor man was trying to get me to hurry up since the dining room was filling up fast. I shook my head and twirled the stem of the glass between my fingers.

"No. There was an emergency back in Los Angeles. The guys are on their way back home to take care of it."

"That is most unfortunate." He bowed his head. "Can I get anything else for you?"

"No." I shook my head. "I'm done. Thank you."

I downed the wine he had given me when I realized what I had just said. I was about to return to my room. I was about to put myself right in the center of a trap. I was nervous. No. Anxious.

By the time I had made it down the hall to my room, I felt like an idiot. After all, there was no guarantee that I would be attacked tonight. In fact, Elliot's little scheme may fall flat. He and Joey would get a good bit of footage of me sleeping. That was it.

I kicked off my shoes and flipped on the television. I tossed the remote on the bed as I busied myself with getting ready to call it a night. But as I headed to the bathroom to change out of my dress, I caught sight of one of the cameras Joey had hidden behind a potted plant.

I flipped it the bird before I slammed the bathroom door. I couldn't understand my sudden anger. Maybe I'd had too much to drink at dinner when I was trying to calm my nerves. Or maybe I was tired of being Elliot's puppet. So I took my time in the shower. I scrubbed off every inch of makeup. I spent twenty minutes drying my hair. Then another twenty putting on my pajamas.

By the time I came back out, it was after eight o'clock. I ignored the small earpiece that Joey had left behind for me to wear. The device was meant to allow them to communicate with me.

I didn't have anything to say.

I went through the motions. I checked the hallway to make sure there was no bottle of wine waiting on me. There wasn't. I almost laughed from my relief, but I didn't want to give Elliot the pleasure. Instead, I picked up my phone and hit the lights.

I was wrong when I said I was exhausted. That was a gross understatement. My bones felt too heavy as I sank into the bed. I pulled up my text messages and used my thumb to pull up my conversation with Cyrus. I hadn't heard from him since he left me three days before. I didn't question it. After all, my keeper was part and parcel of a world I didn't understand. But I didn't like keeping him in the dark about what was going on. No matter how pissed off he would be at me for relenting to Elliot's plan.

I let my fingers hover over the keyboard for a second before I began to type.

I'm an idiot. Don't be mad, Cyrus. Please. I couldn't stand it. But I am in the middle of the most stupid experiment of my life. I let Elliot talk me into being the bait for a nix.

I hit 'enter' and rubbed the sleep from my eyes before I started typing again.

I don't think it'll show up. I didn't get the usual signs tonight the other women had when they were attacked. No wine at my door. And now that I'm waiting, there's no sign of anyone trying to come into the room. I'm fine. I promise. Just don't be mad. Please.

I sat my phone on the nightstand then flipped on my side. I was almost asleep when I heard a creak by the bed. I forced my eyes open to see Cyrus as he lowered himself down to sit beside me. My keeper didn't say a word as he brushed his hand over my cheek. Across my jaw before he leaned in to kiss me.

I groaned against the flash of heat that exploded in my chest. I wanted to hold him closer. I wanted him more than anything I'd ever known. But my movements were too slow. I arched into his touch as he trailed his fingers down my side.

Why hadn't I done this before? Each caress was pure pleasure. The kiss we were locked in left me breathless. I released a gasp as Cyrus' fingers brushed over my stomach. I whimpered his name when he broke away from me.

"You must truly wish for death, mortal."

What? I tried to sit up when I felt my keeper's weight lift off of me. I heard a crash and I struggled to see against the burning in my eyes. Two shadows were locked in a strange embrace. I saw one hit the other so hard, they both fell to the floor under the window. And for the first time, I got a good look at the men fighting.

Both were tall. Both were dark. Both were Cyrus.

I rubbed the back of my hand over my eyes in an attempt to clear them when I saw a flash of gold light the room seconds before the door to my room flew open. I folded over to cover my eyes when one of the intruders turned on the lights.

"Evie!" Joey rushed over to the bed. He wrapped me up in his arms. "Are you alright?"

"Who are you?" Elliot this time. "What are you?"

"No...no one. She invited me over. I swear it!"

A familiar voice filtered through my hazy mind. I let my hands fall to see Cyrus standing over a man I felt I should have recognized. It took a minute, but I got it.

The waiter.

"Drugged." I forced the word out of my mouth, but damn, it was hard. I felt as if my tongue was swollen. "Can't..."

"Lancaster, I would suggest you call the authorities before this man loses his life." Cyrus kept his blade against the waiter's throat. "Now."

Elliot didn't seem to hesitate. I could hear him talking. I struggled against the sluggish feeling that filled my body as more men joined them. It wasn't long after that I saw Cyrus' sword disappear. He jerked the man to his feet then threw him at the others.

"Eva."

Elliot said my name, but I barely heard him. Joey was still holding me. Still trying to shield me from the action I couldn't understand. I heard another loud crack before Cyrus spoke again.

"Leave while you still can on your own accord, Lancaster. If you do not, then I will take great pleasure in ensuring that you do not walk away again."

I felt Joey squeeze my shoulders before he stood. "Cyrus, thank god you got here in time. We couldn't tell..."

"I will speak with you later, Joseph. For now, allow me to tend to Eva."

I started to fall over when Joey released me, but Cyrus was there. He caught me and held me tight against him. He only released me long enough to shift around to lay my head in his lap. My keeper didn't say anything. He just held me. He brushed my hair out of my face. I tried to fight the drug. I tried to stay awake to explain myself. In the end, I managed to whisper a few words.

"Cyrus, I'm so sorry."

"Hush, Little One. Sleep it off. You are safe now."

His tone softened a few moments later as I released myself to the heavy sleep I'd fought off for so long.

"You are safe."

I woke up two days later to pure insanity. That was the only way I could describe it. The news carried the story of my attack. Paparazzi had camped outside the hotel. And the police spent more time asking me questions I couldn't answer than I'd like to admit.

Through it all, Cyrus stayed by my side. He held my hand as I faced the questions. He held me when the trauma of what had almost happened hit me. My keeper was kind. Gentle. And he brushed aside every attempt I made in trying to explain myself.

"There is no need, dear girl." My keeper would tell me. "You were drugged. You had just contacted me. It only makes sense that you thought the beast was me."

His words sounded great. They were the perfect explanation. Except, I couldn't shake the feeling that he was wrong. Surely it wasn't the drug that had made me react the way I had. But I didn't argue with him. I didn't have the words to refute him.

We were at the Black Swan for almost a week before I saw Elliot again. I made a point to seek him out. I needed to talk to him about what happened. I needed to tell him that I was sorry. But most of all?

I needed to tell him I would never let him put me in that position ever again.

Elliot pulled the door open after my third knock. He stared at me before he started to shut it back in my face.

"Elliot, stop it." I smacked the door with my palm to keep it open. "I need to talk to you."

"There's nothing to say, Eva." Elliot's tone was one of ice. "Really."

"Elliot, dammit. Let me come in. I have to know..."

"What?" He snapped. "What do you have to know? Because I know plenty, Eva."

"I need to know why. Was I right? Was this whole episode a way to prove my damned loyalty to you? Because if it was..."

"I heard you." Elliot's voice dropped. "I heard you say his name.

Not mine. I found out real quick where your loyalty lies, Sibyl. And it's not with me."

"Elliot, stop being ridiculous." I heard my own words falter. "You know as well as I do that Cyrus..."

"Is the one you want." He bowed his head and chuckled. "Seriously, Eva. Why don't you just say it? After all, I saw you with him, remember? I saw you betray me for him. So go back to your precious keeper. Leave me alone."

"Listen to me..."

"No." Elliot glared at me. "We are done, Eva. I told you I was in love with you, for God's sake!"

"Elliot," I stared back at him. "I loved you, too, as a friend. If I led you on-"

"We'll finish out the first season in the spring." He interrupted me. "Goodbye, Eva."

"Are you going to quit?" I demanded as my own temper started to flare. "Because if you're considering it, Elliot..."

"Goodbye, Eva."

This time, he was successful. Elliot shut the door and not a moment too soon. I felt my tears start to fall as I turned to go back down the hall. I tried to tell myself that it was for the best. That the past few months were proof that the friendship I had cherished was over. But there was still a part of me that wanted to believe this was all a bad dream.

That I wasn't really the Sibyl. That my entire world hadn't been smashed to pieces over one man's jealousy. I stopped only when Cyrus appeared before me. My keeper didn't say anything. He only watched me. I felt my emotions get the best of me as I thought of how wonderful he had been. How he had been there for me when the one person I had believed in had abandoned me. I threw myself against him as I began to sob in earnest.

I didn't know who I was anymore. I didn't know what I wanted.

And it was killing me.

**** END OF VOLUME 1 ****

Dear reader,

We hope you enjoyed reading The Daughter of Olympus. Please take a moment to leave a review, even if it's a short one. Your opinion is important to us.

Discover more books by Cynthis D Witherspoon at https://www.nextchapter.pub/authors/cynthia-d-witherspoon

Want to know when one of our books is free or discounted? Join the newsletter at http://eepurl.com/bqqB3H

Best regards,

Cynthia D Witherspoon and the Next Chapter Team

ABOUT THE AUTHOR

Cynthia D. Witherspoon is the bestselling author of The Lillian. She has been published in numerous anthologies since 2009. Her work has appeared in several award winning collections including Dark Tales of Ancient Civilizations (2012) and Pellucid Lunacy (2010).

Lightning Source UK Ltd.
Milton Keynes UK
UKHW041849250221
379413UK00008B/466/J